SILENT VIGIL

John Chudley

Grosvenor House
Publishing Limited

This book is published by
Grosvenor House Publishing Ltd
Link House
140 The Broadway, Tolworth, Surrey, KT6 7HT.
www.grosvenorhousepublishing.co.uk

A CIP record for this book
is available from the British Library

ISBN 978-1-83975-490-6

Chapter One

"The lady keeps looking at me."

Will Whitby, the headteacher of Vikant Primary School in Oftness, looked at his daughter Ruth as she sat at the table eating her evening meal.

"What lady, where?"

"The lady at school, in class, standing there looking at me."

Will looked with concern at his daughter of seven. She did not often complain, but this evening strain showed on her young face.

"How long has this been going on? Who is she? You know all the teaching assistants. We haven't inspectors or governors in the school at the moment. Have you spoken to Mrs Mills?"

"She says there isn't a lady."

"What?"

"She says there isn't anyone in the classroom but us children."

"Mrs Mills is the better teacher in your year group. That's why I put you with her."

Will frowned. One of his big concerns in the school, one of any headteacher's for that matter, was the small proportion of children with maladjustment problems or psychiatric conditions, either inherited or induced. Surely Ruth was not exhibiting anything of that nature, most worrying and disquieting? He had no evidence of this before – extremely embarrassing as the headteacher's daughter.

"What about the other children? What's their reaction?"

Ruth looked perplexed. "They didn't seem to notice her."

"Not notice her, have you asked them?"

"Yes."

"What do they say?"

"They look at me in a funny way."

Will could see that his daughter was increasingly distressed and decided not to pursue the matter further but made a note that this was something he must urgently look into. It was seriously worrying.

After much thought, Will decided to investigate unobtrusively, keeping a low profile. In the interests of all, especially Ruth's, the last thing he wanted was a sensation, drawing staff's attention. With that in mind, next day about ten, after the classes had settled down, he left his office, turned right, and walked round the square of corridors outside the classrooms which encompassed the later built assembly hall. These 1930 classrooms had windows opening out onto corridors, added at the same time as the assembly hall, allowing Will to glance into the classrooms as he passed by.

Looking into Ruth's classroom, he saw her sitting uncomfortably at her desk. Will could see no one else other than Mrs Mills. Why was not Ruth relaxed? Other children were. However, this was not the end of the matter. Will would pursue the puzzle further.

Eventually he knew what he was going to do. Telling no one, he would spend an evening quietly on his own in the darkened classroom and see for himself what might occur – if anything.

As dusk fell and the cleaners left, Mr Macnamara, the caretaker, hung about, waiting for Will to go home when he would lock up the school for the night.

Noticing him, Will said, "I will lock up when I'm ready. You can go home."

Mr Macnamara looked as if he doubted whether he could trust the headmaster to do this properly, something he did at the end of every school day and felt was his prerogative.

"All right," he replied reluctantly. "After you've put in the key code you've got four seconds to leave before the alarm goes off."

"I know," Will replied patiently. He did not have to be reminded by the caretaker about the alarm he had a firm install and remembered how suspicious Mr Macnamara was of this new-fangled innovation when first installed, despite schools being broken into in the area. "I won't be caught."

After waiting a while in his office, without putting on further lights, Will walked somewhat sheepishly to Ruth's classroom and attempted to identify Ruth's exact chair and sat in it, facing towards the front of the class, and waited until the last red glow of sunset faded and he was enveloped in complete darkness.

Will did not know how long he sat, his mind wandering. At one point he almost fell off the little seat. He must have nodded off. When he woke with a start, he thought he heard an audible sighing like whispering wavelets on a sandy shore. Surely it must be his imagination. He waited for some time, feeling nervous but at the same time foolish, when he became aware of the emerging silhouette of a woman. He stared in disbelief as her features became clearer. They were immensely sad. He felt he knew this woman but was not sure. She was wearing what seemed to be some sort of uniform. It was smart, fawn, open-necked rather than tunic. She had a knee-length skirt of the same material. Her hair was almost shoulder length, curled upwards at the back, and she was wearing on her head what appeared to be a stylish glengarry – the last person Will expected to see in a school.

Will felt he wanted to speak to her as she stared at him – but could you speak to an apparition? She approached closer, growing in size. Will gave a stifled exclamation and jumped up. Then in an instant, she disappeared. Despite himself, Will was terrified. Had he had a hallucination or what? Blindly he ran out of the classroom, scattering chairs in the darkness.

Down the corridor, he got hold of himself. He did not want Mr Macnamara or Mrs Mills to find the classroom in disarray in the morning. At the same time, he did not want to draw attention to himself by lights going on in the middle of the night, so he crept back and replaced the chairs as best he could in the darkness.

Back in his lit office, Will collected his thoughts together. He did not believe in apparitions. There had to be some logical explanation. Was there something traumatic in the history of the school he did not know about that would throw light on the phenomenon, something perhaps recorded in the old school logs, official accounts of the daily happenings in the school which had to be kept until about 15 years ago? In the next few days, he would look them up. In the meantime, he had better be locking up the school and getting on home before he would have to turn out for school next day.

Though tired, Will realised he must think what he was doing so as not to bungle his leaving and set off the alarm. He put out the office light and felt his way down the corridor to the north entrance, still with 'Boys' cut into the concrete on the outside from the days of segregation of the sexes.

Feeling like some sort of guilty child, he took out a small torch, rehearsed the code in his own mind as he would not have time to put it in twice and took a deep breath. Then, steadying himself, he tapped in the code, walked swiftly to the door, opened it, and got out. With a sigh of relief, he locked the door with his key and walked around the back of the school to pick up his car.

At the front of the school, he had to drag open the big iron gates, drive the car out and put his shoulder to the gates to get them closed again, making a note that he needed to do something about the worn pivots before they wore to a point where the gates would take more than one person to get them open and shut. He winced at the noise as he eventually clanged the gates shut, before driving the 12 miles home with little traffic about at this hour in the morning. When he arrived home, he found Jane Bates, his neighbour from two doors down, babysitting for Ruth, asleep on the sofa. Waking her up gently, Will apologised profusely for being so late and gave her an extra 10 pounds. Jane was an invaluable help. Ruth liked her and he certainly did not want to lose her services.

As he was going off to sleep, Will went over in his mind, as he had many painful times before, the circumstances leading up to his being a widower and

Ruth motherless. Michelle's symptoms and decline were forever etched on his mind. From the time he first met his wife, she was always energetic and vital with a vibrant personality. People were attracted to her. She was much admired and sometimes even envied.

Then, two years ago, she began not to feel herself. She felt tired. Life was an effort. Her tummy felt strangely large and bloated. Will said she should go to the doctor's. Michelle said that was not necessary. It was just one of those things. She would get over it. She must have a stubborn virus. When Will eventually persuaded her to go the doctor's, the doctor sent her straight to hospital. Within a week, she was diagnosed with ovarian cancer. Within 10 days, she was dead. The day before she died, Will took Ruth to visit her. Ruth was very frightened, but Michelle assured her bravely she might have to go away but nevertheless, she would always be with her. When Will visited her the next day, she could only weakly hold his hand but just managed to struggle out with the words, "Look after Ruth." Later that day, she was gone.

Michelle's last words were always with Will. "Look after Ruth." The apparition in Ruth's classroom brought this back to him. Though no one would make up for Michelle, Ruth needed a mother along with himself. She was vulnerable. But Will could not think of anyone he fancied he would like to see as Ruth's mother. However, that was something he must work on. Then, worn out after his late night, he fell asleep.

Chapter Two

Will was tired when he woke up but went into Ruth's room to find her sitting in her bed, getting dressed and looking at the television.

"Teddy's fallen in the creek again on the way to school. Silly Teddy."

"Does he need washing?"

"Not my Yellow Ted," Ruth replied indignantly, picking up her eighteen-inch much-loved soft toy from within her bed. "Teddy on television."

"My Yellow Ted's a good boy." Ruth gave her Yellow Ted a hug.

"I'm pleased to hear it. He might lose his colour in the wash. Start a shower while I get muesli, fruit and drinks ready and then I'll come back up and towel you off."

"Can't you stay?"

"I'm afraid not today. I'm running a bit late – had a late night."

Ruth looked disapproving. "You said late nights are not good for you."

"No, they're not."

"The PTA?" Ruth enquired knowingly.

"Not this time. Trouble with a classroom. The contractor was late. I sent the caretaker home," Will lied.

"Mr Macnamara just sits in his office sometimes."

"I know he does. I'm sorry. We must be getting on. I'll be back up in three minutes. You make a start." Ruth was beginning to know how the school was run and was not going to let anyone not pull their weight or take advantage of her dad. As the headmaster's daughter, she was on his side. It was a responsibility.

When Will went back upstairs, Ruth was out of the shower. He finished towelling her off. They ate breakfast companionably, Ruth chattering away.

"Do you want me to buy you sandwiches at Wallace's Garage or would you like school lunches? I didn't have time to make you a packed lunch last evening."

"School lunches. It's yummy today, sausages and mash and gypsy tart."

"How do you know?"

"I asked Mrs Clark to find out." Mrs Clark was a lunchtime supervisor.

Will realised that Mrs Clark would have gone into the school canteen and asked one of the assistant cooks to look up the six-week school lunch cycle – a bit irregular. Already Ruth was learning how to pull rank. Mrs Clark may not have seen her way to do this for any child who asked but with an eye to her betterment, it could be good policy to please the headmaster's daughter.

Will frowned. "Perhaps you shouldn't have asked."

"Why?"

It was all too complicated to explain why. He did not want to find fault with his daughter. She was a smart girl and learning. "Eat up, my darling, and make sure you've got all your cuddly friends with you. I'll get out the Sunny."

He drove the car round to the front and helped Ruth down the steps clutching half a dozen cuddly toys.

These she carefully arranged them along the back seat and put the seat belt around them.

Suddenly Ruth cried, "Yellow Ted!" and rushed inside.

Will fretted. If you wanted your staff on time, the worst thing was to set a bad example and be late for school yourself. But he knew why Ruth travelled with a string of cuddly toys, Yellow Ted especially. Ever since Michelle's death, she felt insecure. Will gritted his teeth and was patient. This is one of the many things he must do in the future: find a mother for Ruth, not to mention a companion for himself.

When the school was almost in sight, Ruth began to cry. Will stopped the car. After last night he knew why. He took her gently off her booster and put her on his lap. "It's that lady looking at you?"

"Yes." Ruth wiped tears from her eyes with her sleeve.

"Would you like to be in Mrs Sutherland's class?"

"Oh yes, I'd be with Angela."

"I'll arrange it. Stay in my en suite if I bring people into the office."

Will's office had its own washroom and separate toilet. The changeover for Ruth was going to have to be carefully handled. Will ran his school by consultation and negotiation rather than in an authoritarian manner. In that way, he got goodwill and commitment. Having the headmaster's daughter was considered both an honour and a liability, the liability being that everything or anything might be reported on.

Bearing this in mind, Will called Mrs Mills into the office at morning break. Mrs Mills sat down anxiously, not knowing what to expect.

"I wonder if you could help me?"

Immediately Mrs Mills looked more relaxed.

"As you know, Ruth tragically lost her mother, Michelle, two years ago. Bravely, one of the last things Michelle said to Ruth was that she loved her but had to go away. At the time, Ruth assumed that eventually she would come back. Now, as she's got older, she's begun to realise that what her mother meant was that she was dying and could never come back in a physical sense. This has meant that recently Ruth has become very insecure. I'm asking Mrs Sunderland to have Ruth." Mrs Sunderland was the parallel Year Three teacher. "She has Angela McDonald in her class. Angela is Ruth's best friend." Mrs Mills looked relieved. Having the headmaster's daughter in her class was a mixed blessing. She was not particularly put out. Someone else could do a stint.

At lunchtime, Will now needed to diplomatically put to Mrs Sunderland that he would like her to include Ruth in her class. He only hoped no other children saw the same apparition as he and Ruth had in Mrs Mills classroom, and it got about that the school was haunted and parents began to withdraw their children. Up till now, Will had been able to carefully manage his governors who had every confidence that he would always put things right. But a classroom ghost was another thing.

Who was this apparition? Her face seemed familiar. How was he going to get rid of it? It wasn't Michelle but, in some way, seemed to have a connection to Ruth and him as no one else to date appeared to be aware of it. It was a disturbing puzzle, something which Will had no experience of, or any other headteacher to Will's knowledge. He would have to do his best to resolve the puzzle without delay. And in the longer term, there was another matter Will needed to put his mind to: Ruth needed a mother.

Jean Sunderland, with reservations, accepted Ruth into her class when Will put it to her in the way he did. When he told Ruth, she was delighted.

"Goody, I'll be with Angela. The lady won't be there?"

Will hoped sincerely the apparition was not going to follow her around. "Of course not, darling. You'll be fine." With that, Ruth went off happily.

Will looked at his engagement diary to remind himself of afternoon commitments before going over to the canteen to take charge of lunchtime supervision.

Lunchtime could be a fraught period in the school day. With the necessity of two canteen sittings, he could not make the midday break overly short. For years, teachers were rostered to supervise at lunchtimes, but recently new regulations required all workers, including teachers, be given an hour's lunchtime break, which meant schools had to hire lunchtime supervisors.

Will was responsible for everything that happened at lunchtime, like parents entering the playground and taking issue with the lunchtime supervisors, parents and others entering the kitchen to challenge the cooking and menus, incidents like a man being reported lurking in the boys' toilets. He even had to break up two mothers fighting in the playground, their having entered to take sides in their children's playground quarrels, not to mention his having to regularly attend to playground injuries. Lunchtimes could sometimes be a very hectic time indeed. Will had thought of locking all entrances into the school at lunchtimes, but then he would have to employ a responsible adult to stand by the gate to allow entrance to all those with legitimate reasons for coming and going like deliveries.

But his first concern this lunchtime was to ensure Ruth's happiness and to quash potential rumours of his having a haunted school.

After school, as Ruth got in the car with him, Will observed she looked happy. "Had a good afternoon?"

"Mrs Sutherland let me sit with Angela."

"So, you liked the change."

Ruth's face lit up. "Oh yes."

"I wouldn't mention the lady who kept looking at you."

"Why?"

"Not everyone might understand."

"Why?"

Will felt that to try to explain his concerns to a seven-year-old who saw things in black and white would not be understood so decided to change the subject. "I think Yellow Ted's slipping in the back seat."

He stopped the car while Ruth climbed into the back seat and strapped herself in with her cuddly toys, talking to them and sorting them out as she did so.

That evening, after Ruth had played with Patricia, Jane Bates' daughter two doors down, seen a favourite video while eating her evening meal and had gone to sleep listening to him reading her an evening bedtime story, Will reflected on his day and the possible way ahead.

As well as the normal school routine like starting on the termly governors' report and continuing teacher appraisal, Will felt he must research into the history of the school for clues regarding the ghostly apparition which, to date, had only been sensed by Ruth and himself, perhaps a clue in itself, and the pressing necessity for Ruth to have a loving person to care for her alongside himself. There was much to get on with.

Next school day, Will dug out the old school logs, nicely bound but much-worn volumes. To his surprise, the oldest only went back to 1946, though the oldest building on his site, the original all-age gothic-style building, went back to 1901. He began to think of what authority he should consult regarding the history of school buildings in the United Kingdom when he remembered he had authority near at hand in the form of children's grandparents, who would likely know the history of the school through the Second World War. To that end, he sent a letter via the children to grandparents, inviting them to give a talk to the children about Ostness in wartime with particular reference to the school. A few days later, a grandmother called to volunteer.

During Will's interview with the volunteering grandmother, he learnt that the school, to his surprise, was requisitioned during the Second World War, the children being dispersed to surrounding schools, their rolls diminished by evacuation. Will was directed to look at the foundation of the present canteen. He was told to note how massive it was. It was constructed at the beginning of the war as a gun platform. Military personnel occupied the school, male and female. She did not know what they actually did as well as man the ack-ack gun and searchlight but assumed they were there for training purposes. Some were commonwealth and foreign, she remembered.

Hearing this, Will now understood why the apparition he and Ruth saw was in uniform and female.

So, during the Second World War, his school did not operate as a school. He was getting somewhere but in other respects, the plot thickened. Who was this service woman and was why she so traumatised that her ghost remained in the building? He felt he knew her features from a long time ago. And, above all, why did only Ruth and he see it? He had been over this in his mind many times before, was there possibly some family connection? It was as intriguing as it was disturbing. Will knew he must find out more, but how? He asked the grandmother if she knew who any of the women service personnel were and where they came from. She said she did not, but that she had once heard two of them talking in the street with a commonwealth accent, mentioning their home in New Zealand.

At the mention of New Zealand, Will picked up his ears. His eldest brother, Edward, by 15 years, along with his only sister, Zoe, two years younger, migrated to New Zealand in 1938. Will was young at the time. As only Ruth and Will seemed to be aware of the apparition in Ruth's classroom, was there a possible family connection? This is something Will would need to follow up, in the meantime he had the governors' report to think about.

Will always took care preparing this. The governors were supposed to oversee him. The fact was that Will carefully managed his governors. He was a fluent writer and made sure he put a spin on his termly report that showed him in a favourable light, being able, whatever the odds, to surmount any difficulties and put matters right. But exorcising a ghost? That was different proposition, beyond his experience. In any event, it was a very bad idea to have a resident ghost in the first place. It could bring about parents withdrawing their children from the school. It was in his interests that any suspicion of there being a ghost on the premises never got around, one more reason why he needed to find out more.

That opportunity occurred a few days later at the conclusion of the four o'clock governors' meeting when Will picked up Ruth at Gaynor McDonald's, teachers' assistant, who lived in Trelade Avenue, Ostness, with her mother. As Ruth particularly liked Gaynor McDonald, for the last six months, Will had had a private arrangement with Gaynor to look after Ruth after school. This was when he had to stay until about eight in the evening to attend to a governors' meeting which started at four, or a late afternoon meeting with the PTA.

Halfway through Will's headship, the school became its own budget holder. This was when Will's capitation allowance of £6,000 to top up the library was increased to £750,000 from which he had to pay for staff with their on-costs, building maintenance and everything in between. With good management, from this £750,000, Will could afford the recently allowed three teachers' assistants, who he chose from mothers of schoolchildren who had voluntarily helped in the school with day trips away, hearing individual reading or general classroom help and who could be trusted with confidential information.

On arrival, Gaynor introduced Will to her mother. After the usual pleasantries, Will asked if she remembered any outstanding instances associated with the ack-ack gun and searchlight, or military established in the school during the war.

Gaynor's mother looked curiously at Will. "I would like the children to know the history of the school during the war," Will qualified.

After some consideration, Gaynor's mother replied. "As you might have already heard, the school was taken over by the military for the duration. I was only ten in 1940. My mum was huddling me into our garden bomb shelter one evening as a lot had started to happen overhead. It began with the sirens, the searchlight opening up and the school gun firing almost continuously, followed by aerial combat close overhead. It was terrifying hearing the screams of the engines and seeing tracers flying everywhere. Then there was an enormous bang two streets away, which shook our shelter, and terrifying flames. In the morning, we saw the remains of a Hurricane. We weren't allowed to go near it. It was guarded. If there'd been a body inside, it had been removed. It was awful. That's the worst I can remember here in Ostness."

This account was very interesting to Will. A picture was building up. Gaynor McDonald was lucky to have a mother on hand to help her with her children. Will's parents had immigrated to Lockhart In New South Wales, Australia, eight years ago. Four years later, Will and Michelle had visited his parents in Lockhart and found the town to be a quaint, small, old-time town by Australian standards, with a population of about one thousand. Compared with an English village, it had a low, sleepy profile and was known as the Veranda Town. Michelle's parents had split up years ago. Her mother lived in Spain with a partner and a new family. After the split, Michelle's father went to work in the Middle East somewhere. At the time of her death,

Michelle did not know where and so her father could not be informed of his daughter's sad fate. Loving grandparents on hand would have made Will's life bringing up Ruth on his own so much easier. Once again, Will thought he really must see what he could about this.

Chapter Three

Will's life at school was never dull and could at times be quite challenging. He never knew from hour to hour who or what was going to come through his office door. People wanting interviews were supposed to book these at the school office. But really incensed parents would occasionally not observe this procedure, and the first thing Will knew was that his office door was violently swung open and he was being confronted with intruding parents, or a parent's boyfriend, with what the locals called in their quaint vernacular, 'a right attack of the verbals'. As Will could not reply in similar vein, it was his practice to wait until the tirade had died down, the 'effing and blinding' had finally subsided, to then try to achieve, by patient dialogue, a better relationship and understanding. It was the only way ahead. Such people would keep coming back in a similar manner until they were finally won over.

A week later after school, Will had one such unscheduled confrontation. Fortunately, Ruth was not with him at the time. Will thought she was still with her teacher in her classroom. The unscheduled interview, if you could call it that, went on and on with much noisy abuse, threats and shouts. Then, to his surprise, near to what he thought must be the end of a particularly unpleasant encounter, Gaynor McDonald opened his office door without knocking and stood in the room with him, not saying a word, looking squarely at the parents. Taken aback, the equally surprised parents ceased their tirade and left his office muttering.

"I thought you'd had enough, sir, and Ruth was becoming uncomfortable up in the special needs room with me, wondering what was going on."

"I'm very grateful, Mrs McDonald," Will replied, always addressing his staff formally. He was known for his fairness, treating all staff with courtesy and having no favourites.

But Will was nevertheless impressed. Most of the teaching staff were still on the premises and could hear the commotion, including his deputy, but were of the view that it was a headteacher's job to get on with aggressive interviews. That was what he was paid for. But Gaynor McDonald obviously thought otherwise and had plucked up courage to intervene. Will wondered why she was still at school in the first place. Teaching assistants were paid on an hourly rate and generally did not stay after school. Will had not specifically engaged Gaynor privately on this occasion to look after Ruth and wondered about her own children, Angela and Tim, a boy in year six. Maybe they had gone after school to spend the rest of the afternoon with friends, conveyed by Gaynor's mother, Gaynor voluntarily using that time to care for Ruth. Could it be that Gaynor had feelings for him that were more than professional? Gaynor was on her own, her husband having gone off years ago with another woman, the reason for her now living in Ostness with her mother. The possibility was all food for thought for the future.

It was early in the spring term and the days were still short and cold. Owing to the weather, the children were in for much of the time during breaks. The hour was not due to change until the end of March. Along with the usual school concerns, Will was constantly turning over in his mind his ongoing preoccupation with the school ghost or apparition and Ruth's future. In the end, he thought of a way ahead that could solve both.

The "ghost" seemed to be a girl from New Zealand serving with the Auxiliary Territorial Service. Will had always intended to visit New Zealand but had never got round to it before Michelle became unwell and died. Perhaps asking Gaynor and her children to join him, Gaynor, as a paid escort, her two children as companions for Ruth, might prove just the thing. It was always possible that during their time away together a relationship would come about. Will decided, when an appropriate occasion occurred, that he would tactfully suggest this to Gaynor for the long summer term holidays to see what she thought. It would be the New Zealand winter but that could not be helped.

An opportunity occurred to speak to Gaynor away from the school environment when he called at her place at eight in the evening two weeks later to collect Ruth after a meeting of the PTA's summer fete sub-committee. On entering, he found Ruth sitting with Angela and Tim looking at children's television.

After greetings, Will asked Gaynor if he could have a word with her, "Out of the children's hearing for the present, if you don't mind."

Puzzled, Gaynor motioned him into the next room, leaving the door open. "I have an elder brother and did have a much older sister in New Zealand. Michelle and I were always going to visit them, along with a tour, but we didn't get round to it before Michelle died." For the present, Will did not want to mention any other reason like an apparition in his school and possible connection regarding the visit. "I would very much like to undertake a visit to New Zealand in the summer holidays, though it would be winter in New Zealand. Such an undertaking, nevertheless, would require most of the six-week summer holidays period. But I'm concerned about Ruth. She would need the security of another adult in the event of my falling ill, and children companions. I was wondering if you would like to accompany us as a paid escort along with your children, all costs involved being paid by me, other than a little personal spending money. This would be nothing to do with the school, and the less the school knew about it the better."

Gaynor looked surprised. "Really?"

"I see more of the teaching assistants during the school day than the teachers as they're busy in their classes. Having got to know you at school, as well as through your looking after Ruth after school on many occasions, you seem the best person to ask. Ruth likes you and your children. She feels secure with you. I hope you don't think I'm taking a liberty, but I can't think of any person being better suited to help us. I'd be really grateful if you could consider the idea. I don't expect an answer now. I just ask if you could think about it."

Gaynor continued to look surprised. "Well, I must say—"

"And I don't want you to think I'm in any way propositioning you," Will interrupted.

"Oh no, I don't think that for a minute. You're always so correct with us all." Gaynor looked embarrassed.

"I think it's important to get everything straight right from the start." Will was older than Gaynor. He had married comparatively late. Michelle was near the end of her childbearing time when Ruth was born, as a consequence, Will was unusually old to be a father of such a young child.

"Of course. I understand."

Will was relieved to see Gaynor's embarrassment change to amazement.

"Well, it's a big undertaking. Something I never expected would come my way. I'm honoured you've asked me."

"You'll keep it confidential for the present at least?"

"Of course."

"And think about it?"

"I will."

"I will look forward to your decision. Shall we join the children?"

Gaynor showed him and Ruth to the door, briefly putting her hand on his shoulder, a thing no staff member would ever do at school, but this was a private occasion. It would be nice if, while away, a successful relationship came about. Ruth needed a mother nearer the age of the other mothers in her year group.

The next few weeks were very busy for Will at school. There was secondary school selection, the 'eleven plus', which Will had to enter a proportion of his fourth-year children for, always a contentious undertaking. Will's school catchment consisted of two areas, a council house area to the north, where two-thirds of his children came from, and the Comber Heights district to the south, a much newer, 'upwardly mobile' area where a third of his schoolchildren lived.

His Comber Heights parents were ambitious, always wanting their children entered and expecting them to be successful. The fact that Will had, in fairness, to tell quite a percentage of them that, on their academic showing over the last four years, their children were not likely to be successful brought great resentment and unpleasantness, the parents saying they must be entered anyway, and it would be the school's fault if their children failed, as many would. On the other hand, the larger Ostness council house parents to the north had no such expectations. Every year Will had to persuade a few such parents to enter their children, as school records showed that a small number had every chance of success, their parents never anticipating that academically their children could possibly be in the grammar school league.

Chapter Four

Will heard a bang and children's laughter as he tapped on Gaynor McDonald's door at eight fifteen in the evening a fortnight later to pick up Ruth after a governors' sub-committee meeting.

"Sounds fun." Will did not know quite how to greet Gaynor when she opened the door, ushered him in and shut the door behind him. He took her hand warmly. She looked pleased.

"Mum gave the children a board game at Christmas. It's noisy but a great success." But instead of calling, 'Your father's here, Ruth,' Gaynor motioned Will into the sitting room, leaving the door open so they could see the children. "I've talked it over with Mum. She says it's the opportunity of a lifetime. Tim, Angela, and I can join you for your trip to New Zealand in the summer. Thanks for the kind invitation. I'm so excited but apprehensive."

"Apprehensive?"

"Our going together, what will your governors think?"

"There's no law against it. It's a business arrangement."

"But people will talk?"

"Would that worry you too much?"

"I suppose not."

"Well, if you're sure about it, I'll book return flights via Singapore, leaving as soon as the summer holidays begin?"

"Via Singapore?"

"I know you can go via Los Angeles, but when Michelle and I visited my parents in Lockhart, New South Wales, we travelled on Singapore Airlines via Singapore. These international hubs are vast, like carpeted cities. At Singapore, we got what they called a Sky Train from one terminal to another."

"Sky train?"

"Elevated railway, we'll just have to keep an eye on the children in crowded places, we don't want them lost. OK if I go ahead? I'll keep you informed. I suggest we don't tell the children until the summer holiday begins."

"Very sensible." Gaynor's face clouded over. "I just hope I can cope. I've never done anything like this before, never left the country."

Will put his arm gently on Gaynor's shoulder. "I'm not particularly adventurously myself. I like security. But together we'll manage."

At that point, Tim ran into the room. "Angela's knocked over the flower vase. There's water everywhere!"

"Children," said Gaynor, making a face at Will as she hurried into the other room. "At least it's water."

Will thought it might be a good time to call Ruth and take his leave.

At school, Will liked to lead from the front. He found that he got more respect and co-operation if his teaching staff knew that he was prepared to take a turn along with the rest of them on playground duty and have a teaching programme where he taught every class in turn in the course of the year, during which he demonstrated he was a good and effective teacher.

Monday morning before school his staff found the most difficult playground duty of all, so Will did it. But he did not lose by so doing. Parents bringing children into the playground and the children themselves often gave him much useful information about what had been going on in the home during the weekend and their hopes and fears in general.

While he as in the playground, children might complain that their teacher had been awful to them, had a grudge against them, always after them. Will, in turn, would ask such complainers what they had been doing and would hear that they were only doing this and that, to which Will would respond by saying something like, “And do you think what you were doing was helpful?” to which he invariably got a not very convincing reply.

On this particular Monday morning in late March, there was frost on the ground and puddles were iced over. The children were not supposed to slide on the ice but invariably did, fell over and occasionally injured themselves quite badly. Before long, Will noticed an injured child lying where he fell. The child eventually got up himself but looked shaken. Will called for a teaching assistant to take him inside where Will would need to check him for concussion as soon as he came in. It was Gaynor who responded to his call, took the child in then came out again.

“What’s the weather like in New Zealand in midwinter?” she asked Will quietly away from the hearing of others.

“I think I once remember brother Ted saying in a letter that it was like our midseason. Apparently, there’s no ice or snow in Auckland where he lives. But then Auckland’s latitude is about 47 against our 51½ north where we live. Why?”

"I was just wondering what to pack." Then, as a parent approached Will, Gaynor moved away.

During the Easter holidays, Will saw nothing of Gaynor or her family but during the summer term, he saw quite a bit of her, what with the sub-committee meetings associated with events like the school sports, the school fete, and the swimming galas, keeping Will at school till near eight many evenings. Although she was paid to look after Ruth and for Ruth's evening meal, Gaynor always seemed pleased to see him and to enjoy his company when he popped in to take Ruth home.

On arrival, Will was invariably taken aside into the drawing room to be told how the evening went with the children. On one such occasion halfway through the summer term, Will said to her, "There's no need to call me 'sir' out of the children's hearing. Call me Will. When we're away, I certainly don't want to be known the way I am in the profession."

"I feel a bit awkward."

"Try it. You'll get used to it."

Gaynor gave a faint giggle. "OK, Will." And they both laughed.

On the next occasion Will visited, he told Gaynor he had booked their flights which he believed would be leaving from the new terminal four at Heathrow, formally used mainly by British Airways. He also said he was looking into transport to and from the airport and insurance which they must have, including the children. He also asked Gaynor if she had passports for herself and her children and told her how to go about getting passports if they had not. It was all very exciting. He sat with Gaynor at the dining room while the children played until they both realised it was getting late for the children.

"I think we need more time together to get all the details sorted out," Will observed. "On a weekend before long, my place at Peckingly might be better a place to meet than at Ostness near the school, be less gossip. I'll tell you how to get there. I've a large, sheltered garden for the children to play in including a trampoline."

Gaynor made a face. "People always gossip and what they don't know they make up."

"Precisely, that's human nature. You're still prepared to take it on, our trip... as a business arrangement, that is?"

Will thought the term 'a business arrangement' caused Gaynor a little discomfort and decided from now on not to mention their venture in that way.

They had a happy day, discussing all the details they both felt they needed to go over and watched the children on a new trampoline Will had recently bought for Ruth. Tim was the more confident, but then he was three years older than the girls.

"I think they need to be supervised while using it," Will observed. "They could get hurt if they bounced off. I know a place in Southend-on-Sea where I've bought gym mats for the school from school funds rather than invoicing County Supplies. The trampoline could do with nets round it and gym mats in the area the children get off."

"I see what you mean now you mention it," Gaynor agreed.

"It's an important aspect of my job, ensuring children's safety. Would you believe it? I found a kiln on a wooden floor when I first came to the school. Of course, I wouldn't allow it to be used until it was mounted on a concrete base with a screen around it."

"Unbelievable."

"But a fact, quite a while ago now. Let's go inside and have an evening meal."

They trooped inside into the kitchen-dining room. Will switched on the stove. Then he bought out an assortment of vegetables and filleted salmon to cook, switching on a timer.

"Vegetables in first, when the timer pings, the oven will be the right temperature."

"An efficient cook?" Gaynor smiled at him.

"I've got better with practice. The children can sit round the low table. I'll put on the television. I needed to get with basic cooking after Michelle died.' Will brought out food from the fridge.

"I'll lend a hand." Gaynor began taking the tops off the strawberries.

"We'll be away in a few days now," Will observed as they worked together. He noticed Gaynor looked anxious.

"I only hope I..."

Will leaned across and put an arm on her shoulder. "I know how you feel. It's a big undertaking for both of us." The timer pinged and he put the vegetables in the oven. "The fish fillets only need four minutes. I'll put them in later. We haven't been together like this before. We'll need to be able to have trust in each other, take the good with the bad. But we'll be fine. I've been overseas once before, to visit my parents in Lockhart, New South Wales, with Michelle. I'll ring you daily from now on. Keep you informed of every detail." Gaynor turned to face him, looking grateful. Will felt already a bond was forming, though he too felt a little anxious.

He heard Ruth calling, "When's the meal ready, Dad? We're hungry."

Will withdrew his arm. Gaynor looked at him gratefully. "I'll see if the vegetables are ready. If they are, it won't be long before I feed our hungry lot."

While the children were eating at table and Will and Gaynor were doing likewise on high stools behind them, Will said, "I should be getting our tickets any time now, which we'll have to present at the booking-in desk in exchange for boarding cards when we arrive at the airport, one for each leg of the journey. I'll tell you the number of bags allowed and the weight limit when the tickets arrive. The new wheeled suitcases are much better. I'll help you with the cost if you haven't any. Then there's size limits for cabin luggage. I'll tell you that as well when I get the tickets. Best to travel as light as possible. We can always buy anything else we might find we need, such as warmer clothes for the South Island, when in New Zealand."

"There's a lot to think about, especially with children."

"I can come over to your place and give you a hand if you like?"

"I think I can manage, thank you all the same. Mum has been abroad in her time." Gaynor gave Will a grateful look as she got up to attend to her children. Will hoped they would get on well and all would be fine.

Tickets arrived a few days later. They were to leave at eight in the evening on the 26th of July on a Boeing 747. Will would need to ensure that by then everyone had passports, tickets and insurance and the adults enough

New Zealand dollars for immediate use on landing for such things as taxi hire. He would need credit cards for motel bookings and a hire car. And, of course, he must remind Gaynor not to forget to bring her driving licence, and likewise to remind himself, also to take his newly acquired Nokia mobile phone. He needed to confirm his transport to and from the airport as well. There was much to be getting on with.

Soon the exciting day of the 26th arrived. The long school holidays of six weeks had begun. The airport car was going to pick up Gaynor, Tim and Angela at 2pm, come on to Ruth and Will's at Peckingly, after which it would take two hours to the airport, with a built-in two hours' contingency time in the event of a hold-up on route, to be at the checking-in desk two hours before take-off. That was the timetable Will had made out. He only hoped all went to plan.

Chapter Five

Ruth had observed suitcases being packed for a number of days now and had asked Will why. Will had told her that they were going on a long summer holiday but not where and with whom as it would be all round the school in no time. However, as soon as the term came to an end, he would tell her all about it. So today she knew. They were going to New Zealand with her best friend, Angela, her brother, and mother. It was all wild whoopee!

At twenty-five past two in the afternoon, a people carrier swept into their drive with Gaynor, Tim and Angela aboard. "We're going to New Zealand for the whole of the summer holidays!" Angela shouted to Ruth as soon as the door opened.

"Only it won't be summer," Tim added.

"As soon as these suitcases are aboard, I'll lock the house. We've got to keep a move on. Got everything – passport, driving licence, money, all that?" Will called to Gaynor as a way of greeting.

Gaynor looked worried. "I hope so. The children were so excited they wouldn't go to sleep last night. I feel exhausted already."

"Once we've taken off there'll be 13 hours when you can make up for it if you don't want to watch onboard television. All in!" Will rushed back into the house, returning out of breath. "Seat belts on!" They were off.

It was a long ride. There were inevitable delays on the way. They picked up the A12, M25 north, exiting the M4 and bearing left for Heathrow.

"Where are you going?" the driver asked.

"New Zealand!" the children shouted.

"Going for a bit of bungee jumping then?"

"What's that?" Ruth asked.

"I don't think so," Will answered. "A bit scary. There'll be plenty of other exciting things to do and see."

At last, the driver turned right towards the long tunnel leading to the terminal where they began unloading, making sure nothing had been left behind. "Careful Yellow Ted doesn't escape from your hand luggage," Will reminded Ruth as she scrambled down the long step from the vehicle to the pavement. "You know what he's like!"

"He's here." Ruth patted her hand luggage reassuringly.

Will did not want a hiatus before they had even started. "Let's see if we can find trolleys." He looked around him.

Tim saw them first. "Over here, sir."

Grabbing a couple, Will thought he did not want to be addressed as school 'sir' for the whole trip, but he'd attend to that matter later. Looking across to the vast terminal then down to the ticket summary, he was reassured that they were at least at the right terminal before proceeding further.

Gaynor was dismayed by the vast throng of people. "Hold Angela's hand tightly, Tim, and then the pocket of my coat. Don't let go. I need two hands to push the trolley."

Wise advice, Tim thought as he took Ruth's hand, put it on his trolley handle with his own hand over the top. "Let's go!"

At the terminal they looked around. "One floor up for departures. Need to take the lift." Will led the way.

Departures was cathedral-like in size with areas for each airline.

"I want to go to the toilet," interrupted Angela looking uncomfortable.

"I'll take the girls if you'd take Tim." Gaynor looked around. "Over here."

So right from the start, Will thought, *there was the demonstrated need for two adults, one of each sex*. He had been correct in steeling himself to ask for someone to accompany them, as well as providing child company for Ruth. He took Tim's hand. "Come on, Tim, this is our entrance."

Meeting up outside, Will looked around. "We need to find Singapore Airlines booking bay. There's a sign saying it's someway right over to the left." They began pushing their way through the milling crowds, holding on to the children. Eventually their checking-in desks were found. "Got your passports ready?" Will got out the tickets and his and Ruth's passports.

When it was their turn to step forward, Ruth dutifully put her bag on the hold luggage transport rollers as the suitcases were weighed and their destination bands affixed. "Not hand luggage, darling," Will said to Ruth. "The big suitcases go right through to Auckland. We keep hand luggage with us. Careful. Yellow Ted's peeping out. You don't want to lose him." Ruth certainly did not and snatched her little pack off.

As they trekked off to security, Will turned to Gaynor. "Keep the first-leg boarding passes handy. Put the second ones away securely for the Singapore/Auckland leg."

"How do you know all this?" panted Gaynor as they struggled on, keeping a firm hold on her children.

"I may have told you; I went to see my folks in Australia not long before Michelle began to show signs of what we later found was the beginnings of her terminal cancer."

"Of course," Gaynor looked embarrassed.

"Don't be. The travelling was all a mystery to me first time. Follow the signs to security."

At security, everything they carried had to be packed on individual trays including their coats. To Gaynor's dismay, hair-cutting scissors were seized and she was given a ticket saying the scissors could be retrieved in Auckland. No blades over four inches were allowed. Will took out Yellow Ted and gave him to Ruth, knowing she would not want to be separated from her precious teddy-bear companion.

"It's owing to recent hijacking incidents and the Lockerbie bombing," Will said as they took their turns through the screening arch. He turned to Ruth. "This arch will only ping if you have on you a metal object." Will always thought one should explain things to children if it was within their understanding.

They trooped into the departure lounge, staring up at the flight departure monitors, looking for their flight and departure gate which, when it eventually turned up, proved to be a long way. Threading through the duty-free shops, Will stopped to make sure they were going in the right direction. "Got all your bits and pieces?" He looked carefully at what Ruth was carrying, relieved to see the head of Yellow Ted peeping out from her little pack.

Approaching, at last, their departure gate, Gaynor looked out to see their aircraft up alongside the entrance covered ways. She was amazed at its size. To her it looked like a gigantic prehistoric bird, surreal in the night light. "It's enormous!" she exclaimed.

"We'll need passports again, along with our boarding cards when we're called to board." Will began to search for what was needed.

"I want to go to the toilet!" Angela called, jumping about holding herself.

"Again! Oh no. Stay with sir, Tim."

"Don't be long." Will strained to hear what categories were progressively being called to come forward with growing concern.

"Our boarding group's been called but we can board with the last passengers," Will said, giving a sigh of relief as Gaynor finally arrived, fumbling frantically for her family's first-leg boarding cards and passports.

Down the covered boarding ramp, Will observed, "We're the second left turn, the first seems to be for business and first-class passengers." After they had all stepped aboard, he explained, "I booked five seats next to the aisle in a row right at the far end of the aircraft. On my trip to Australia with Michelle, I noticed, on that version of the Boeing, there was an aisle behind the last row with access to toilets, somewhere the children can run around without annoying other passengers. I hope this aircraft's similar."

After some jostling with other passengers, they all got seated. Will looked about. Their plane appeared similar to the one Michelle and he had travelled on.

Eventually, the milling around ceased. They checked that they had found their right seats, stowed their hand luggage before sitting down with a sigh of relief.

All done. While waiting for take-off, Will leaned over and whispered to Gaynor, "I can't be called school 'sir' for the next five weeks. Everybody will think I'm some sort of lord. Call me Will, children as well."

Gaynor looked concerned. "Should we, children and all?"

"Yes please, if you don't mind. It'll be awkward otherwise, especially with my relatives. They'll be casual, down-to-earth, no-nonsense New Zealanders after all these years. I don't want to be thought of as a stuffy Pom."

"All right, if you think it will be easier."

Will gave Gaynor a grateful smile.

They waited expectantly for take-off. Eventually, after the children were getting restive and impatient, constantly asking when, an announcement came over that they must see their seatbelts were on and hand luggage properly stowed. Then the engines roared up. The suspense was palpable.

The plane taxied to the top of the runway and waited. Then it was off, vibrating, hurtling down the runway. Will became aware that Gaynor was trembling. He changed Ruth to the other side of him, took Gaynor's hand and squeezed it. He too was feeling apprehensive. Michelle had been a strong, confident personality. Only now was he beginning to realise how much he had depended on her, especially when travelling. With her, he never felt apprehensive. But Gaynor was different, she was younger and less experienced. On the other hand, she had ability, and Will felt she would soon find her feet and develop confidence which, as time went by, proved correct. As the plane took off and rapidly gained height, features on the ground becoming increasing small and distant. Will continued to hold Gaynor's hand. They needed each other.

Eventually he said to her that, as for the present the children were still too excited to sleep, they'd better take them round to the back aisle, walk them about a bit, take them to the toilet after which, when taken back to their seats, they might be able to get them off to sleep.

Will was right. After some running about, the children were getting tired. Ruth and Angela, sprawled out in their seats, soon fell asleep, Tim following 20 minutes later. Only Will and Gaynor remained awake. "I wonder where we are?" Gaynor fidgeted restlessly in her seat.

"There's a programme available on the screen in front of you that will tell you. I'll show you how to get it up when I can locate the handset."

"Only over Wroclaw. Where's that?" Gaynor asked.

"Poland. We're going east via Singapore. If you go via Los Angeles, you go west over Greenland. The first leg is a 13 flight either way. I suggest you stretch your legs and freshen up in the toilet. I'll look after the children. When you come back, I'll do the same."

Finally, they tried to settle down, children asleep on each side of them. It was at that point that Will realised Gaynor was breathing over fast, anxious, hyperventilating, she would get ill if she continued in this way for too long. He took her hand and stroked it. She did not mind. "I'll find your headset and see if I can locate some soothing music. Like that?"

Gaynor nodded. Will put the headset gently on her and continued to hold her hand. Eventually her head fell on his shoulder and her rate of breathing slowed. Will felt relieved. He didn't want her unwell before they had hardly started on their five-week trip together.

It was Ruth who woke them up. She wanted to go to the toilet. Gaynor stirred, her normally well-groomed light brown hair tousled. "I'll take her."

"No need to on the plane," Will replied. "I can manage."

"That's what I'm here for."

Will did not argue further. It was nice to hear her positive, wanting to help. When Ruth came back, she wanted to sit on Will's lap. Gaynor got up as if she should be doing something. With his left arm, Will pulled her gently towards him. He found her closeness comforting. It was a long journey. They needed to relax.

When they finally all stirred again it was still dark. "It's one long day and one long night going this way. Two quick days and nights coming back. You can see on the flight progress screen the arcs of daylight and darkness and where the plane is in relationship. I'll show you." Ruth was interested, too, and they all looked. "We're over Turkmenistan. Where's that?" Gaynor observed.

"About halfway. We'll be out of the arc of darkness before long. I can hear activity in the galley. They'll be serving breakfast soon. Better take the children to the toilet now. The toilets will all be engaged for some time after breakfast." Will stood up. "There're still green lights showing on most toilets behind us. Come on, Ruth."

Round in the back aisle, Will turned to Tim to take him into a toilet. "I don't need you to be inside with me. I'm 10 and can manage on my own."

Will was about to say, "All right, but don't lock the door," but Tim was already inside, locking the door. Will shrugged his shoulders and waited. Meanwhile, Gaynor came out of another toilet with the two girls. "Where's Tim?" she asked.

"In the toilet. He said he was 10 and didn't need me."

"And you let him?"

"He was in there in a flash before I could do anything. Are you all right, Tim?" Will called. They heard a muffled cry and the door shake.

"Are you OK, Tim?" Gaynor inquired anxiously.

"Can't open the door!"

"Pull the knob on the door to your right, away from the opening," Will called back.

"I can't. It won't move." They heard the door shake frantically and repeated banging then hysterical shouting. "Let me out. Get me out of here!" Followed by crying.

"Why did you let him?" Gaynor turned on Will.

"I didn't let him!" Will replied, hurt and a little annoyed.

"Well, do something!"

"I'll get a steward. They must have means of getting people out of toilets if they fall ill. Hang on, I will be as quick as I can."

Within three minutes, Will was back with a male senior steward carrying a gadget which he clamped on the door. Within seconds, the was door opened. Tim rushed out, clung to his mother, and glared balefully at Will as if it were his fault. Sometimes, Will felt, one just could not win.

When breakfast was cleared away and they were all back to normal, Gaynor turned to Will. "I'm sorry I shouted at you. I was upset. Sometimes Tim can be headstrong."

"I could see you were. Never mind."

"Thank you." Gaynor looked relieved. They said no more on the subject.

It was now daylight. People stirred and began moving about. Food was served. Six hours later, the pulse of the engine changed. The plane began a sweeping turn to the left. Looking down, Will saw a long, green strip of land and islands. Soon they were told to turn off electrical devices, put their seats upright, stow luggage securely and prepare for landing. It was exciting. The long first leg of their trip was coming to an end. They were beginning the glide into Changi Airport, Singapore.

Descending to lower altitudes, the plane began to buck and swoop in turbulent up and down draughts, and they were told to ensure their seatbelts were tight. The children were torn between excitement and apprehension.

Will put his arm around Ruth. "Like a funfair ride, dear."

Ruth was not so sure. "My ears hurt."

"Try to yawn. It will help."

The rollercoaster ride continued for what seemed a long time until they were aware of the plane rushing amongst the treetops. Next moment they were over an airfield, the tarmac tearing by, then a jarring bump, and another. Gaynor gave a stifled cry. Will took her hand and held it tight.

"It's OK. Hold on, brakes will come on in a second."

They did, along with reverse thrust, followed by shuddering. Anything not secured was thrown to the floor. They had landed. An announcement came over that everybody must remain in their seats until the seat belts signs were finally turned off.

When the signs were off, Will and Gaynor stood up, making sure they got all their hand luggage from the overhead lockers before joining the long queue to disembark. Stepping into the tunnel leading up to the terminal, they were greeted by a rush of hot air to remind them they were now in the tropics.

"Where are we?" asked Gaynor as they followed the crowd up into the air-conditioned terminal building.

"Our second leg tickets say we depart for Auckland from Terminal Three. We need to find out what terminal this is." Will looked around him.

"What's a Sky Train? Is it a train in the sky?" asked Ruth, pointing to a sign ahead surrounded by blinking lights.

"Good girl. That's what we're looking for, 'Sky Train for Terminal Three'. No, it's a light railway on a raised railway line. Make sure you don't lose your little pack with Yellow Ted. Like me to carry it for you?"

"I want to carry Yellow Ted. A train in the sky?"

"You'll see. Hold my hand tightly."

"Can you wait a minute!" Gaynor called. "Tim, you've let go of your sister's hand! Come on, Angela. We don't want to lose you."

God forbid we lose anyone, Tim thought to himself. *That'd be the last straw!*

The elevated railway took them on a tour of the airport, leaving them looking down at areas of lush tropical garden and airport support activities as it sped along.

Suddenly Will was aware of an automated announcement. 'Terminal Three next stop.' "Got your hand luggage, Ruth? Everyone ready to get off."

"Hear that!" Gaynor echoed, swaying on a shoulder-high support strap.

Bundling out, they found themselves in what seemed like a carpeted street extending into the far distance. They followed the surging crowd, eventually coming to numbered departure gates, shops and airport lounges. It was a long walk. They were all tired after their flight. As they had a four-hour wait until their next flight, Will thought that a comfortable airport lounge with eating and toilet facilities would be just the thing. He suggested they looked out for Air Singapore Lounge. Eventually, on the left, a sign appeared saying Singapore Airways Lounge was up chrome stairs, or passenger could take an adjacent elevator or lift. "This way," Will said.

At the top, they found they were in an extensive glassed foyer leading to a luxuriant lounge where they glimpsed tables of food and relaxing seating areas. There was a desk in front. Will went up to the desk where he was asked for their onward flight tickets. These were examined and he was quoted a large entrance sum.

"So much?" he protested.

It was then patiently explained to him that the lounges were for business and first-class ticket holders, part of what they paid to travel in classes costing five times or more that of economy. They were welcome as well but at a cost. Since Michelle had died, Will had saved quite a bit as he did not have the heart to holiday on his own with Ruth but, after paying for them all including return fares, he could not outlay a lot more, bearing in mind there were five weeks in New Zealand ahead.

Embarrassed, he turned away. "For first and business-class travellers," he muttered to the others. "Let's find our departure gate. We'll wait there. We might find a reasonably priced restaurant on the way. In any event, food will be served when we're in the air again."

Unlike Heathrow, they did not come across any cheap and cheerful cafes, only exotic and expensive regional restaurants. They would have to wait.

On the way, Angela said she needed to go to the toilet. She seemed to require the toilet more often than the other children. Frustratingly there was not one to be seen. Will knew there were always toilets at departure gates. "Hold on!" They hurried to find their departure gate.

As predicted at their gate plenty of toilets were signposted. Gaynor took Angela to one of the toilets while the others waited not far away. There they waited and waited.

Suddenly they were startled by a piercing scream. Gaynor rushed out shrieking, "I can't find Angela! One moment she was beside me at the basins washing her hands. I looked up to put lipstick on. When I looked down, she was gone! Disappeared completely! Have you seen her? We've got to find her!" Gaynor was beside herself.

Will rushed forward. "We haven't seen her. We were chatting, waiting for you both to come out. You wait by the toilet where she was last seen while I go to the information desk to ask for an immediate search. I'll give the authorities her description, including what she's wearing. She'll be found."

When Will, Tim and Ruth returned, Gaynor was pacing up and down, beside herself with anxiety. "I've looked in all the unoccupied closets and hammered on the doors of the occupied. She was with me at the handbasins one moment. I looked up at a mirror to put on lipstick, when I looked down, she was gone! How could that be? She just vanished into thin air?"

"There'll be some explanation. She can't leave the terminal. She'll be found."

"She's been abducted in somebody's suitcase. You hear of these things." Gaynor began to shake uncontrollably. Will put his arm about her while Tim grabbed his mother and took her hand. "I can't leave here without her!"

"And I wouldn't think of travelling on to New Zealand without you. The authorities will find her. Singapore is a small island. Until she's found, everybody leaving will have their suitcases searched." Will did his best to console Gaynor.

Gaynor wrung her hands, still pacing frantically about. Will took hold of her again. Gaynor could not be pacified. Time stood still. Tim and Ruth fretted. They were upset, tired and hungry. Will looked around desperately, searching for inspiration, for someone to help, anything. He felt so helpless, especially in a foreign country. At least the airport staff spoke English.

After what seemed an eternity, Will heard their names being called over the public address system to report to the information desk. Running desperately towards it, they could see two smart paramilitary Chinese or Malaysian policemen in beige uniforms holding between them Angela, who did not seem too greatly distressed.

"Angela!" Gaynor shrieked. At the sound of her mother's voice, Angela began to cry. "Where have you been? What happened to you? We've been out of our minds!" She took Angela into her arms.

At the sight of the reunion, the policemen smiled. They turned to Will, looking pleased. "We need to see your passports and travelling documents."

"Of course," Will replied, greatly relieved.

"So, this is—?" indicating Angela.

"Angela McDonald."

"And you are?"

"Will Whitby. Gaynor McDonald is the mother."

The policeman looked curious but made no further comment. *Good job*, Will thought, *that we weren't in some strict Islamic country otherwise we might have been in real trouble.*

When the policemen left, Gaynor turned to Angela, still sobbing big tears. "Whatever happened to you, darling? Where have you been?"

Angela clung to her mother emotionally, unable to explain what happened. They learnt subsequently, from what they could put together that, acting on impulse, Angela had decided to run out and join the rest of them waiting outside while her mother was doing her face. Not immediately seeing them owing to groups of moving people, she had kept on running and got herself inextricably lost in the vast milling terminal, seeming even larger to a child. It appeared that someone, noticing her distress, had taken her to the patrolling paramilitary police.

Eventually, after much tearful hugging, Will led them to an information screen featuring departures to find out how much time they had to check in. To their utter dismay, they saw that their departure gate had now closed. They had missed their onward flight.

Depressed, they trudged back from the departure area to where, in the vicinity of the Singapore Airport Lounge, Will had noticed a Singapore Airways booking desk. He produced their tickets and explained what happened. The operative at the desk, who had heard about the lost and found child, smiled at Angela, who pointed to herself, not at all abashed.

"I can get you on the next flight to Auckland. It'll land at three in the afternoon, New Zealand time, business class."

Will's face fell. "I can't afford business class for five."

The operative again smiled. "Oh no, you won't be paying any more than you've paid already. It's only business class that has the space. It's better you take the seats than they remain empty."

"Really?" It was Will's turn to smile. "Well, in that case, we'd be delighted. Thank you very much."

Will was over the moon. This was luxury he had never dreamt of. Though tired, he walked away with a spring in his step.

They were told that their new departure gate was nearer this time and in the opposite direction, designated by a large, red-lit number where, when it opened, they would have to present their tickets at a bureau in exchange for boarding cards, after which they must go through security before proceeding to their departure lounge.

Will felt that he didn't want the embarrassment of going up again to the Singapore Lounge, though with the new tickets they held they would have had the right to do without further payment but wait instead in the vicinity of their departure gate.

On the way they had time to marvel at their surroundings. To their right were magnificent indoor gardens, complete with shimmering pools, trees, waterfalls and banks of flowers of bedazzling colour. Will thought it nothing less than a version of the Hanging Gardens of Babylon. Interspersed were glittering boutiques and shopping malls.

"A magic forest!" Ruth exclaimed as she looked in wonder.

"A garden of enchantment," Gaynor echoed.

Fascinating as it was, though they had three hours to put in, Will felt they'd better not linger too long but be at their boarding gate in good time, to be ready when it opened, particularly in view of what happed last time. He did not want any further of his party lost, locked in toilets, or doing something else daft that he so far hadn't envisaged.

When their gate eventually opened, they were they one of the first up to the bureau to show their passport and tickets in return for boarding passes. Then it was on to security. Everything portable was to be put in trays, including Will's belt and shoes. When Ruth's little pack was put in a tray, Yellow Ted was taken out of her pack and given to her.

As they assembled at the boarding gate, their boarding passes were looked at. Observing them to be business class, they were beckoned to the front, behind first class and those with special needs. They felt most important.

Before long, they were beckoned to the boarding desk. Here their passports and boarding cards were again examined, the children having to take off their hats. Angela did not want hers off, feeling it was going to be taken off her for good and refused. Will groaned inwardly, *Not another scene*. Fortunately, Angela was convinced that it would be given back to her and relented. Beyond the examining desk, in the boarding tunnel, Will was keen to direct them to the first entrance on the left leading to the first and business-class compartments where cabin attendants, the women in long sinuous dresses, led them to their seats, addressing them by their names, which the attendants were expected to remember.

Their seats turned out to be seating and sleeping consoles, luxurious and ingenious. They were each ushered into their own and shown where to stow their hand luggage and were asked if they wanted their coats taken. The children were delighted and jumped about in their consoles as if they were play areas. Two were near the window and three were opposite across the aisle. Gaynor smiled across at Will. This flight was going to be very different from the last.

It took a while for the remaining passengers to board, but eventually they were ready for take-off. The pilot's voice came over the public address system, introducing himself and giving a flight resume. After that they were told to fasten seatbelts and ensure their luggage was safely stowed. Flight attendants came round to check. It was all very novel and exciting.

After take-off and the islands had faded from view, attendants came round to take dinner orders. Will and Gaynor helped the children. It was to be a five-course silver service. They had to cut out some of the hors d'oeuvres. By the time the food began to appear, the children had fallen asleep. It had been a long day.

The children had to be woken up to eat. They had eaten little all day, and, in any event, their beds needed to be made up properly. Trays were pulled out, tablecloths and table napkins arranged before courses were slowly served, ending with fruit or desserts of choice, at the end of which Will and Gaynor asked if the children's beds could be opened out and made up. Fascinated, they watched as the beds were pulled out from the top of the seats, leaving a triangular cut-out to stand in beside chest-high doors opening out into the aisles. Blankets were produced. Will found the flight rather cold. The children were more than ready for sleep and snuggled down in their compartments that could have accommodated two adults or up to four little children. When the children were asleep, Will and Gaynor looked at their television sets. Before long, they too felt tired and asked for their beds to be made up.

When all was quiet and lights dimmed, Will went across to Gaynor's console, asking if he could join her for a bit. She opened her door and beckoned him in. He lay down beside her. She snuggled up close to him contentedly.

"Were you really going to stay with me in Singapore if Angela couldn't be found for a number of days?" she whispered.

"Of course. Anyway, I'm not much good on my own."

Gaynor snuggled closer and sleepily murmured. "Me either?"

"It was very worrying."

"You were a brick."

Gaynor's head fell on Will's shoulder. Will let it lie there.

Suddenly Will woke up. He must have fallen asleep as well. He should not be found here by the cabin staff or the children. Putting Gaynor gently aside, he crept quietly into his own console where he fell quickly asleep, lulled by the throb of the engines.

Unlike the last long flight when sleeping proved difficult, especially for the adults in normal plane seats, on this leg, in proper comfortable beds, Will could have gone on sleeping longer when the cabin lights were put on. Flight attendants came round and began packing up beds and serving breakfast to those already up, based on orders taken the night before.

At one point during the early hours, which was not actually night where they were in the skies, passengers having been asked to keep their blinds drawn to allow for a period of sleep, Will checked on Ruth only to discover she was not in her bed. Choking down panic, he took a deep breath. There was no way Ruth could have left business class. All the cabin attendants knew her. Looking around, he noticed every toilet was displaying green lights so she could not be locked in a toilet. Will got up, checked the toilets only to discover Ruth snuggled up with Angela. Gently, without waking either girl, he lifted Ruth into her own console and covered her up, giving a sigh of relief before going back to sleep in his own comfortable console.

In the end, next morning, Gaynor and Will had to wake the children up to eat their breakfast and get ready for landing, breakfast being served in the same silver service manner as dinner the night before. Breakfast had hardly been cleared away when an announcement came over that everyone had to return to their seats, ensure landing and agricultural cards had been completed, make sure seats were in an upright position and prepare for landing. There was a last-minute scramble to find a vacant toilet – there was always a great demand for toilets after meals, especially breakfast.

As the plane noticeably lost height and the engine beat quietened, cabin attendants circulated to see everyone was back in their seats, belts on and hand luggage stowed safely. Looking out, Will could see a long strip of green land, white surf beaches, followed by an extensive turquoise harbour. Landing wheels clumped down. The plane slowly circled, seemingly preparing to land on the water. At the last moment, a landing strip appeared beneath their wheels, extending out into the water. Next instant, the plane bumped down, rushing headlong forward until abruptly brought up by the roaring reverse thrust of the engines. Then it coasted up to a long grey/white building. They had at long last reached their destination.

Passengers began removing their seat belts. To their surprise, they were all commanded to stay in their seats. Then abruptly the end cabin doors opened. Two flight attendants slowly walked the aisles, holding up cans of hissing aerosol disinfectant which made some passengers cough. They learnt later that this was bug spray.

Suddenly Ruth shrieked out that she did not have Yellow Ted. She tried to struggle out of her seat to find him. A cabin attendant came over to her. On no account was she to leave her seat until instructed, but if the party stayed after the rest had left, the plane toilets would be searched, and Yellow Ted would be found. Will thought that he could strangle Yellow Ted. But could a teddy bear be strangled? He would probably survive the ordeal to haunt him for the rest of his life. Due to the errant ways of Yellow Ted, they were going to be last off the plane to collect their luggage!

Chapter Six

Fortunately, Yellow Ted was soon found. Clutching him separately, Ruth and Will led the way up the disembarking tunnel into Auckland Airport's International Terminal. Their fellow passengers were nowhere in sight. Angela and Ruth could not walk quickly owing to their age; however, there being no others about, they could not get lost either. It was a long way to baggage reclaim during which they had time to take in the arresting paintings of New Zealand scenes and life covering the walls as they walked by.

Ultimately the passageway opened out into a tax-free retail hall which they made their way through, looking for the sign to baggage reclaim, only to find their carousel going round and round empty with no one about. Concerned they looked about for their hold suitcases to eventually discover them lifted off to one side. Will then searched for airport trolleys, having to walk some way before two were discovered. When found, he brought them over after which they all headed for the border control desks. With the other passengers having gone through there was no waiting, the smallest of their party having to be lifted up to be seen while passports, landing cards and prohibited food and plants forms were examined.

"Remember what I said, absolutely no food of any sort like crumbling biscuits or fragments of chocolate in pockets," Will announced.

"No, sir," Gaynor replied with a grin.

"There's a lovely dog," Ruth exclaimed as they approached another check area signposted 'Agriculture'.

Ruth was right. There was a small, eager dog on a lead pulling a handler, darting amongst people and their luggage, whether pulled pushed or on trolleys. Will thought it was sniffing out drugs but later found out it was sniffing for food or plant products. Unexpectedly it appeared quite interested in Will's big hold suitcase which was marked before it went into the scanner with the others. When all their luggage was through, Will's suitcase was selected to be carefully examined, and an attractively boxed present was brought out. To Will's embarrassment, it had to be opened to reveal a traditionally clad corn dolly. To his further embarrassment, he was told it must be steam fumigated and would be posted on to the intended recipient, brother Ted, Will having to provide the address and pay the cost, meanwhile being watched by the others suppressing grins. *Sod's law*, he reflected bitterly, *it would have to be me!*

After all that, they were now free to proceed to the hall where friends and relatives waited for arriving passengers. As most arrivals had now left, Will looked across at the few members of the public still waiting, trying to identify his brother. Scanning the crowd, he could not recognise anyone with a family resemblance or his New Zealand wife, Layla, who he had seen in photos.

"Where have you been? We were beginning to feel you weren't being allowed into the country?"

Startled, Will looked back over his left shoulder. He had not noticed the small group standing on the other side of the roped-off oval behind them.

"I'm Ted and this is my wife, Layla."

Will was confronted by his brother, who he hardly recognised, not having seen him since he was a young child. Ted was bigger than him, in his seventies, a little overweight, with a shock of grey-brown hair. Beside him was as a small, slim woman with long straight hair, of similar age, in brown slacks and a tight red top, who Will took to be Layla. Will envied Ted's abundant hair. Though he was 15 years younger, his own dark, slightly wavy hair was beginning to thin.

Will extended his hand but instead was grabbed round the shoulder and given a bear hug. "We don't do Pommy handshakes here, mate. Introduce us to your girlfriend and the children."

"This is Gaynor McDonald. She is not my girlfriend but a colleague – just a friend. We have pooled resources, so to speak, to make the trip possible. Gaynor's son, Tim, her daughter, Angela, and my daughter, Ruth."

Gaynor smiled but stood back. She did not want a bear hug. In her smart blue trouser suit with carefully groomed brunette hair, she was in marked contrast to Layla's rather worn appearance. Being 10 years younger than Will, in relation his cousin and his wife, she was of a younger generation.

Ted looked as if he did not believe a word about Gaynor not being his girlfriend but did not comment further, turning his attention to the children instead saying, in an avuncular manner, stretching out his arms, "And these are your children."

The children's response was to stand back, uncertain. They did not want a great bear hug either from a big man they did not know. In time they would get to know and like Uncle Ted, finding him to be generous, big-hearted and fun to be with and their response would alter accordingly. "You, Will, stay and look after the luggage. The others come with me while I get the Holden and bring it round." Away from the airport, Gaynor found the air surprisingly warm and humid for wintertime. They walked along a covered way, signed as short-stay parking, to a square beige Holden which proved to have just about enough room for them all and their luggage. Back at the entrance, Will leant to help Ted still struggling to fit the remainder of their luggage into the vehicle.

All packed in, sitting back with Gaynor, Will looked around as the car drove away. His first impression was of space and luxuriant green growth. Tall palms lined the wide carriageway leading away from the airport terminal buildings. Suddenly he remembered that they had forgotten to retrieve Gaynor's confiscated long hairdressing scissors but decided not to mention it as they could soon buy another pair if required.

"We turn left at the first major roundabout heading for the city," Ted announced in his acquired Kiwi drawl. "There's a modern bridge over the Tamaki at Panmure these days. Takes no time to get into the city compared with when there was an old swing bridge." Looking about him, Will became aware of arms of water. Later he learned that at high tide there was barely a third of a mile separating the Waitemata Harbour on the east with the Manukau on the west, hence the name Tamaki Isthmus.

After another 10 minutes, Ted turned sharply right at a roundabout then left. Will noticed that they were now in a verdant suburb featuring elegant homes set back in large gardens.

"When I was young, in Auckland there were no downtown city buildings over three stories owing to earthquakes but in the sixties and seventies, the Japanese showed us how to build skyscrapers on flexible foundations. The city's skyline looks different these days. We're approaching Newmarket then Parnell." Ted continued his guided tour as they swept into the city.

Gazing about them, they noticed signs like Britomart Place and Viaduct Basin. Then they observed Ted was joining what was signed 'The Northern Motorway' and glimpsed water on the right which Ted said was St Marys Bay. A promontory appeared ahead. "Westhaven," Ted announced. "The Harbour Bridge." Soon they were over bright blue water.

"What a superb view!" Gaynor exclaimed.

"Got to keep to the second to left lane. We leave the motorway at the Esmonde Road interchange. The bridge connecting the city to North Shore was completed in '59. Before long, it couldn't meet demand, and Japanese contractors added two additional outer lanes known as 'Nippon Clippons' making it eight lanes in all," Ted's commentary continued.

Will looked up at the great central arch towering above him and down at the water far below. It certainly was an impressive structure and the breathtaking view up and down the harbour, as Gaynor had observed, simply superb.

"We turn south to our right into Lake Road for Narrow Neck and Devonport. I live in Merani Street,

Narrow Neck. It's called Lake Road as it used to run up to Lake Pupuke, a freshwater crater lake between Takapuna and Milford. Now the road goes right up the East Coast Bays and beyond."

Will looked about. They were passing through well-off suburbs with especially beautiful homes on rising ground to the left. Looking at a detailed map before he left, Will knew that the southern end of North Shore was in fact a narrow peninsula between the Waitemata Harbour and the Hauraki Gulf, ranging in width from a mile to three or four. Owing to its narrowness in places, only one through road ran its entire length leading to congestion in the rush hour which they were now experiencing.

"I want to go the toilet," Angela announced.

"The nearest toilet is at the southern end of Takapuna Beach, dearie," Ted said. "It'll take longer to try to turn round in this traffic and go back than it will to go on to my place, we're already up to Hauraki Corner. You'll have to wait."

"Can't wait," Angela responded.

"Hold on!" Gaynor fumbled in her hand luggage stuffed under her legs and came up with an empty plastic ice cream carton complete with lid.

Holding Angela in one hand on her lap and the ice cream carton under her, Gaynor said, "Go into that."

"Angela's Ice Cream Special," Tim joked.

"Not in front of sir!" Gaynor was embarrassed and indignant.

"You told me to call him Will while we were away," Tim replied flippantly.

"Sir William is it now," Ted drawled, entering the conversation.

"School speak," Will mumbled. The whole episode was getting out of hand.

"We're turning into Old Lake Road now, Old Lake Road as it was the first road north until the causeway was built from Mount Victoria," Ted continued.

After four hundred yards or so, highlighted in the sunset, a beautiful beach appeared, backed by what Will learnt later were pohutukawa trees.

"That's Narrow Neck Beach ahead, but we're going left into Merani Street, second street above, our house is two-thirds of the way up on the left."

After three hundred yards, Ted stopped at an off-cream painted bungalow. They were invited inside. Pausing on the veranda, looking back over the Gulf, they were awed by the spectacle of the setting sun highlighting conical Rangitoto Island, two nautical miles offshore.

"We'd invite you to stay with us while you were in Auckland, but we haven't the room for two families. Layla's got an evening meal ready for you after which I'll take you to a villa I've hired in your name at the Gulf Horizons motel on the Takapuna foreshore. It's in a stunning location and has plenty of room. I'm sure you'll enjoy it."

Will was sure he would, but he felt that he might not find the cost of paying for it such an enjoyable experience and would have preferred to have been consulted. But then he supposed Ted meant well in taking the time and trouble.

Stepping inside, they were led past what appeared to be two front bedrooms, with a sitting room on the right into a large kitchen/dining room. They were invited to sit round an equally large table on which Layla placed a quiche Lorraine and what Will learnt later was a kingfish quiche, along with a huge salad to which everyone was asked to help themselves. Sitting down, Will observed smaller study, computer and needlework rooms off to the right.

"Does that soft toy have to accompany Ruth to the table?" Ted queried.

"He's not a soft toy," Ruth responded indignantly. "He's Yellow Ted!"

Ted was about to say something like, 'You could have fooled me,' when Layla put her hand on his and motioned him to be quiet.

The visitors seized on the food and quickly ate. They were very hungry. While eating, Will had time to observe Layla and the way she related to Ted. It was obvious that Ted did the talking for both of them. But what was not so obvious was that Layla, in her own quiet way, was a force to be reckoned with. Unlike Ted, she came from an old, well-established New Zealand family. She had confidence in her identity and thought Ted a bit over the top with his overtly Kiwi image but was fond of him, appreciating his caring warm heart, but wincing at times when he came out with sayings like 'I'm a box of birds' for professing he was feeling well, which she felt was out-dated and wouldn't be understood by visitors to New Zealand, or even young or new New Zealanders for that matter.

It was quite dark when Ted came to drive them to their waterfront villa, with lights from the shore twinkling in the harbour though it was still early in the evening. Of course, it was winter, Will realised.

"After Hauraki Corner keep in the right-hand lane or you'll find yourself going off to the city and won't find it easy to turn back," Ted advised. A mile or so later he announced, "Now here at Halls Corner take the second road right at the junction into Hurstmere Road, follow along"—Will noticed they were now driving along a pretty tree-lined street with shops and businesses either side—"until you'll turn right at the Mon Desir here." Will felt he would never remember all these instructions but, come the time, he would use a detailed map. "Turn left at the very bottom by the boat ramp. Don't go further or you'll drive into the sea."

Will thought he would be unlikely to do that. "Your villa is three or four along on the left. You can't miss it. It has a lychgate. Trying to be old-worldy, if you know what a lychgate is?"

Will did but he wondered if Ted really did. Lychgates seemed inappropriate before a private house, being designed in times long gone by to shelter coffins at the entrance to churches prior to a burial. However, as they slowly approached, Will observed in the car lights that it did indeed have an imitation lychgate. "You'll find tea and coffee, milk, welcoming biscuits and probably chocolates. It's tradition here in New Zealand," Ted continued. "In the morning, once we've picked up your hire car at Albany, there's a bonzer food mall in Anzac Street, drive there. You'll find fruit from the Islands you've probably never heard of. Call for you at ten. Hooray." With that Ted and Layla were off.

There were seven or eight steep steps up to the front door with no handrail on either side, making getting up the luggage difficult and dangerous for the children. Will found a note under the porch light telling them where the keys were and how to turn off the alarm.

Inside, the place was a dream with spacious rooms and more than enough accommodation for two families. Ted had explained that it was not the usual, large New Zealand-style villa but a replica of a Cape Cod mansion, complete with balcony and widow's walk. In the fridge in the kitchen in the rear of the house, they found fresh milk and nearby tea, coffee and drinking chocolate. On a table big enough to seat 12 or more was a welcoming note, a large box of chocolates and an equally large bouquet of lovely blooms. Beyond the table, the kitchen merged into an extensive conservatory area reaching out into a garden.

After drinks and chocolates, Will and Gaynor went about to agree on rooms, the children, excited to explore, following. They went upstairs.

"What a spacious room!" Gaynor exclaimed, looking all around then going out onto the balcony. "And the view!" Will joined her, staring out at the vast Hauraki Gulf, dark and mysterious in the moonlight, with Rangitoto Lighthouse flashing red every 12 seconds. "It must be breathtaking in the light of day."

"I'm sure. We'll see in the morning." Will went back into the room to examine the adjacent en suite. "Look at the size of that bath. Ruth could swim in it. We would have had to watch that she didn't drown in it when she was a toddler!"

"I've never seen anything like it." Gaynor leant down to examine the tiling.

"Neither have I," Will admitted. "Would you and your children like the upstairs?"

"No, I couldn't. You're paying for the place. There's at least three bedrooms downstairs, a very large one to the left of the sitting room. There are three of us."

"All right, shall we go downstairs? The children are getting tired," Will agreed and they trooped into the sitting room. Will tried the television. After fiddling he got a number of stations, very few compared with Britain.

The children were weary, beginning to flop about. "Time we got them to bed," Gaynor observed.

"OK," Will concurred, sweeping up Ruth and Yellow Ted and taking them upstairs. "See you in the lounge later."

"I won't be long," Gaynor yawned, "my lot are asleep already."

Gaynor was back in the lounge when Will came down. He was going to sit in one of the unoccupied sofas or easy chairs, but the way Gaynor looked up at his entrance drew him instinctively into sitting alongside her on a sofa. Then it felt suddenly strange. Here they were, sharing a home with a growing family as if they had been married for 20 years. But the fact was they did not really know each other, owing to the arrangement they had, meeting when Will came to collect Ruth when he had to stay on in the evenings. Gaynor had been employed by Will for approximately two years as a teachers' assistant, having formerly been a voluntary parent helper. It was not as if she had been Will's deputy or principal secretary, in which position they would have worked together closely and would have got to know each other well, professionally at least.

"It's been an exhausting 24 hours," Gaynor said, stretching.

"It certainly has. It's this time change, what it does to the body clock. I doubt I'll sleep, even though I feel worn out."

Without quite realising it, they found themselves sitting shoulder to shoulder, companionably supporting each other. Time went by.

Abruptly Gaynor sat up. “I’d better go to bed. Your brother Ted is coming for us at ten.”

“I guess I should do the same,” Will agreed yawning, getting to his feet.

Instinctively, he put out his hand to help Gaynor up, perhaps being used to doing this for Michelle.

Whether it too was by instinct or not, Will did not know, but what he realised was Gaynor had lightly kissed him on his cheek before she stumbled off to her bedroom, leaving Will with a warm feeling as he felt his way upstairs. Though tired, Will tossed and turned before finally falling asleep to the murmur of the waves below.

He felt he had been only asleep 10 minutes when Yellow Ted was thrust in his face followed by a gentle kiss from Ruth who had squirmed across from the other side of their enormous bed. It was light, and the alarm said five to eight. He had better get up pronto. They had to be away by ten. If he had his own way, he would not have engaged a hire car until the following day, but Ted had meant well in setting him up with a rental home and car in advance. After Will had shaved and showered and Ruth had what amounted to a swim in the enormous bath, they stumbled downstairs to find Gaynor and her children already in the kitchen.

“I’ve found some muesli and we have milk.” She handed him a bowl. “Ruth like the same? Tea or coffee?” To Will’s surprise, she leant over and gave him a light kiss before bending down and giving Ruth a good morning hug, humouring her by administering

Yellow Ted a peck when he was thrust in her face. "Sleep well, dear? Comfy in that enormous bed?"

"Yellow Ted got lost."

"I'm glad he was found." Gaynor turned to Will. "Do you think I could ring Mother to tell her I've arrived safely in New Zealand?"

Will took out his newly acquired Nokia mobile phone. "I don't really know if this would connect with Britain. I could try, though I've not really got the hang of it." He got out his phone and began to fiddle.

"There's a phone on the wall in the sitting room," Gaynor observed.

"Yes, try that." Will was relieved. He did not really want to demonstrate his lack of technical knowhow.

"What about the cost?"

"It'll go on the bill. Don't forget, there's a 12-hour time difference, 13 hours, in fact, as Britain's on summer-time." Will looked at his watch. "Nine o'clock, it'll be eight in the evening back home. The code for Britain is 44, leave out the first nought."

"Not too late then."

"Not too late." Will turned to take Ruth upstairs. They had better be getting on. "I'll take Yellow Ted and your muesli."

Back up in their great room, while Ruth ate the remainder of her muesli, Will went out on the balcony to take in the view in daylight. He gasped at the panorama before him. To his right, below the tops of exotic palms in the foreground, lay the curving sweep of mile-long Takapuna Beach, backed by what he learnt were evergreen pohutukawa trees. In front of him, the deep blue Gulf, reflecting the blue of the sky, extended out to a distant horizon, interspersed with islands great and small. Nearer, the thousand-foot volcanic Rangitoto Island dominated the scene.

While he was gazing, he became aware that Ruth had joined him. "I wondered where you were."

"I've read that Rangitoto Island, remembered in Maori tradition, rose from the sea only six hundred years ago."

"The sea?"

"The seabed, there were earthquakes, the sea began to steam and boil, and Rangitoto Island appeared. It grew and grew until it became the size it is today. I'd like to visit it while we're here. Have you finished your muesli, dear?"

"Yes, I'd like a proper breakfast."

"That reminds me, we need to get food later. We must get moving. It's twenty to ten. I'm told there can be sudden sharp showers in Auckland. We'd better include in your day bag, along with Yellow Ted, a light cardigan and raincoat. I'll carry your bag."

Downstairs he found Gaynor ready with her children. "Good, I'd really rather spend the day loafing on the beach. The children don't appear jet-lagged but I do. But I guess we need the car today to go out to that food mall Ted described."

"We've a lovely kitchen. I've just been looking at it," Gaynor said enthusiastically.

"I didn't ask you to accompany us just for your cooking skills. But I always appreciate good home-cooked meals, that's for sure. If you'd care to take the children outside and wait on the top step, I'll duck back and put on the alarm. By the way, got light raincoats, it can be cold during showers. You'll need enough to keep warm."

Gaynor said she had. Will quickly went inside, put on the house alarm and equally quickly returned, shutting the front door before the alarm went off. On the top step, where they had a good view, they waited for Layla and Ted.

More or less on time, their car hove into view. Shepherding the children down, they waited under the lychgate. *Good job we aren't elderly*, Will thought, *those steep steps could prove a problem.*

"Good-day, folks, a box of birds this morning, not crook with jet lag?"

"I'm a bit jet-lagged," Will admitted, "but the children seem fine, they're more adaptable at their age. Thanks for coming."

They scrambled into Ted's car. Ted turned right and drove up into the town. Part way up, indicating to the left, Ted observed. "When I was young, on the Shore, I'd great times drinking in the old Mon Desir pub, its lawns swept right down to the water's edge. It'd been there for 90 years or more, gone now for up-market apartments. Those were the days."

"A fair dinkum pity," Layla observed. "It was a traditional place, built in old colonial style. It should have been given heritage status – money!"

Partway down Hurstmere Road, Ted turned unexpectedly right and, after innumerable intersections, joined what he said was the Northern Motorway before turning left off it again. Will had no idea where they were. Ted explained that motorways were mostly restricted to Auckland, though there were a few short lengths in and out of Wellington, the capital, in the south of the North Island. In the sixties, seventies and eighties an ambitious system of fast urban motorways was planned and developed for greater Auckland, including 90 bridges in all, some spanning parts of suburbs situated deep down in narrow gullies.

Will knew from reading up before he came that the population of greater Auckland was disproportionate to the rest of the country, being nearly 1.3 million compared with Wellington, the capital's, 400,000 and Christchurch, the largest city in the South Island's, 300,000. In fact, the whole population of the South Island was only a little over a million.

"We're in Albany," Ted announced. "Now to find Cars-for-All Rental." He stopped and took out a map. "Ah there's one in the Colonie Centre off Latham Road."

Will looked about him. Built around an early settlement, it was now greater Auckland's newest urban area to the north, planned as a spacious mix of businesses, shops, apartments and entertainments within a created environment of parks, lakes, tree-lined streets, paths and cycleways. It was immensely spread out by English standards but, Will considered, lacked character.

"Layla's found the Colonie Centre," Ted announced, indicating Layla who was map-reading beside him. "You'll need passports, driving licences and, Will, your credit card."

Inside the smart, new Cars-for-All Rental office, Will took out his recently acquired North Shore street map and asked the trendy female operative to mark where they were as he would have difficulty finding their office when it was time to return the car. To Will's surprise the girl replied, "Don't worry, sir, just ring us from where you're staying and we'll come and collect it," at which

Will felt annoyed, as it seemed the car would have been brought to them instead of having to go all the way out to Albany. However, he reminded himself, brother Ted meant well. In all probability, he rarely would have had an occasion to hire a car himself and therefore would not have known that a car could be brought to where they were staying. He consoled himself he had seen a bit of Auckland that otherwise it might not have occurred to him to visit and further, out at the site, he could at least pick and choose a car from what was available.

"How about this spacious Toyota Vienta, six cylinder, roomy, ideal for the lot of us and our baggage?" Gaynor suggested, looking around.

Ideal, but for the price? Will thought. *But we do need a spacious car, like brother Ted's Holden.'*

In the end he had to admit that Gaynor's smart blue Toyota Vienta had a lot to recommend it but found the only model available was automatic. "I love automatic cars," Gaynor said enthusiastically.

"I've never driven one," Will admitted.

"I'll soon show you how. They eliminate the whole dimension of gear change, easy." Gaynor's enthusiasm was infectious.

In the end, Will was persuaded to opt for the Toyota Vienta. When it became time to hand the car back, he was not disappointed. He had always intended having Gaynor on the hire agreement as an additional driver in the event of his not being able to drive owing to some temporary problem. After the completion of the paperwork, he felt it might be wise for Gaynor to give him the benefit of her experience before he drove off.

"To start off with there's no clutch. Your left leg is redundant. Automatic cars have what I call a built-in creep. Once you engage a drive, the car moves slowly off so you must always have a brake on to start with. You just pick up speed by releasing the brake and using the accelerator. Start the car, it won't start unless you're in neutral, brake on, select a drive. Give it a go," Gaynor said encouragingly.

Having driven twice round the extensive compound, Will pulled up alongside Ted and Layla to thank them for helping them get the hire car.

"You're on your own now," Ted drawled. "Ask directions to the motorway, making sure you drive south. Remember, your last turning off is the Esmonde Road interchange. Miss that, you have to take the first off-ramp on your left over the bridge and work out how you can get back on the motorway again driving north. We'll invite you back for a day with us at Merani Street in two or three days' time. Maybe you'd like a sail over to and land on Rangitoto Island."

"I certainly would," Will said enthusiastically. "Thanks for all your help since arriving."

"You're welcome."

With that, Will cautiously drove off. After half a mile, he stopped and asked for directions and was told that he needed to make sure he went under the motorway, turning right onto the southern on-ramp. With Gaynor's guidance, using their detailed road map, he made it. "I'll keep an eagle eye open for the Esmonde Road turn-off, it'll be on the left." After two or three miles, Gaynor saw it coming up on the road signs. "Next slip road on the left."

"Wilco," Will acknowledged, relieved. "Now what?"

"Takapuna left, Devonport right," Tim suddenly observed.

"Smart boy," Will responded. "You remembered what Uncle Ted said. Left-hand lane then."

"Uncle Ted and Yellow Ted," Ruth interjected.

"I think you'll find his real name is Edward, Ted for short," Gaynor corrected.

"That's right," Will confirmed. "His proper name is Edward. He just likes to be known as Ted."

"Not like Yellow Ted," Ruth maintained.

"Nobody could be like Yellow Ted," Will agreed with feeling, suppressing dark thoughts about what he could do at times to Yellow Ted.

"Hall's Corner is coming up," Gaynor said, looking at the map. "Remember, Ted said the second road right is Hurstmere, two roads on the right come together at the junction."

"Right oh," Will acknowledged.

"Then straight through the next roundabout. After that, down to the right at the Mon Desir apartments."

At the waterfront, Will said, "Why don't we turn round and go to that food mall and stock up with food for the week? Then we're done for the day. I seem to remember Ted said it was on Anzac Street."

Retracing their route, they found they could not go straight on at the first roundabout but had to turn right into the back of Takapuna. Ever resourceful, Gaynor eventually found a huge food store in Anzac Street where they were confronted by a range of food such as they'd never see before.

"If you keep an eye on the children, I'll choose the food. Anything in particular you want?"

"You know more about cooking than me. I'd probably miss something essential like cooking oil as we're starting from scratch," Will agreed.

Although quite crowded, the supermarket was nothing like an international airport for congestion. Will found looking after the children the easier option. The bill came to 250 dollars, about 125 pounds for the two families, starting from nothing. Will considered the amount more than reasonable.

When all the food was taken inside and stored, Will drew a sigh of relief. Still feeling jet-lagged, he felt he had done enough for the day. But it was two thirty and they had had no lunch. Gaynor said she had better get going and rustle up vegetables quickly in the microwave while pan-searing teriyaki fillets on the oven top in a frying pan, which would take about 12 minutes, six minutes a side, in butter or olive oil with appropriate seasoning. Will was asked to heat a pan and watch it, keeping it covered, telling her when the oil was hot enough. "Turn on to medium to high heat." Will felt a bit like King Alfred and the cakes but felt, unlike King Alfred, he had better watch what he was doing and get it right. "Get a paper towel and dry the fillets. We'll season with sea salt, adding lemon then garnish with dill and parsley, OK?"

It was OK by Will. He examined the pan. "The oil looks hot and ready."

"Season, then pop the fillets in skin side down. I'll put five plates under the vegetables, nice to serve onto hot plates." Will felt happy that they could cook together companionably, a good sign for the future, he felt. "Poke the fish, see if it's ready to turn over." Will felt it was. Gaynor then skilfully turned the fish with a spatula. "Come and sit down, children, lunch is about to be served."

"I don't like fish," Tim said.

"You've never tasted this fish. We don't get it in England. Try it. You must be hungry."

Along with everyone else, Tim ate eagerly. They were hungry.

"How do you know to cook teriyaki?" Will asked after everyone had fallen silent.

"I don't," was Gaynor's simple reply. "The fillets looked like salmon fillets, so I thought I'd try that way, giving them an extra minute a side in the event of their being tougher."

Will was impressed. Gaynor might not have high academic qualifications, but she certainly had practical skills, which for everyday purposes were much more useful.

After washing up, they thought they would go on the beach at last. Will reminded them about the advice he had been given about taking light raincoats. They had only been five minutes on the lovely wide sands when they were buffeted by driving rain. They ran for the shelter of the pohutukawa trees.

"I don't like this," complained Tim.

"Yellow Ted's getting wet," chimed Ruth.

"We're all getting wet," Gaynor reminded them. "But I expect it'll soon be over."

She was right. After 10 minutes the rain stopped as quickly as it came and the sun shone, after which they continued southward along the beach.

With the end of the beach still about half a mile away, Will reminded them that they had the same distance to walk back to their holiday home, and that it fell dark early and quickly, being wintertime though not cold. Somewhat reluctantly they turned back for the northern end of the beach.

It was just as well he did as the children were lagging at the end. In the sitting room they flopped down exhausted. Will put on a radiant heater and the television.

"I guess I'd better get us all something to eat." Gaynor got herself slowly to her feet. "Sandwiches and a salad perhaps?"

"Sounds ideal, need a hand?"

"Keep the children amused, won't be long."

After their meal, Will told the children a story about an inane soft toy, always in trouble, bucking authority, which made Gaynor laugh along with the children.

"I didn't know you could be so much fun," Gaynor commented.

"I haven't always been a headteacher," Will countered. "I enjoyed my time as a class teacher. I used to lighten the school day with a bit of fun on occasions."

"You're not a stiff headteacher now." Gaynor sat down beside him.

"Thank you." Will appreciated the compliment.

The children lay about contentedly, showing they were ready for bed.

"I think I'll take my two." Gaynor put her arm round Angela and extended her hand for Tim. "Come on, darlings, time for bed."

Will decided he would do the same with Ruth. "See you later." He nodded to Gaynor.

Gaynor was in the sitting room when Will returned. She turned off the television. "No need to switch off if you're watching something," Will said.

"It's all right, not the variety we're used to."

"I found CA News the most informative."

"The National News seemed a bit hyped."

"Sort of."

They sat in silence. The end of the day was when their situation together came to the fore. Here they were, middle-aged people, both having been married before. Both would ideally like to marry again for themselves and their children if the right person came along. But they were cautious. They were not in a rush. For a start, Will was 10 years older than Gaynor. Will wanting to see New Zealand with company and support seemed logical, and Gaynor's mother was right in saying it was an opportunity of a lifetime. But was it an opportunity for anything else, or was the unique romance of the holiday tempting them into a relationship they might later regret? They would take their time, see how it all worked out. In the end, events would determine their future.

It had been a long day for adults and children alike. Will was still suffering from jet lag, his body clock not yet synchronised. He felt tired but he knew if he went to bed, sleep would not come. It was comfortably warm by the radiator. Without realising it, he slumped into the corner of the sofa against Gaynor. He didn't know how long he'd been asleep but when he woke with a start, he found he had his arm around Gaynor, and she was asleep with her head on his shoulder. He sat Gaynor gently up.

"Look at the time, two in the morning. If Ruth wakes, she'll be wondering where on earth I am!"

"Mine too," said Gaynor, rubbing the sleep from her eyes.

"Good night, sleep well." It was Will who kissed Gaynor lightly on the forehead this time before hurrying quietly upstairs.

Perhaps it was the warmth of Gaynor's body still with him, plus Ruth snuggling up against him when she sensed Will was in bed, but to his relief, he fell asleep quickly.

Will woke with the alarm at eight. Ruth was still asleep. There was no rush to get up and get away this morning. No one was coming. They had the day to themselves. Will gently drew aside the curtains and opened the glass doors leading onto the balcony to once again to be confronted by the breathtaking view. How glorious it was. There were so many places to visit and things to do. He had better make a list of priorities – consulting with Gaynor. Then he thought how long and easily he had fallen asleep with her on the couch and concluded they were compatible together.

After Ruth's usual swim in the enormous bath and Will had shaved and showered, they went downstairs. Gaynor and her children were in the kitchen beginning breakfast.

"Morning, you two. Sleep well?" Gaynor looked up and instinctively Will kissed her on the forehead before Gaynor bent down to give Ruth a kiss to again have Yellow Ted stuffed in her face to be kissed equally.

"If my friends could see me kissing a teddy bear, they'd think I'd completely lost it," Gaynor observed.

"What we do for children. Sleep well?"

"OK, and you?"

"Better for the first time," Will confirmed. "After breakfast, we could discuss what we might like to do today?"

"OK, after breakfast – cooked, cold or both?" Gaynor moved quickly from stove to working top.

"What's cooking?"

"Sausages, eggs and bacon."

"Sounds delicious. I'll start with the cooked please."

When the children had finished breakfast, Gaynor suggested they put on jackets, go out through the kitchen patio windows and explore the garden, looking across at Will for his agreement.

"Good idea, look, Ruth, Yellow Ted has toppled into the remains of your cereal, sponge him off, dear. I'll get your anorak."

While the children were outside and they were washing up, Will suggested that today they should explore the local area to see what it had to offer, before sightseeing elsewhere. He did not feel, at this juncture, it was the time to explain that, while in the country, he also wanted to find out more about his sister Zoe, who went off to New Zealand with her brother in 1938 when she was 20. That he was hoping, in some way, he might be able to resolve the mystery of the school ghost. Will had heard nothing of her for many years. Gaynor had no knowledge of his disturbing classroom vision. It was going to be a delicate matter explaining it to her when the time came.

"There's a stunning lake nearby, Lake Pupuke, I got a glimpse of it from the car. After exploring the length of the beach perhaps we could take a look at it. It's not far away." Gaynor glanced about to see where she could hang a damp tea cloth.

"Good idea," Will agreed, who was feeling back on form after a better night's sleep.

Down on the beach, raincoats on, they started walking south on the firm sands near the water's edge. "Don't be caught by the last of the waves sweeping up on the sands. It's a bit too chilly for bare feet!" Will advised.

"A bear with bare feet," Tim joked, trying to jerk Yellow Ted out of Ruth's pack.

"Leave Yellow Ted alone, horrid boy." Ruth put Yellow Ted on the other side of her.

Will turned to Gaynor. "Would you and Tim like to walk to the far end of the beach, Tim's a good walker being three years older than the girls. I hear there're changing rooms there, including a toilet. I think the distance might be rather a challenge for the girls. I feel they might prefer to play in the sands up by the pohutukawas, warmer and more sheltered. We could meet back in the villa at twelve?"

"If you don't mind it sounds a good idea, see you about twelve at the villa, hope we don't catch a shower. Enjoy yourselves." With that, Gaynor and Tim strode off.

It was a good idea. Will took a few photos with his newly acquired Fuji digital camera, hoping he had got the operational procedures right. He found new technology difficult, accepting that Gaynor was rather better at it than him.

Near twelve, the skies suddenly darkened and the wind rose. Realising that a shower was imminent, he got the girls to their feet and they ran to the villa, getting there just in time before the skies opened up unleashing a driving shower for 10 minutes. Inside, Will turned on the radiant heater in the lounge. Five minutes later, Gaynor and Tim arrived, gratefully standing by the heater for warmth.

"I'll get lunch in five minutes after we've changed out of our wet clothes." Gaynor took off Tim's wet coat, gently flipping the water to the side.

Will helped Gaynor off with her coat. "You don't always have to cook. I've noticed plenty of restaurants up on Hurstmere Road."

"Kind of you, Will, another time. I think on this occasion the children are better here, they can be themselves, spread themselves around." She turned to the children. "Let's look in the food store, shall we? What would you like?"

"Sausages and chips!" Tim shouted.

"I'm sure we can do better than that. We've got in lovely food, some things we don't get readily or at all in England."

Typical, Will thought, coming into the kitchen behind them, *you shouldn't have asked them what they like.*

"I found this *New Zealand Woman's Weekly* with recipes amongst the magazines in the lounge. How about this sesame salmon skewers recipe with brown rice salad? We've got most of the ingredients or similar. You'd like something tasty, munchy and crunchy off sticks, wouldn't you? Let's see, help me find sesame seeds and oil, I can remember buying them, sea salt, brown rice, salmon pieces, cucumber we can peel into ribbons, bean sprouts, peppers, lime juice or something like it, olive oil and some sort of seasoning." The children scrambled to see what they could find, Tim reading off some of the ingredients to the girls, proud to show off his superior ability. It turned out to be a messy and chaotic business with the children helping, but it kept them occupied. They began to lose interest during the cooking process, but the exercise served its purpose and Will had to admit that the end product proved rather good.

Will washed up while the children sprawled about in the lounge. Gaynor offered to help but Will insisted that the cook should not have to wash up as well. Joining them 15 minutes later in the lounge, Will said, "You were saying after breakfast that you'd like to visit Lake Pupuke. I was looking at the map. You were right. It's not far away. We turn right when we get up onto Hurstmere Road, OK? I think the children have worked off their lunch and are ready for a change. Raincoats again and jerseys! I'll see you, Gaynor, when you're ready, with your children on the top steps."

Will took Ruth upstairs, suggesting she wash as she was sticky helping with the cooking and then they were hurrying downstairs, extra jersey and Yellow Ted as usual in Ruth's little pack.

"Right, we're off!" Will was getting more expert at putting on the alarm and locking up.

Once up on Hurstmere Road, turning right, Gaynor observed, looking at the map, "We bear left at a bend called 'Black Rock', must be a prominent feature, the coastline is just off to the right, and then turn left up Sylvan Avenue, about a mile further along, which leads to the lake. It looks at this point as if there's only about two hundred metres separating the lake from the sea."

At the 'Black Rock' left bend they could see nothing that looked like a black or another sort of rock but what the children did spot, on the other side of the road, was a bungalow in the form of a miniature stone castle complete with crenellations and slit windows. "A dear little castle!" they shouted.

"We'll stop by on the way back," Will answered, "we'll be on the right side of the road then," wondering how anyone got planning permission to build a dwelling in the form of a folly. What he did find out later was that it was built in the early days of settlement, before modern planning laws.

Sylvan Avenue was a gentle climb of about two hundred metres before dipping down to small parking strips between trees. Everyone eagerly got out and walked through the trees towards the water. Bursting into the lake area, the children ran towards the dark lake edge where a number of small yachts and canoes were tied to a wharf, Gaynor urgently running after them.

"Wait for me! The water will be very deep!"

Equally concerned, Will puffed in her wake. On the wharf they took the children's hands. At that moment, a dark cloud appeared overhead with strong gusts rippling across the water which caused sailing dinghies and windsurfers, caught off guard, to whip over or capsize at the same time. The children thought it a funny scene and fell about laughing as rescue boats buzzed out from the shore.

When they had seen enough of the lake shore, Will suggested a stroll in the extensive park to the north. Before turning away, he took a few photos of the lake scene, noting the lovely homes and gardens bordering the lake.

The park or domain, as the locals called it, consisted of undulating grassland interspersed with individual stands of native trees around which the children had fun running around. Eventually, noting the time, Will suggested they had better be moving back to the car. To his surprise, Gaynor said she would like to drive, handing Will the map. At the non-existing Black Rock, Gaynor stopped the car and they got out to view more closely the battlemented bungalow.

Noting the heavy stonework, Gaynor shrewdly observed that it would be no place to be in in the event of an earthquake. Remembering that this was earthquake country, Will agreed.

When they got back to their beachfront home, they got a surprise call from brother Ted saying that good weather was forecast for tomorrow and would they like a sail over to Rangitoto Island, which was just two nautical miles off their Narrow Neck Beach. Will was delighted and agreed. Bring a change of warm clothes, Ted said, just in case.

That evening, for quickness, Gaynor served ready-made meals from the freezer after which she thought she would experiment with red tamarillo fruit. Will thought the fruit originated from Argentina but he noted that, along with passionfruit, they seemed to be grown plentifully locally. Gaynor used the blender and make smoothies. The children watched fascinated as she cut the fruit in half and invited them to scrape out the inside. She then took out milk from the fridge, added strawberry jam and gave the resulting concoction a whirl. Finally, choosing pretty glasses, she put in straws and passed the smoothies around. They proved very popular. She said she would keep half for the morning and next time the children could try their hand at making smoothies themselves, perhaps using passionfruit. Observing all this, Will thought he had made a good choice in asking Gaynor to accompany him to New Zealand. She had a knack of involving the children and keeping them amused.

That evening the children needed no persuasion when it came to bedtime. They had had a long, active day. When Gaynor and Will met up again in the lounge, sitting on the sofa in front of the radiant heater, watching television, they soon felt sleepy. Will put off the television and instinctively they cuddled up at the end of the sofa, putting their feet up on the other end, neither of them wanting to make the first move regarding taking closeness further. The children knew where they were. Will dimmed the lights.

"You're marvellous with the children," Will said.

"You can be fun with them yourself," Gaynor replied.

"We make a good team."

"There's just one thing."

"Yes?"

"I know you're doing the paying."

"I haven't had occasion to spend money since Michelle died. I have the resources."

"That aside, I don't mind going to Ted's tomorrow."

"Yes?"

"But as an equal team member..."

"Yes?"

"Perhaps I should have been consulted."

Will paused, Gaynor was right. "Sorry, I apologise, you should have." With that, Gaynor sighed contentedly.

Next morning, Will woke up early, full of expectations. While Ruth was having her usual morning swim in the enormous bath, Will packed for her a change of warm clothes, doing the same for himself before shaving and showering. Taking Ruth downstairs, he found Gaynor had already got a hot breakfast going. "Good morning, help yourselves to the smoothies I made with the children yesterday, breakfast won't be long."

"Good morning, lovely day." Will gave Gaynor a light kiss on the forehead before greeting Tim and Angela. "Got changes of clothes packed?"

"I hope we won't be needing those."

"Well, just in case." Will thought he noticed a slight terseness in Gaynor's voice and decided to pursue the subject no further.

"I've made sandwiches as I didn't know what we'd be doing for lunch."

"That's very good of you." Will began clearing up in the kitchen preparatory to doing the dishes. He did not want to be late, the prospect of visiting the magic island was an exciting prospect.

By nine they were on their way. After Hauraki Corner, which in reality was just a bend, the road descended steeply to rise up again.

"Slow down," Gaynor was peering at the map, "Old Lake Road is coming up on the left. Turn into it. Merani Street is the second on the left before the beach."

Ted and Layla were waiting on the veranda for them. Ted stepped down to the car as they swung into the drive. "Good-day, nice weather for a change, high pressure, fine and sunny, settled conditions, just right for a sail. I take it you can sail, all Whitbys can sail."

Will doubted very much if all Whitbys could sail. "I can sail a dinghy," he replied cautiously.

"Just the job, I hadn't entered you for the Hobart Race." Will wondered what on earth was the Hobart Race. "I belong to the local sail racing club. But along with my Zephyr, I also have a vintage 1930s sixteen-foot sailboat, carvel built, renovated it myself, re-fixed planks to the frame in places, caulked it, replaced the decking, ideal for family sailing. Come inside, Layla has something for you to eat before you get decked out and then we'll go down to the beach."

On the way to the beach in Ted's Holden, they were given a full account of Narrow Neck. "When I first came here right up to the sixties Narrow Neck was a causeway. The first settlers describe Devonport at times of very high tides as being temporarily an island. Woodall Park, on your right, up to the Waitemata Golf Club and, on the other side of Lake Road, Ngataringa Park, bordering Ngataringa Bay, was all mangrove swamp. In fact, when I first bought *Karoro*, after spending a couple of years doing it up on my section, I used to keep it in the mangroves to the right of the causeway, hauling it across the road on a wooden beach trailer, which I also kept tied floating in the mangroves. I couldn't afford the few corrugated iron boat sheds in those days. People now say the mangroves should have been left, all part of the natural environment."

"What does the name of your boat mean?" Tim asked.

"*Karoro*, it's the name of one of the largest gulls in these parts. They fascinated me when I first came here. I used to feel they were free, winged spirits, wheeling around to see what we mortals were up to."

Ted parked the car in a large car park opposite children's play apparatus, kiosk and boat lockers. Will, Gaynor and the children followed Ted up a path onto the original causeway where there were toilets and changing rooms, overlooked by a yacht racing command tower, evergreen pohutukawas shading the foreshore.

"You couldn't see a lovelier beach than this," Ted said proudly, surveying the wide sands, white breakers rolling in, the aftermath of the gusty conditions of the last few days. Two nautical miles offshore, conical Rangitoto Island, brooding, mysterious, beckoned.

"Right, let's get out good old *Karoro*."

They followed Ted back to one of the lockers. He opened the doors, and Will helped him pull out the vintage yacht. It was in beautiful condition, white hull, gleaming brown varnished quarter-decking edged by red splashboards.

"Impressive," observed Will, "about the size of a Wayfarer."

"I don't know what a Wayfarer is but *Karoro* is 16 feet, large for a dinghy."

"A Wayfarer is the same size without quarter-decking. I used to sail one."

"We'll get it down to the beach. We need to be careful on the ramp. It's heavy compared with the Zephyr. We don't want it to run away with us."

Will and Gaynor struggled to help hold it down the steep wooden ramp before continuing to assist Ted to pull the boat to the water's edge where he swung it into the wind which was blowing straight into the beach.

"It's slow to rig up compared with a modern dinghy." Ted unlashed the mast, slotted in the halyards, sorted out the stays and then lifted the mast upright, staggering around as if about to toss the caber, causing everyone to jump out of his way before he managed to insert the mast into a slot in the foredeck, "Layla says that I look like a drunken circus act doing this."

Will thought she might have something there.

"She hasn't got modern stay tensioning devices. There're brackets on the ends of the stays and similar attached to the outer decks. A light line goes round and round between the two which you pull to get the tension right, not too tight as we need to give the mast some flexibility. Now attach the sails to the halyards, slotting the luff in the mast, sail battens in their slots, sheets attached with bowline knots and up we go!" Once up, the sails flapped about wildly. "We'd better secure the sails a bit. We don't want the children hit by a bowline knot. Can be painful."

Gaynor looked concerned. Will shared her thoughts. It was indeed something they needed to watch out for.

Ted continued with his flow of information. "There're paddles strapped on the inside of the hull; orange smoke flares taped in the stern locker. I've got yellow floatation jackets to fit everyone from the yacht club, I'll help you on with them. I'll assist you out as far as I can go in the surf and be there for you on your return."

"You're not coming with us?" Will asked in alarm.

"Wouldn't be wise, three adults and three children in a boat of this size. Two adults and three children will be just fine. *Karoro* is a lovely cruising yacht. Once clear of the surf, you'll really enjoy sailing it. Roll up your pants, Will, we'll run it out into the surf."

Will did as he was directed. The water was cold. "Hold the stem to the wind while I slip away the cradle. The wind is slightly to the north of directly on-shore. You'll go off on the port tack." Ted leant over and put the daggerboard in place, leaving two-thirds of it sticking up out of its casing.

"But—" protested Will.

"What's the matter, you said you can sail."

"But not out through surf."

"Three breakers and you'll be away, a piece of cake, just keep straight into the breakers, you don't want to be rolled over. Take in the main sheet immediately to power up, daggerboard down as soon as you can. Never mind the foresail halyard until clear, you need the centre of effort aft to beat. I'll put Gaynor and the children in." With that, Ted strode ashore and, to Gaynor's surprise, swept her up into his arms and carried her out into the boat. "Sit on the port side, the left, and hang onto the children when you hit the breakers, you don't want them thrown overboard."

Gaynor was about to speak when Ted rushed back ashore, picked up the two girls, gave them to her and, wading back, did the same with Tim. He then went to the stern of the boat, eyeing the breakers ahead. "Come round to the stern now, Will, on the windward side." He paused. Will felt his legs trembling. "Go for it, push run! Get aboard, Will!" Will scrambled over the stern. "Take up the main sheet, ready with the daggerboard, keep straight into the waves, hold on to the children, Gaynor!" Ted's voice grew fainter as he continued to shout advice from the shore.

They were off, Will too appalled to speak. The first breaker loomed ahead, a tearing white wall roaring down on them. They hit it, the boat shooting up in the air. Gaynor held on frantically to the children who looked terrified. There followed a period of calm sailing. Will pushed the daggerboard three parts down before another wall of water was on them. They were more ready for it this time. After another period of calm, the third breaker was less severe, not yet breaking. After the final shooting up and banging down, they found themselves in a long, gentle swell and gradually began to relax, Gaynor releasing her hold on the children.

For a while no one spoke. It had all happened so quickly. Beyond the breakers, the yacht, heeling to the wind, surged smoothly ahead, the wind sighing gently through the sails. Relaxed, Ruth left her seat and sat on her father's lap at the helm.

"That was exciting," Will finally said.

"Too exciting," Gaynor replied with feeling.

Will put Ruth's hand on the helm along with his. "You push the helm away when you want to go up into the wind, go left that is, like this, opposite to what you would do in a car, pull it towards you when you want to go off the wind, turn a little right."

Ruth experimented cautiously with her father's guidance. After a while, Tim asked if he could have a go, the children changing places. Before long, Will found that Tim, being that much older, had natural ability, being able to sense the everchanging pressure on the sails, essential to maintain a constant heading.

"Head a little to the left of the lighthouse to compensate for leeway."

Will found this a good move in every way as Gaynor felt proud of her child's achievement, lessening the impact of the unnerving experience of going out through the breakers.

"I thought brother Ted was coming with us," she eventually observed.

"So did I," was Will's rueful response. "It'll be better coming back as we'll be with the breakers which are supposed to lessen with the better weather."

"It'd better be."

Will noticed in the distance a large container vessel approaching the Rangitoto Channel. "Steer for the stern," he advised Tim. A few minutes later, Will said quietly so not to raise alarm. "I'd better take over; a large vessel will produce a sizable bow wave."

"Not again!" Gaynor moaned.

"It won't be a breaking wave but hold on to the children."

They soon heard the thudding of the engine, and it was not long until the vessel was upon them, passing about six hundred yards ahead, after which they soon saw the bow wave running rapidly towards them like an advancing tsunami.

"Here we go!" called Will as they rose up and down a number of times.

They'd been sailing for three-quarters of an hour, the island drawing close. From this distance, they could see what from afar appeared a green island was in fact terrain composed of large and small lumps of jagged scoria rock from which pohutukawa trees contrived to grow and thrive from cracks in the rock. As they drew closer, Will could see no landing beach but between menacing scoria reefs, extending out into the water, he observed narrow coves, two dinghy-widths wide, with sand at the end. He selected one, ghosted in, bumped up on the sand after which he jumped into the water and carried the children ashore.

"I'll carry you ashore, too," he said to Gaynor, "keep your feet dry."

"You sure you can manage, I'm quite a bit heavier than the children." Gaynor looked doubtful.

"I'm not as big and strong as brother Ted but I'm sure I can."

The children looked on with interest as Will staggered ashore with Gaynor in his arms.

"Don't go off this bit of sand without shoes, the rocks look lethal, you could get your legs stuck between the cracks." Will went a few paces inland behind a large stand of rock. "There's a dry piece of sand here, out of the wind too, a lovely place to have lunch."

He went back to the boat's stern locker and took out the lunch Gaynor made up last evening wrapped in a plastic bag, along with two bottles of mineral water. On his return, they took off their buoyancy jackets to prop themselves up on while relaxing having lunch. Will sat back. He could hear nearby the trill of a bird he had never heard before and further off a beautiful deep bell-like call sounding like fairy music.

"Ted said that when he first came here as a young man, he saw wallabies on the island which had been introduced by early settlers, but which have now been culled as the island is a public reserve and the authorities want to return it to its original state. He also said that baches, holiday homes, built by early settlers, are being progressively removed."

"What are wallabies?" Ruth asked.

"They're like small brown kangaroos," Will replied.

The scene was enchanting. Will closed his eyes. Gaynor carried Angela off to take her to the toilet. He could hear Ruth and Tim chatting as they played nearby in the sand.

Suddenly something made him open his eyes. He blinked. "Bloody hell!" he suddenly shouted, jumping up and running round the corner towards the boat. The tide had come in and the boat was floating off, its speed increasing as the top of the mast and brailed-up sails caught the wind. He tore off his clothes frantically down to his underpants and plunged in after it. He thought he could retrieve it, but he found himself out of his depth before he could reach it and began swimming desperately, the boat's speed increasing as it caught the wind.

In the distance he could hear Gaynor calling. "Will, are you mad? The tide will sweep you away!"

Will swam with all his might. He could see Yellow Ted in the stern getting smaller as the boat drifted further into open water, speeding up as it caught the wind. He gasped for air. With a start, he heard splashing behind him. Turning on his side exhausted, he saw Gaynor in a yacht's small tender rowing urgently after him.

"Get in!" she commanded. As Will struggled over the stern, she rowed on strenuously for the drifting sailboat, eventually coming up to its stern. "Get in and sail it back!" With that, she turned and began to fast row back to their tiny cove between the rocks.

Struggling aboard, shivering violently, Will freed the roughly brailed mainsail, took the tiller and main sheet, and bore away in an attempt to come about. He tried twice to get up enough speed to turn up into the wind but was blown back on each occasion. In despair, he paid off and gybed about, ducking his head just in time as the boom crashed over. The water was calm and clear, only the top half of the sails catching the wind. As he was pulling tight the mainsail, he glimpsed the remains of microlight aircraft on the sea floor. In the end, he got the boat moving sufficiently to be able to beat back up the coast. Now he must locate the cleft in the rocks where he had left the others. He was finally helped by Gaynor waving her maroon jumper from the bough of a pohutukawa she had climbed. When he finally brought their yacht up to the water's edge, he collapsed onto the sand. Continuing to shiver violently, he got to his knees.

"If I hadn't found that tender, you'd have been swept away and drowned," Gaynor scolded as she dried him off with her jumper.

"Brother Ted's antique boat and you all marooned on the island," Will managed to stutter out.

"Never mind Ted's boat. He knew where we were. He'd soon have raised the alarm. Ruth would never recover from the loss of her father as well. You were utterly stupid, impulsive! It was just luck that someone visiting the island from a larger yacht anchored offshore had left their tender up the next cleft and I know how to row."

The children stood around amazed to hear their headmaster being thoroughly dressed down by a very junior member of staff.

"I'm sorry," Will replied weakly, "I didn't think."

"Didn't think's right! What have you got a brain for?" Gaynor was still incensed.

"Dadda rescued Yellow Ted," Ruth said in her father's defence.

Gaynor didn't bother to reply that she rescued Yellow Ted along with Will but instead threw a spare pair of her pants at Will saying, "These won't fit but they'll have to do. Put them on along with your clothes. We'd better be going. It gets dark early."

Still shivering, Will ruefully struggled into his clothes, to his embarrassment, Gaynor and Ruth helping him. He noticed Gay's left foot had a nasty bleeding gash where she had torn it running about on razor-sharp scoria in sandals. He fished out a clean handkerchief and gave it to Gaynor who wrapped it around her foot. Dressed, he just managed to push the yacht around in the narrow space to face open water. "Get in over the stern," he said to the others, "then all move forward, and I'll be able to push off."

Getting away was the complete opposite to taking off from Narrow Neck Beach. They sailed very gently, picking up the wind as they moved further away from the island. "Look, Dadda," Ruth suddenly called, pointing at the water three feet astern, "a little blue penguin!" They all looked where she was pointing to see a charming iridescent blue-green penguin darting and tumbling just below the surface. After a fleeting display, it disappeared.

"Can you identify Narrow Neck Beach from this distance, it should be a reciprocal course?" They all looked around at the long coastline opposite. "Look for a break in the shoreline. Takapuna Beach to the right will be much longer, two miles further to the north." Will peered ahead.

"I can see the beach, there're sails of boats being taken down the ramp," Tim responded.

"Good boy, sharp eyes. Would you like to take the tiller for a bit? Aim for the boats on the ramp. With the wind backing north against the tide, bearing straight for the tower should be about right."

As Tim took his seat beside him, Will hoped, as before, that the invitation at least might be an action meeting Gaynor's approval. As they got further out into the channel, the wind increased, backing further north. Meeting an opposite flowing tide, a vicious short chop arose. The yacht, already heeling, began to bounce and sway about.

"I think I'd better take over," Will said to Tim. "Sit up on the windward side with the others. You did well, show promising ability."

Will began to slip the main sheet, spilling air in response to the strengthening gusts to control the angle of heel. Brother Ted inferred it would be a steady force two all day, but the wind had increased to a force three, gusting force four at times, Will could even see it increasing further. At least it was getting them back quicker than when they came over. Spray began to sweep over the boat as it hit the steep seas.

"We're making good progress," Will observed encouragingly.

"Yellow Ted's getting wet," Ruth complained.

"We're all getting wet," Tim replied.

Will began watching the approaching waves carefully, trying to ride over them as skilfully as possible. He had little experience in wild water conditions but was learning. In mid-channel, with the tide at its strongest, waves began to slop over the stern where there was no splashboard. As the water aboard increased, sloshing about inside, Will said to Tim, "Do you think you could slip down and hand me the bailer, it looks like a dustpan attached to a light line."

Gaynor held his collar as Tim carefully climbed down from his windward position and handed the bailer to Will, who contrived to throw water to leeward when water slopped his way, holding both mainsheet and tiller in one hand as he did so. "And while you're down there, Tim, do you think you could slacken off the foresheet, that's the line attached to the trailing edge of the foresail, attached to that cleat on the lee side, the low side at the moment." He could not ask Gaynor as he needed her up to windward for balance and to hold onto the girls in the bucking boat.

It was not so much the height of the waves that was causing the problem but rather their confused nature, banging against each other, throwing spray in all directions. Will was concerned that with much more water aboard they would founder. He continued to bail madly as he sailed.

"You're throwing water over me!" Angela complained.

"Water's coming from everywhere," Will muttered.

"I don't like it!"

Will felt she was saying what everyone felt and looked around in despair. Then he noticed he was bearing down on a large green buoy, a starboard channel buoy marking the edge of the deep water for shipping. They were through the main channel after which the speed of the tide would progressively weaken. And it did, before long they were taking less water aboard and were sailing fast towards the shore. Will could see the breakers ahead but, in contrast to the morning, the remnants of the big seas from away out had decreased along with the breakers.

He headed for what he thought was the middle of the beach. He had heard that he must not allow the boat to surf on the breakers as it would go over the top, broach to and roll over. As the first breaker approached, he let go the mainsheet, taking the power off the boat, allowing the wave to surge harmlessly underneath in a tumble of white foam before powering up again. He did this with the second and third wave, before suddenly realising he was near the beach but, with the slackening effect of the tide and increased wind speed as it blew along the shoreline, he found he was almost under the cliffs to the left of the beach. Desperately, Will pushed the daggerboard down again to stop the leeway when there was an enormous bang. He had hit a reef at the far left of the beach, breaking the daggerboard right off. At that moment, he was aware of Ted, waist-deep in water, getting hold of the stem of the boat, pulling them to the right, away from the rocks towards the beach.

"Let go the sheets and help me pull the boat along!" he yelled.

Will jumped out of the boat, and together they pulled the boat towards the sands, dragging it up as far as they could in the remaining waves.

"Now push it round facing the surf and hold the stem," was the next command.

Will did as he was bid while Ted grabbed the two girls and rushed them up the beach, followed by Tim and then Gaynor. "Hold the boat where it is for 10 minutes, I'm just going to run Gaynor and the kids home, I see Gaynor has a nasty gash on her ankle. Layla will give them hot showers. I'll be straight back with the beach trailer."

While his brother Ted was gone, Will thought he would try to do something useful. Contriving to hold the boat pointing seawards, he went round to the stern and struggled to take the rudder off its pintles, finding he had to hold a tension spring down so that the rudder did not ride up and off in rough weather. Concentrating on what he was doing, a larger than average wave hit the boat and before he could get back round to the stem, the boat had rolled over, the mast hitting the sand with a whack, the raised sails filling with sand. If only he had tried to get the sails down rather than bother with the rudder. With hindsight, that would have been the more useful thing to do. He wondered what on earth Ted would say when he got back to his precious yacht.

When Ted did come puffing back with the beach trailer, he was very good. "Rolled over has she? I've done that myself coming in. Let's get the sails off her so that we can get it upright again to un-step the mast. Broken off the daggerboard as well? I'll soon make another. I've done the same on the same reef. You don't really notice the rocks at end of the beach from the boat ramp."

Will held the top of the mast at waist height while Ted got the sails off, dismayed at their sandy state. "Don't worry, we'll hose them down and spread them over the yacht to dry. We'll need to swing the yacht towards the surf. Hold the stem while I detach the stays."

On the beach with everything roughly secured, they began tugging the yacht towards the ramp, the rusty beach trailer bearings squeaking in protest. "The council says that the old wooden ramp will have to be replaced before long, it was old when I first came here, by a cutting. It was built when there was only the causeway. No need for a ramp now."

"What happens when the next big earthquake and tsunami strikes? In 1855, in the early days of settlement, a tsunami demolished the Wellington waterfront, swept across where the airport is today?"

"Now that's a thought. You're very knowledgeable about New Zealand's early history?"

"I've been reading up. A tsunami would sweep right through the landfill."

"You're right. I'll have it brought up at the next council meeting. We've got tsunami warning procedures and coastal evacuation plans but, as you say, Narrow Neck is particularly vulnerable," Ted replied between puffs as they dragged the yacht towards the wooden ramp. On the ramp, late beachgoers rallied around to help them pull the laden beach trailer up, the remnants of the water taken aboard pouring out of the open bung hole in the stern.

In the boat locker area, Ted hosed *Karoro* down, inside and out, then its sails, after which he edged the yacht into the locker, rigging on top, draping sails overall. "With the door shut, sun on the roof, it gets hot in the boat lockers. *Karoro* will soon dry out."

"I'm sorry about the damage," Will apologised.

"Don't worry about it. I'm sorry for you that the weather report turned out wrong. As long as you enjoyed the sail, old boy." To Will's embarrassment, he put his arm round his shoulder and gave him a friendly hug. Despite his hearty and expansive nature, which tended to put Will off, being quieter and less demonstrative, brother Ted was a real good sort, kind and generous. Going the short distance uphill in the car, he put the car heater on full as Will was still shivering, anxious to get into dry clothes.

In their Merani Street home, Will found Gaynor and the children sitting round the kitchen table eating, Gaynor's ankle carefully bandaged. Will picked up his dry clothes and gratefully accepted the invitation to have a hot shower. Never had he found a hot shower more welcome.

Coming out, warm at last, Will joined the others at the table and was offered baked kingfish and kumaras along with an assortment of vegetables. Like the others, he was ravenous.

"How did you enjoy the island?" Layla asked as Will sat down.

While he was thinking about a suitable reply, Tim blurted out, "Will was stupid, didn't use his brains."

There was an appalled silence at the table at such a remark from a child. "I thought you could sail, Will?" Ted eventually responded.

"Nothing wrong with his sailing," Gaynor replied.

There was further silence. Ruth leant against Will in sympathy. Layla, noticing the tension, said, "Like to look at the evening news on television?" pushing a television on a stand in front of them in an effort to change the subject.

"Better still, why don't we go all go into the living room, put on the heater and look at the large television there. It'll be more comfortable on easy chairs?" Ted followed up, realising that Tim had brought up a sensitive subject the adults did not want, for some reason, to discuss.

After the news with tension eased, the children playing happily on the carpet with a board game Layla gave them, Gaynor and Layla talking animatedly together, getting on well. Ted asked Will if he would like to see his sporting gear in the garage.

The large back of Ted's garage, as well as a being set up as a fully equipped general workshop, was an area displaying an array of sporting equipment, fishing rods for fresh and sea fishing, every imaginable lure and river fly, snorkelling gear, spear guns, throwing nets, hunting crossbows, targets. Since coming to New Zealand, brother Ted had become the archetypal outdoor Kiwi sportsman.

"And there's my hunting rifles. I have to keep them inside in secure locked cabinets. Come indoors."

Will was taken to Ted's study/computer room to the right of the kitchen. Ted took a key from behind a picture and unlocked the gun cabinets. "There's this Sako Vixen 222 with a beaut sight, nice and light, this Tika T3 308 rifle with Bolthorn chassis, very accurate but not so handy, and this 308 Remington 700 ADL with Leupold scope. I've stopped a big tusker with that charging straight down a track at me, quick and easy to use, just as well on that occasion."

"Where to you go hunting?"

"The Kaimanawas mostly, I've got a mate in Turangi from army days."

"Where are they?"

"A little east and south of Lake Taupo." Will decided he would have to look at a map when he got back to Takapuna. While in the study, alone with brother Ted, Will thought he would ask him about their sister, Zoe, who came out to New Zealand with him in 1938. "Now that's a strange, sad story, a bit of a mystery really. As soon as the war started, she went back to Britain, she'd only been here a year. I certainly didn't. I'd come to make a new life here. When I had to, I joined the New Zealand army and, as it happened, very luckily, had a lovely war, if you could excuse the trite expression. After basics, I was assigned to a coastal defence unit, just the job, ended up a captain monitoring a great line of coast from Dargaville right round Cape Reinga to Bream Head out of Whangarei. What I got to know about Northland in those days!"

"About Zoe?"

"Ah yes, a lovely sister, came out with me to New Zealand to start a new life. Unfortunately, we'd only been here a year when the war began. She could have stayed and joined the New Zealand forces, but she'd fallen madly in love with a fellow in the local flying club. When we first came to New Zealand, we went up to Paihia in the Bay of Islands as we heard the weather up north was warm and there were jobs in the expanding fruit growing industry in the Kerikeri district – the town wasn't in existence then.

"Well, to cut a long story short, this guy, a fair dinkum handsome and dashing fellow, was an enthusiastic and experienced flyer, a third-generation New Zealander by the way, not a Pom like us. Right at the beginning of the phoney war period, he dashed off with a mate to join the British Royal Air Force, though New Zealand did have an air force at that time, part of the Empire Air Training Scheme, consisting of planes like De Havilland Tiger Moths. Airspeed Oxfords and North American Harvards. Zoe was devastated. Though I cautioned her, she decided to follow him to Britain with the idea of catching up with him there. After that, the story becomes vague and I never learnt really what happened, but it appears that her presence wasn't welcome by this guy, which disillusioned her no end, after which she became involved with another guy, an airman I think. She never would talk about any of her time back in Britain during the war, which resulted in some sort of tragedy for which she considered herself in some way responsible. The upshot was when she came back to New Zealand, she was in a state of shellshock, after which she was never her former happy self. She became eccentric and reckless, taking on crazy challenges as if she were trying to escape from something, memories, I could never fathom it out. She stayed with me after I was discharged and had got together enough money to afford this Merani Street place, but when I got married to Layla, she decided to strike off on her own, went back up to Northland again, somewhere on the Hokianga, I think, or in that region. Then 10 years ago, she disappeared. The authorities never knew what happened to her."

"Did you make inquiries?" Will asked.

"We did, Layla and I went up to Paihia where I learnt she was last staying."

"Did she have a close friend who might know something of her last movements?"

"Yes, she did. Woman named Tawhaitu Tahu."

"Did you try to locate this woman?"

"Yes, we did, we heard she was a half-cast Maori. I'm sorry, I'm told I mustn't use that term anymore, not politically correct, you know, a mixed-race woman of high reputation, mana as the Maoris put it, Rangatira background, Rangatira being hereditary local leaders, lawyer by profession. But I found she was on an extended holiday in Indonesia, of all places, Arata Beach, 23 kilometres from Pariaman, left before Christmas."

"Have you her address?"

"Yes, I have, I'll look it up, just a minute, ah yes, right to the north of the town, high up, in a pole house, Te Haumi Drive, set amongst lovely native bush apparently."

"A pole house?"

"Yes, that's what they're called, the houses are built on the side of steep ridges, the downward sides supported on long poles. They have magnificent views."

All this fascinated Will. Zoe may have told this close friend what really happened during her return to Britain in the early years of the war which so disturbed her. Her account could be the answer to the apparition, the school ghost, something only Ruth and he knew about, but which was extremely worrying and disturbing. While in New Zealand, as well as seeing as much as he could in the time at their disposal, Will's aim was to go up to Paihia, locate this woman and hear what she had to say, which might help put her disturbed spirit to rest. He knew he would have to tell Gaynor more but felt that this was still not the time, not yet.

Chapter Seven

Back in the sitting room with the others, Will found the children tired, beginning to loll around and fall asleep on the carpet. It was warm in the room with a large radiant heater on. It seemed with no frost and snow, Auckland homes did not have central heating, residents tending to put on electric heaters on what, for them, were cold winter evenings. After a few minutes, Will went over to Gaynor. “Do you think we should be getting the children home to bed? They’re beginning to fall asleep on the floor?”

Gaynor, who had been absorbed in a conversation with Layla, looked around. She nodded in agreement. “Come on, children, it’s time to take you home to bed, gather up what’s yours. Don’t forget Yellow Ted, Ruth, I’m sure your father doesn’t want to have to drive straight back again as soon as we reach home.”

Listening to her, Will felt, not for the first time, she sounded like the wife of a couple who had been married for years rather than two separate people who were cautiously endeavouring to find their way together, neither in a hurry to make the next move.

“Can I go sailing with you in your racing yacht, Uncle Ted?” Tim asked as he got to his feet, obviously in no way fazed by the day’s experience.

“Tim’s a promising yachtsman, he soon picked up how to helm,” Will commented, then wondering if he had said the wrong thing as after today's experience, Gaynor may not have wanted him sailing.

"Zephyrs are small, one-person racing dinghies with no foresail. They're quarter decked which reduces the cockpit area, though I suppose it would accommodate another of your size. I can't reduce the sail area, reefing down as in *Karoro*, a family cruising yacht. In shore with a gentle breeze, I guess we could manage. You'd have to ask your mother."

"Can I, Mum?" Tim asked eagerly.

"We'll see," Gaynor replied. "We mustn't forget our wet clothes. Layla's kindly put them all in a big plastic bag by the front door."

On the porch, Gaynor and the children allowed themselves to be given a goodbye hug by Uncle Ted, now they had got used to him, appreciating his kindly intentions. Will was given the same when it came to his turn.

"You won't be able to get into Lake Road from Old Lake Road at this time in the evening owing to the constant flow of traffic. You'll need to go left up Merani Street when you leave. Turn right towards Seacliffe Avenue, then right along Seacliffe until you come to the raised planters in the middle of the road. Turn left at this point down Winscombe Street. At the bottom, with Belmont Intermediate School on your right, you'll find traffic lights. Turn right into Lake Road. You'll know your way after that. Good luck. Looking forward to seeing you all again soon. Hooray."

"What does 'hooray' mean?" Gaynor asked as they drove off. "It sounds as if he's pleased to see the last of us which he obviously isn't?"

"It seems another word in New Zealand for 'goodbye'. It's all part of Ted's persona, of being a full-blown New Zealand guy."

After that there was an awkward silence. "Right-hand lane, if not you'll end up in the city," Tim said pertly from the back seat beside the girls who were fast asleep. "Second right at the junction at Halls Corner."

"All right, Tim," Gaynor interrupted. "I think Will knows his way from here."

"He's got a good memory," Will muttered. "It'll serve him well when he does exams in the next few years, something I never had."

Turning right down towards Beach Road, the reflection of shore lights in the water and the arc of stars twinkling overhead were of a clarity Will had not before experienced, reminding him they were now in the unpolluted air of the South Pacific.

Inside their Takapuna holiday home, Gaynor and Will took their respective children straight to bed. When Will came down to the sitting room, wondering what reception he would get when on their own, he found the lights and fire on with a note on the settee saying, 'Shattered, gone to bed. See you at breakfast'.

This was the first evening away they had not spent the first part of it together on the settee. Will wondered, after his debacle on the island, whether it would be their last. A coolness between them would be awkward for the rest of their time away and would defeat one of his aims in taking Gaynor with him, that Is, to build a relationship with a person Ruth liked with the possibility, ultimately, of marriage and a mother for Ruth. Will would have to wait to morning to find out.

After Ruth's bath swim, which seemed to take longer than usual, he found Gaynor in the kitchen, bustling around, "I'm making bacon, sausages and egg, and putting out cereal and yoghurt, set you all up for the day." She appeared not to notice Will at first but bent down to kiss Ruth and Yellow Ted who was thrust in her face. "As I've said before, if my friends back home could see me kissing a teddy bear each morning, they'd feel I'd lost my marbles!" at which Will laughed, breaking the ice.

"After breakfast, I'd like to discuss possible day's activities with you," Will said to Gaynor as they sat down.

"OK," replied Gaynor replied lightly in a manner suggesting this was a new day and a new start, putting yesterday behind them. Will hoped fervently his interpretation was right.

When all the breakfast was cleared away, Will brought out a map of greater Auckland. "I thought you might like to spend the day city side. People say the Tamaki Marine Drive along the opposite shore is spectacular. Halfway along at Okahu Bay, near well-known Mission Bay Beach, here," he pointed to the map, "I was reading there's a fabulous aquarium, Kelly Tarlton's Sea Life, where people walk through transparent tunnels with fish, big and small, swimming overhead and all around them, and then there're the volcanic mounts like Mount Eden and One Tree Hill and Domain, a large park, with spectacular views. And over here at Western Springs," Will again pointed to the map, "there's a fascinating zoo where animals are featured in a large area of varied terrain, so I was reading. Children like zoos, we've got to keep them interested and give them an opportunity to run about. What do you think?"

Gaynor took the map. "Good thinking, interest for all, eh?"

"I hope so. I want to keep off the urban motorways if possible."

"Layla was telling me you keep to the right on them, there's passing both sides in laned situations in New Zealand, until you get near your exit. We'd need to leave the motorway just south of the bridge at the Fanshawe Street exit, here." It was Gaynor's turn to point at the map. I'll drive if you like?"

The last remark surprised Will. Though Michelle was a good driver, when they were together, she always preferred Will to do the driving. "If you want to."

"OK, I'll make up the lunches."

"Need a hand?"

"You can bring over to the working top what I'll be needing, beginning with film wrapping then bread."

Gaynor got on efficiently. Will thought, not for the first time, what a good decision he had made in asking her to accompany him. He bustled to do her bidding before taking Ruth upstairs to get her ready for the day. Out on Lake Road, Tim said, "Right-hand lane for the city."

"When I want driving directions from you, Tim, I'll ask, thank you very much," which met with Will's approval as he thought Tim, on occasions, had too much to say for himself.

At Esmonde Road, Gaynor observed the signs overhead and bore left towards the city and Harbour Bridge, Will watching on the map on his lap. "Fanshawe Street is second exit off, first major one, look out for signs, Custom House, Ferry Terminal, after which keep bearing left for Tamaki Drive."

"Thanks," Gaynor looked in her mirror. "Can you sort out the girls behind, they seem to have got themselves in a bit of a tizzy?" Will turned round to attend to the children.

"I suggest we stop at Kohimarama Beach or Mission Bay to give the kids a run about. There's more space at Mission Bay Beach Reserve, and fountains, I suggest Mission Bay."

"Mission Bay it is." Gaynor parked the car and they all bundled out, the children running about in excitement, fascinated by the dancing jets of water from the fluted fountain flying 20 metres into the air. "Don't get into the pool," Gaynor shouted. "I haven't a change of clothes for you!"

Will and Gaynor sat on a seat together, looking across the sparkling Waitemata towards Rangitoto which looked the same from any angle. Eventually, Will felt moved to say, "I'm sorry I acted impulsively yesterday, not using my loaf, something I tell my schoolchildren never to do."

"You could have lost your life."

"I realise that now. Thank you for saving me. I didn't know you could row so well."

"Before my husband Allan left, he used to travel abroad for his firm's exporting business accompanied by his secretary. After a while, he started coming home to our nice house beside the sea in Devon less and less, claiming he had to remain at his headquarters in London. Finally, we began not to see him at all. It was then I realised he preferred life with his secretary rather than with me and the children. During his increasing absences, I bought a blow-up yellow dinghy and used to take the children fishing on the sea water lagoon below the house, sometimes venturing out to open water beyond the shingle bank to troll for bass over a nearby reef. That's when I taught myself to row. When he started to give me just the bare minimum legal child maintenance, I had to sell our Devonshire home, come to Ostness and move in with Mother."

"It must have been very hard on you," Will observed.

"Yes, it was. Which reminds me, tonight I'll have a go at trying to get your mobile phone going. We're in the 1990s now. There's not much use taking it to New Zealand if you don't know how to use it."

"I've had it going back home on occasions with a bit of help."

"We'd better try to get it going here then. I think the first step would be to get it connected to New Zealand telecom. I'll try this evening if you like."

"OK, that'd be good of you." Will was realising more and more what a smart and able girl Gaynor was.

Will looked at his watch. "Perhaps we should make a move and go along to Kelly Tarlton's Sea Life, the aquarium, it's not far from here, after that we could have lunch up on Mount Eden or One Tree Hill."

"Good thinking. Come on, children, we're off to the aquarium to see all sorts of sea creatures swimming all around us."

"Are we going into the water?" Tim asked.

"No, come along. You'll see."

And they did see, to their wonder and amazement. It was not a conventional aquarium. After paying, they were ushered into a series of transparent tunnels, the aquarium being up above and all around them, sea creatures great and small gliding overhead and alongside. Tim was delighted, rushing to have a close encounter with a huge shark 10 times his size just the other side of the transparent tunnel. The girls, on the other hand, hung back, overawed and wary. Will was astonished by the strength of the material supporting the underwater walkways as there must have been hundreds of tons of water above their heads. They all found it a fascinating experience.

"Are all these creatures found in New Zealand waters?" Gaynor asked, observing some fantastically coloured octopuses nearby. "They're sinister-looking creatures."

"Your guess is as good as mine, I suspect many are. This is what viewers would expect. There's probably plenty of information available in the galleries surrounding," Will replied.

Though there was a large amount to see, if they were going to keep to their proposed itinerary, it was soon time they moved on.

"Who knows what our car number plate is?" Will asked when they got outside."

"TX7693," Tim shouted eagerly.

"Smart boy," Will observed.

"It starts like Tyrannosaurus, T-Rex."

"With such a smart brain as yours, don't forget to do your teeth before going to bed tonight as you often do," his mother retorted.

"Looking at the map, Mt Eden appears nearer, we'd better go back towards the city, round by Auckland Domain and up Mt Eden Road unless you want the Southern Motorway," Will observed, looking at the map.

"No, Mt Eden Road looks better. On the motorways you blast along and see nothing," Gaynor responded, looking over Will's shoulder at the map." She turned to Tim. "OK, Tyrannosaurus Rex, get in."

"You wouldn't want Tyrannosaurus Rex in the car," Tim replied, laughing. "He'd eat you all up!"

"Perhaps not. Tim, get in then and put on your seat belt." Gaynor saw all the children aboard and went round to the driving seat. "Happy to navigate?" she said to Will.

"You're doing fine."

Gaynor smiled and drove off back the way they had come.

As they wound up Mt Eden, a dormant volcano, one of many scattered about greater Auckland, they got a stunning view of the Waitemata Harbour and the Hauraki Gulf, as far out as Great Barrier Island on the far horizon. At the restaurant they found they could drive no further but, if they wanted to go right up to the top, they would have to walk. After discussion, they decided to walk, Ruth sitting on Will's shoulders and Angela on her mother's.

"What a view!" Gaynor exclaimed when they reached the top.

"And the city behind, you can see our next venue, One Tree Hill, not that far away." Will looked down at the crater, seemingly about a hundred feet deep, with grass and rubble at the bottom. "To think that flames and molten rock burst out of there quite recently in geological time."

"I hope it doesn't happen again while we're here!" Gaynor observed.

"In the time the dinosaurs?" Tim asked.

"No, it happened in comparatively modern times, but if it were to reoccur there would be signs, like when Tarawera blew its top last century."

"Tarawera?" Tim queried.

"We'll no doubt be visiting Rotorua on our New Zealand trip and we'll all find out about it then," Will concluded. "There's not a lot of room for a picnic lunch on Mount Eden. I understand One Tree Hill is in an extensive domain, Cornwall Park, if the children can last out that long I think it might be better to have lunch there, room for them to run around. I'll look up the map." Back at the car, Will took out the map. "If we keep going along Mt Eden Road and turn left at Balmoral Road we should get there."

As Will assumed, there was plenty of room in Cornwall Park. After lunch, to get to the mount itself, they needed to drive, bearing left as they approached the one-way route to the top marked by a huge obelisk. From the 182-metre summit, they could see the two harbours, Waitemata to the north and Manukau to the south.

"Amazing!" Will exclaimed. "I was reading there are actually three craters and those terraces," he pointed to the concentric formations around the peaks, "were cut by hand by the Maoris in pre-European times to form fighting platforms, the outer edges of which had high wooden stockades. These stockaded forts were called 'pas'."

"'Pa', sounds like father?" Tim said.

"Nothing to do with father," Will responded. "It's the Maori word for fort or fortified village, I understand."

"You certainly have been swotting up your facts," Gaynor replied, looking around her.

"I look up brochures in advance, if possible, so that I come informed, to have some idea what I'm looking at."

"Very commendable. Shall we go to the zoo, time's getting on?"

"The zoo!" the children cried.

Come all this way to see a zoo when there're great zoos back home, Will thought to himself, *but then that's children, the exotic animals at a zoo are always spectacles that attract kids. I should know, having worked with children all my life*, he reasoned. "OK, it's the zoo next, back to the car," Will announced, chasing after the children as they ran enthusiastically towards the parked car.

In the car, Will picked up the map. "It looks as if we have to cross the city. If we go back to Balmoral Road we should get there eventually, providing we can discover a way under the North-Western Motorway, otherwise it's take the motorway back to the city and out again."

"We'll take the advice of the navigator. Everybody in, seatbelts on," Gaynor agreed cheerfully. "Here we go!"

It took a while to work their way through to the zoo, but they eventually did, finding parking in Motions Road. At the zoo entrance, Will bought a map. Looking at it he realised there was so much to see. It was a complete day's visit. The zoo was spread over a wide volcanic terrain with animal types grouped in locations suited to their species. With what time they had, they would need to choose the animal group they wanted to see the most. Predictably, Tim opted for lions, but the girls said they wanted to see darling little monkeys, which Will saw were featured in the far end of the South American sector. It was quite a way round to the left, contrary to the recommended route to follow.

"Little monkeys would like to see little monkeys," Gaynor observed laughing.

"You're right about them being little monkeys," Tim mocked.

"Don't be like that, Tim. Will and I would like to see sweet little monkeys too, lions will have to wait until another visit. It's a long way, we'd better get moving," Gaynor added crisply. Will and Gaynor took their seven-year-olds onto their shoulders. When they eventually got to where the little squirrel monkeys were, they found they were living with capybaras, large docile rodents only found in South America. To the girls' delight, they saw that some of the monkeys were on capybaras' backs.

"I don't think the squirrel monkeys are riding those odd creatures," Gaynor observed.

"Capybaras," Tim interrupted.

"All right. Capybaras, know-it-all," Gaynor continued, "but sitting around on them."

If the girls were intrigued to see squirrel monkeys on the backs of capybaras, some of the nearby squirrel monkeys appeared equally intrigued by the shoulder-riding girls, swinging alongside excitedly in their large chain-linked enclosure.

"Run!" Ruth commanded her father. Will ran. To her delight, the monkeys followed, squealing loudly. "The other way, faster!" Obediently, Will ran the other way faster, the excited monkeys turning and following. Ruth shrieked with delight. "Now the other way, faster!"

After four or five hectic spurts in each direction, Will stopped exhausted. "I think that's enough," Gaynor intervened. "You'll be giving your father a heart attack."

"Well, that was fun!" Will gasped.

"We'd better be going, if you lark about here like that much longer, we'll be getting complaints from the keepers that you're overexciting the monkeys. Anyway, we should be making a move, or we'll be driving back home in the dark."

Back in the car, Will said, "I'll drive," not wanting to be seen leaving the more challenging city driving all to Gaynor.

"If you wish," Gaynor got out the map. "The quickest way would be to get onto the North-Western Motorway, once I find an on-ramp, as Layla describes the slip roads onto motorways, and then at the Karangahape Interchange bear left onto the Northern Motorway and head for the Harbour Bridge. Layla says keep right on the motorways until nearing your exit as traffic passes both sides and cars on left-hand lanes will be positioning themselves for leaving the motorway before long, not like in England where it's antisocial to hug the outside lane."

Will did not have much experience of using motorways in England as, especially since Michelle's death, he had little reason for leaving East Anglia. "OK, I'll leave the navigation to you. I think from memory we come to the Great North Road first, after that I'm in your capable hands."

Looking out for the signs, Gaynor found an on-ramp and they were soon speeding along with the rush hour traffic. Before long, Gaynor was advising Will to work his way to the left of the traffic to bear left onto the

Northern Motorway. After that it was amazing how quickly, as they descended the long winding incline, the lights of the Harbour Bridge appeared ahead. Crossing the bridge, with the sun setting to their left in a golden ball over the Inner Harbour, Gaynor advised Will to get into the second to left lane, preparatory to leaving the motorway at Esmonde Road.

Once on it, Tim called out, "Right-hand lane."

"Tim, dear, it's nice you can remember what Uncle Ted said but it's off-putting for Will to have us all directing him."

"He's not my real Uncle Ted."

"No, he's Ruth's, but it seems appropriate you call him that as well," his mother replied.

Will remembered he needed to take the right-hand lane as that lane, joining others, swept up and over the motorway to Takapuna. "Ted was telling me that in the South Island, out of the towns, we might only see another vehicle once in half an hour, especially in wintertime," Will observed, "which will be more like it."

Approaching Lake Road, Will was waiting for one of them to advise him to turn left but nobody did, respecting what Gaynor said. He knew Ruth would not butt in as she expected her dad to be in charge, to know it all, except when they were home alone together when she was in charge. Along Hurstmere Road, Will said to Gaynor, "Like me to stop and get take-aways, it's been a long day and you must be tired."

"It's thoughtful of you, Will, but I have something quick in mind, better for us than take-aways. Once in, if you'd like to attend to the children, I won't be long."

Inside their holiday home, Will put on the large electric heater and the television while Gaynor hurried out to the kitchen. After taking off coats, he then got on all fours, going around the room with a girl in turn on his back, pretending to be a capybara, Tim disdainfully seeing what he could find of interest on the television.

Before long, Gaynor returned, smiling at the scene. "If you'd like to serve the vegetables and kumara from the microwave onto hot plates you'll find underneath, I won't be long pan-frying the fish, the stove-top element is hot," she said to Will.

By the time Will had the children organised at the table and vegetables served, Gaynor was ready to add the fish. It was a great meal and quick. Will again marvelled at Gaynor's efficiency.

After the meal in the sitting room, it was soon obvious the children had had a long day as they began to fall asleep on the carpet at which Will and Gaynor took their respective children off to bed.

Back together in the sitting room, Gaynor said, "I was going to get your mobile going."

Observing her and feeling tired himself Will suggested, "It's been a long day, why don't we leave it until tomorrow? I have only one activity in mind for tomorrow."

"What's that?" Gaynor asked sleepily.

Taking care how he phrased his reply Will said, "There are ferries running from one of the Custom House quays at the bottom of Queen Street, Auckland City, over to Mackenzie Bay, Rangitoto Island, from where a wide walking route leads to the top. It attracts tourists from all over the world and is considered one of the most unique and worthwhile things to do while in Auckland. I thought you and Tim might like to walk to the top while I amuse the girls by taking them round the numerous rock pools and walkways featured in the shallow bay. The girls would never make it to the top unless we carried them on our shoulders. They'd be happier playing about beside the sea."

"That's very kind of you, Will," Gaynor replied. "I wouldn't want to sail over there again in a small yacht."

Will thought that this offer would, in some way, make amends for his bungled and embarrassing episode when last on the island and allow him to see features beyond what could be observed from a tiny bay. For some reason, he was attracted to Rangitoto Island as if, for him, it stood vigil over a mysterious past with which he had some connection but could not understand why. "I suggest we take the ferry, a twenty-minute journey I have found out, from Devonport to the bottom of Queen Street in the city for the experience, where a ferry leaves from one of the Custom House quays on a regular timetable for Rangitoto and then return directly to Devonport, leaving the car at Devonport."

"It sounds good, I'd be happy with that. Tell me in the morning what ferry you intend catching so I have the children and packed lunches ready in time."

"I think we should all help with the packed lunch. I've got the times here. It's all in this brochure, one of the many on the mantlepiece I've been looking through."

Gaynor yawned. "You're very efficient," she said as Will moved to the end of the sofa, putting his feet up as she leant against him.

"And you're a very efficient driver."

"Ah, well, before I took the part-time job at your school, I had a part-time job for an airport call car firm based at Ostness, taking clients to Heathrow, Gatwick, City and Stansted Airports in luxury automatic cars.

Mother looking after the children. But I like working in a school better. The driving job was on my CV."

"I'd forgotten," Will admitted. "No wonder the Auckland motorways didn't bother you."

"I had to adapt to the different procedures, passing both sides, which Layla told me about."

Will was embarrassed he had forgotten what was on her CV. It was quite a while back and, what with all he had to keep in mind at school, such a comparatively minor matter had long been erased from his memory.

Gaynor yawned again. Will felt sleepy too. Before they knew it, they both fell asleep together, Gaynor waking up with a start and slipping away to her own bed at three in the morning, at which point Will put off the heater and stumbled sleepily upstairs to join Ruth.

Downstairs next morning, Ruth and Will found Gaynor already bustling around in the kitchen. After the usual round of greetings, including accommodating Ruth's Yellow Ted, Will said, "I'm looking forward to the time when Ruth's not so emotionally dependent on her teddy. Perhaps this trip with you all will make a difference, increase her sense of security."

"I hope so, I'll have your breakfasts ready in a jiffy," Gaynor replied, bustling around, giving Will a brief kiss in passing.

After breakfast Will remarked, "As I said yesterday, I think we should all contribute to the packed lunches, it's good for the children to do what they can, tell us what you want in front of you."

"All right," Gaynor replied, "thoughtful of you, Will, but I doubt it'll make the process quicker."

"I thought we could try and make the ferry to the city. Ted said we'd need to park back along King Edward

Parade where the parking is free and walk down the diagonal pathway through Windsor Reserve to Marine Square. We want the second, covered wharf, the first is the redundant vehicular ferry wharf, now used for recreational purposes. We should leave by nine fifteen at the latest."

"OK, we all need to get a move on," Gaynor agreed. "I'll tell you what I need for the packed lunches."

With Will at the wheel, they left for Devonport in good time. "We'll go by Narrow Neck," Gaynor said, looking at the map, "after that carry on along Vauxhall Road, turn left at Tainui Road past North Head, you can drive up there, it's called Hauraki Gulf Maritime Park."

"Ted said that for years it was a military fort, no one could go there," Will interrupted.

"Well, you can certainly go there now, why don't we drive up for the view on the way back?"

"Why not," agreed Will, "we'd need to be back before dark."

"We're taking a ferry back directly to Devonport, we'll make sure we get one that makes it possible."

Will nodded in agreement.

They could only get parking quite a way back near Torpedo Bay, having then to proceed on foot. Just past the yacht club, Angela wanted to go to the toilet. Fortunately, there was a public toilet Devonport side of the yacht club after which it was a further scamper for half a mile along the footpath beside the water parallel to King Edward Parade to arrive at the toll booth beyond the shops at the end of the wharf with the ferry about to sail.

"We only made it!" Gaynor gasped breathlessly. All agreed it was a lovely twenty-minute sail across the busy waterway, bow spray glittering in the morning sunshine. Only too soon the tall, city buildings loomed up close and they were slowing down approaching Custom House quay. Scrambling ashore, they turned right to look for the Rangitoto Ferry departure quay. When they found it, they discovered it was a fifteen-minute wait for the next ferry. After catching their breaths, they strolled around the immediate area. There was much to see including ships of all sizes along with busy waterfront activities.

The journey to Rangitoto took 30 minutes in a smaller twin-hulled ferry. As they drew near the island, a very a different panorama from the precarious landing near the lighthouse met their gaze. Their shallow draft vessel was about to enter a wide bay with a scattering of exposed rocks. Seated passenger stood up for a better view, the many Japanese tourists aboard jabbering excitedly as they aimed their cameras. Will and Gaynor, each holding a daughter's hand, followed the crowd onto the long wooden wharf. Tim, as always wanting to be independent, jumping off ahead of them. Ashore there were dining and resting facilities to the left of the wide gravel pathway leading to the summit. Here, on a sheltered seat set back out of the wind, they had their lunch. Overhead a scattering of fair-weather cumulonimbus clouds suggested a fine afternoon. Before them was a unique scene, lush vegetation squeezing out from every rocky cranny while to seaward, shallow lagoons merged into the bay.

"The weather looks settled for your walk to the top. There's plenty of small inlets and rocky pools for the girls and I to explore while you're away," Will said. "Shall we all go to the toilet first and meet right here in a little less than two hours' time to catch the three thirty ferry directly to Devonport?"

"It's very good of you, Will, you're sure you don't mind?"

"The girls would never make it there and back unless carried. They'll be happier poking into rock pools and exploring the walkways here."

"All right, both girls have a spare pair of pants and waterproofs in their bags. Don't lose Yellow Ted!"

"Now that would be something," Will replied grinning. "Good luck, don't get lost!"

Gaynor bent over and gave Will and the girls a brief kiss before striding off with Tim up the pathway.

After a few photos, some including the children, Will took the girls' hands and they moved off right towards the rook pools and walkways.

It was fascinating, so many varied pools and inlets with small sandy beaches interspersed with rocky outcrops. Will looked across to observe where they had come from to make sure they did not get lost. Looking out to sea, he observed a pod of dolphins blowing and diving. Will wondered about the tidal range and thought he must be careful not to be cut off by the tide. The girls were enchanted, running this way and that, calling to each other excitedly.

They had been away exploring for over three-quarters of an hour when Will became aware of a sudden deep rumbling, at the same time the ground began to shake under his feet and the water in the rock pools splashed about erratically. He froze with fear, an earthquake! He had no knowing if it came from the mountain or from far away! He looked out to sea to observe if a tsunami was sweeping landwards. He thought he saw one far out but realised it was probably the bow wave of a passing vessel. But he knew what he must do, get onto higher ground as quickly as possible! The girls looked at him, frightened. "What is it, Daddy?" Ruth called.

"Come on, take my hand, run!"

"Where are we going?"

Will realised he must not panic. Though the rumbling and shaking had ceased, it only lasted for seconds, there was no time to lose. The children could only move so fast and with their light shoes he did not want their ankles going over and being gashed on the sharp scoria like what happened to Gaynor. Taking care, he made their way as quickly as he could back along the rough pathways towards the wide route leading from the wharf up the mountain, looking every so often over his shoulder out to sea as he did so. He noticed people still eating in the restaurant but nevertheless he felt he should get at least 30 or 40 feet above sea level to be on the safe side.

Four or five hundred yards along the pathway leading up the mountain, he stopped for them to catch their breaths. "What was the shaking, why are we running?" Ruth asked again.

"I want my mummy!" Angela cried, sensing the tension.

"Your mum and Tim will be coming back down this path towards us before long," Will replied to Angela. "Don't worry, dear," feeling for the first time he might have over-reacted. But then he thought that it was better to be safe than sorry. "There's been an earthquake," he explained to the children.

"What's an earthquake?" Angela asked.

"It's when the ground shakes, it happens in New Zealand."

"Why did we run?" Ruth followed up by asking.

"Sometimes a huge wave can follow. It's wise to go for higher ground I've been informed," Will replied, beginning to feel even more that he might have over-reacted as some descending Japanese tourist passed them, chatting happily to each other, appearing not in any way fazed by an event everyone on the island must have experienced. After 20 minutes, more groups passed them to wait for a return ferry, some foreign, some New Zealanders and some Australians. He was beginning now to distinguish the slight difference in accent between Australians and New Zealanders. Will overheard a group of Australians saying to each other that this was the shaky isles so what else could you expect. At least Australian tourist felt the earthquake was an event to talk about. Rather sheepishly, Will suggested to the girls that perhaps they could begin to stroll back to wait for Angela's mum and Tim at their agreed rendezvous point. He checked to ascertain that Yellow Ted was still in Ruth's bag. Will felt Yellow Ted was making him neurotic.

A little before time, Gaynor and Tim arrived out of breath. "The earthquake," was Gaynor's first words, "I thought the mountain was going to blow its top! Bits of loose rock hurtled past, it was terrifying! We were in the ash cone area at the time on our way down with a lot of Japanese tourist. To them going to the top seemed like a pilgrimage. When the earthquake struck, some of them stopped and bowed. They didn't seem bothered, it was strange." Gaynor spoke quickly, obviously upset.

"Are you all right?" Will asked.

"Yes, but I can't wait to get off the island. I don't want that experience again!"

"I was concerned," Will admitted, "I brought the girls up away from the water in case there was a tsunami."

At that Angela hung on to her mother crying, "Mummy!"

"It's all right, dear," her mother replied reassuringly.

"But I don't think the earthquake's anything to do with the island. Its epicentre could well be hundreds of miles away. We'll look at the news this evening. New Zealanders don't seem bothered but I overhead some Australians talking about it who appeared a bit concerned."

"I was alarmed when you hear how the volcano was formed."

"Handed down Maori accounts say there were a lot warning signs at the time."

"It frightened me, let's take our place on the ferry."

"It frightened me too," Will admitted.

"It didn't frighten me," Tim announced.

"Brave boy," his mother replied sceptically.

On the ferry, the earthquake did not seem to feature in passengers' conversations that Will could overhear, though some were speaking other languages. On the way to Devonport, to the children's enchantment, a pod of dolphins joined the ship for a period, leaping and swooping through the bow wave. Will ducked about, trying to get a photo along with dozens of others.

After bumping alongside the wharf at Devonport and waiting their turn to disembark, it was a long trudge back to the car, entertained as they were by vessels of all sizes sailing in each direction along the busy waterway separating Devonport from the city.

They took the opportunity of taking the children to the public toilet near the yacht club before getting in the car, which was not far away on King Edwards Parade. Reaching it, they sank into their seats gratefully.

Within three minutes of starting back, they were passing North Head. "Like to whip up and see the historic reserve, Hauraki Gulf Marine Park. There should be fabulous views from the top. We've got half an hour before dusk," Will reminded.

"If you like," Gaynor said. "I know I suggested it this morning, but I don't feel like much more walking."

"Neither do I," Will admitted, even though he had not walked up Rangitoto. "Just a brief look." With that, he swung right and began a steep ascent in the car. Within two hundred yards, they passed ornamental gates, turned right, and continued to climb steeply until they had to bear off left into terraced car parks, not far from the top.

They got out of the car. The view was superb, a panorama of the outer harbour and gulf, the sails of yachts catching the glow of the setting sun. "Where's Tim?" Gaynor suddenly inquired.

"He's run off going up that pathway!" Angela replied, pointing round to the left above them.

"Come back, where are you going?"

"It's not far from the top!" Tim called back.

Reluctantly, as it was not too far, they followed Tim up the steep incline. At the summit, there was an even more superb view through all points of the compass comprising inner, outer harbour and gulf. Around the levelled rim were distributed a range of late nineteenth-century cannons with a huge one in the centre designed to retract down into a massive circular chamber, once part of the crater. The whole top of the mountain, they found, was a labyrinth of old defensive tunnels dating back as far as Maori times. Tim was enthralled, wanting to see everything at once.

"The park closes in 10 minutes time," Gaynor observed, "we'd better be getting back to the car. We don't want to be locked in."

Nobody did, so tired as they were, they hurried back to the car. Passing Narrow Neck Beach, Gaynor said, "If you take the first right up the hill, Hamana Street, which leads into Seacliffe Avenue, you'll avoid Merani Street. If Ted and Layla see us, they'll wonder why we didn't call in. I don't feel like company. I just feel like getting home and getting our own meal in our own time."

"I couldn't agree with you more," Will replied.

"If you remember, we turn left at the raised planters in the middle of the street into Winscombe Street to get our turn at the traffic lights to turn right into Lake Road, otherwise we'll never get out with the constant traffic at this time of day. It seems odd coming all this way to such a sparsely populated country to be held up by traffic."

"It's just because at Belmont it's a squeeze point where the peninsula narrows, leaving only enough room for one through road. Where Old Lake Road and Lake Road join, there're two routes to Devonport and the populated suburbs and bays beyond."

"I guess so," Gaynor agreed. "You know your way after that."

"I do. It's been an eventful day."

"You can say that again," Gaynor replied.

Back at the villa, with the television and fire on, the children were too tired to need amusing, freeing both adults to make a quick evening meal. After that it was children promptly to bed.

Coming down for the nine o'clock news, Will was right about the earthquake. Its epicentre was at a depth of 25 kilometres in the Bay of Plenty, north of White Island, a constantly erupting volcano which had seen increasing activity of late, the earthquake measuring four point three on the Richter Scale, felt widely over a large part of the North Island. No damage was reported.

Sitting together at the end of the sofa with their feet up Gaynor said, "I was frightened today by the earthquake."

"So was I," Will admitted. "It's just that we're not used to them."

"I suppose so," Gaynor replied sleepily, after which they both nodded off, cuddled into each other on the sofa, once again struggling off to their respective beds about two in the morning to be there for their children.

Next morning after breakfast, Will, who felt that he'd been calling all the shots, said to Gaynor, "So far, I've suggested what we might do but, if we want to see more of New Zealand before we go to the Bay of Islands for the last four or five days, we can only spend one day more here before we'd better tour south. Many attractive places still to visit are featured on brochures on the mantelpiece such as Auckland Memorial War Museum, Waiheke Island, Eden Gardens, Piha, Tiritiri Matangi Island, Kitekite Falls, Auckland Domain, why don't you let Tim look through them and see what he would like, the girls chose little monkeys at Auckland Zoo?" Will took a handful and gave them to Gaynor.

As she began flipping through them, Tim picked them up and began to do the same. "I'd like to go to this

MOTAT place," said Tim, showing Gaynor a brochure she had just put down.

Gaynor took the proffered brochure. "Museum of Transport and Technology?"

"There are all sorts of brilliant cars and aircraft. You can get inside them, look."

"Spread across 40 acres, MOTAT will take you on an interactive journey to explore and discover the achievements that have helped shape New Zealand," Gaynor read aloud.

Reading over her shoulder, Will added, "It's located close to the Western Springs Stadium, Auckland Stadium and Western Springs Park. The museum has large collections of civilian and military aircraft and other transport vehicles. I think I'd quite like to go there, and I'd take Tim, while you have other venues nearby that you might like to take the girls to as they probably wouldn't have the same interest in MOTAT at their age. It would be straight there and back on the same route we took when we returned from the zoo at Western Springs last time, ending up on the North-Western Motorway. You're good on the urban motorways, perhaps you'd like to drive?"

Gaynor was obviously not enthusiastic. Will wondered if he had done the right thing in involving Tim without consulting his mother on her own first. They were living, in a way, like man and wife but were in fact two independent people who needed to negotiate as such. In future, Will felt, he would plan a negotiating strategy in advance like he did at school, rather than talk off the cuff. In the end, Will said, "When I come to think about it, I feel we can only afford the morning. If we're going on a whistle-stop tour down south, we need the afternoon to plan, pack, pay off the villa and otherwise get organised."

"Precisely," Gaynor agreed. "We'll all go to MOTAT for an hour, an hour and a half at the most, get back here for lunch, plan and pack. At least it will be a novelty for the girls."

"Agreed, I'll get Ruth ready and the car out."

While waiting on the top step for the others, Ruth asked, "Where are we going?"

"This morning we're going to see early flying machines and other forms of transport not used these days like trams."

"What are trams?"

"Likes buses on rails."

"Yellow Ted doesn't like trams," Ruth replied.

"I'm sure Yellow Ted will be fascinated. He likes new things."

"Not trams."

Will was relieved when the others appeared as he could see his conversation with Ruth was getting nowhere.

Along Lake Road, Tim suddenly said, "I did like all those old guns on the top of North Head."

"Make up your mind," Gaynor said. "We turn to the city and the Harbour Bridge in a minute. Devonport's straight on."

"Planes and thing."

"Right, city!" With that, Gaynor swung to the right. Then she turned to Will who was sitting beside her with the map. "Can you give me warning of interchanges and exits please?"

Will smiled to himself. If only his staff at Vikant Primary could see him taking orders from this most junior staff member who was not even a teacher, they would have never believed it. But that was life. In changed circumstances, the conventional order of things could be turned upside down. While he was musing, Gaynor suddenly said, "I'd like to go the hairdresser's in Takapuna this afternoon, there'll be time, if you wouldn't mind looking after the children."

Will suddenly felt he had taken little notice of how Gaynor was turned out but there she was beside him, her brunette hair well groomed, dressed in a smart, fitted light-blue trouser suit. When he thought about it, he had been married long enough to know that women always liked to go to the hairdressers!

"OK, of course," he replied.

Once parked, walking towards the entrance, they were passing one of the innumerable stone walls built of the rock that littered the larva field Auckland was built on when Ruth's attention was drawn to an attractive cat perched precariously on the rough stonework. As she came up to stroke the cat, she suddenly jumped back. "Tiny dragons, look!"

What Ruth saw, and what the cat was looking at, were three or four-inch skinks or geckos, Will did not know which, running about where the sun, shining on the stones, had warmed up their metabolism. He learnt later the skinks and geckos were the only true lizards found in New Zealand. They were indeed fascinating little creatures, lithe and agile, like miniatures of the Jurassic age, projected into the present and grown small. Will got out his camera to see if he could get a closeup. Tim's imagination was fired too, and he began looking for other stonework in the sun, searching for lizards.

In the end, Gaynor became exasperated. "When all you lot stop playing about looking for lizards, we might just about have time to see what we came all this way for!"

"Sorry, I got a bit carried away," Will said somewhat sheepishly.

Gaynor felt like saying, 'Not for the first time' but held her tongue.

Having paid a family entrance fee, they headed for the Pioneers' Aviation Pavilion. Inside they were met by a boys' own aircraft collection, starting with relics and reproductions of Richard Pearse's first 1903 aircraft, right through to 1930s Fox and Tiger Moths, a 1930s Rapide, New Zealand's first commercial passenger-carrying aircraft, a Short Solent 1940s double-decked Flying Boat from New Zealand's first international airline, TEAL, a Short Sunderland marine patrol flyboat, as well as a De Havilland wooden fighter bomber, as well as a restored 1940s Avro Lancaster bomber, a De Havilland Vampire 1950s jet fighter and advanced jet trainers. Even Gaynor and the girls were impressed. Where exhibits were interactive, Will and Tim were in having a go. Gaynor led the girls about by hand, explaining to them, as best they could understand, the wonders around and, in some instances, suspended over them.

Only too soon it was time to leave for home and lunch. "Must we?" Tim implored.

"If you'd hadn't spent so much time messing about hunting lizards, you'd have had more time inside the museum," Gaynor pointed out.

"I haven't seen them on stonework on the Shore," Will observed.

"You were as bad as the rest of them," Gaynor remarked.

"Has Will been stupid and thoughtless again?" Tim inquired, assuming studied innocence.

"And I don't want any more remarks like that from you, Tim, my lad. Regarding the event you're alluding to, Will acted with the best intentions without thinking of the possible consequences. It's a lesson you could well learn. The incident is over and done with, and I don't want it ever mentioned again. Do you understand me?"

Tim knew by the tone of his mother's voice that she meant what she said. "Yes, Mum," he replied, subdued.

Wisely, Will kept out of the discussion but felt grateful Gaynor had taken the stand she had. In their present circumstances, it was difficult to reprimand the other person's child while the relationship between them was at an early and evolving stage.

As usual Gaynor managed the motorways back with confidence and efficiency, Will content to give her warning of approaching interchanges, marvelling once again at the breathtaking panorama as they crossed the Harbour Bridge.

After his dressing-down, Tim made no attempt to give his mother advice about what lanes to take and ways to turn as he knew she needed no reminding, as did Will, once they were back on the Shore.

Inside their villa, having taken off their outdoor clothes, everyone, according to their age, played their part in preparing vegetables and kumara, which they discovered they all liked better than potatoes, for the microwave while Gaynor pan-fried snapper. Will noted Gaynor seemed to prefer fish to red meat like he did, much better for one was his opinion.

"OK," Gaynor announced with a flourish. "Grub's up!" Hungry as usual, everyone fell to eating, Gaynor leaning across to cut some of Angela's food smaller. Ruth, with Yellow Ted at her side, however, liked to show independence, taking her time, pretending to give Yellow Ted a nibble, which could test Will's patience.

After lunch there was much to do and organise. Will needed to go up to the office of the Gulf Horizons Motel to pay for their time at the villa with his credit card. He knew it was going to be expensive. For the rest of their time in New Zealand, he intended to stay in motels and travel lodges. He needed as well to check the car's oil and tyre pressures, work out how he was going to store the food Gaynor would be buying to take away with them and then to organise the car in such a way that what they would require during the day was at hand. While out shopping, Gaynor said she was also going to have her hair done.

"If you intend shopping in Takapuna, Ted was telling me that, up from Halls Corner, there's a large car park in the grounds of what was the first wooden church in the area. He said it was where he and Layla got married in 1956 but was later pulled down. He said it had probably been demolished due to extensive borer."

"What's borer?" Gaynor inquired.

"Some sort of wood termite, I understand, hence its name."

"OK, anything you need while I'm at the shops?"

"Remember snack bars for the kids while travelling, safety razors and shaving gel for me please. Got enough money?"

"I'm all right for the moment."

"I might be on the beach with the children when you come back. I'd better give them a run around as they'll be travelling tomorrow."

"I'll give you a wave when I'm back."

"Right oh, good luck." Gaynor gave them all a brief kiss before she dashed off.

It was surprising how quickly the children had adapted to the idea that, as far as they were concerned, they were a family and went off happily with Will in light raincoats as they knew by now a shower could come and go quickly at any time in Auckland. Will realised that the weather would be cooler further south and they would need warmer clothes. He had bought in advance and packed for Ruth warm tights, a warm woolly polo-necked jumper and woolly hat with a bobble on the top, plus a doll's size one for Yellow Ted.

Gaynor came back in good time, giving them a shout from the top of the steps before she went inside, after which it was Will's turn to take the car and do what he had planned. While out he called in at the post office to buy a stamp for a letter to his parents in Australia. He was of two minds about the wisdom of letting his parents know he was presently in New Zealand as they might have expected him to stop over to see them, made more difficult by having Gaynor and her family with him, but then equally they could be offended when he eventually told them he had been to New Zealand but did not let them know at the time. It was one of those decisions where the pros and cons more or less balanced out.

When he came back, Gaynor asked Will what he thought the temperatures might be like at this time of the year in the South Island. Will replied that if they were to see the popular resort of Queenstown, go down to Te Anau and up through the Homer Tunnel to Milford Sound, there could be snow at times. Out of the car, they would need warm coats, gloves, leggings and woolly hats over their ears. This evening he said they would need to discuss their itinerary in relations to the number of days at their disposal. Gaynor's reply was that she would now go and pack what they had but would likely need to buy more before they got far south. Will said it was likely he would need to do the same.

About five, the families gathered in the lounge to watch early evening children's television. Will was anxious to note the Upper North Island weather forecast for tomorrow on National TV One *News at Six* at the end. In the following international news, they learnt that Saudi Arabia's King Fahd had issued a decree replacing all members of the Council of Ministers who did not have ties to the royal family.

"Where's Saudi Arabia?" Tim asked.

"It's a big country in the Middle East that produces a lot of oil," Will replied, "not a democracy like Britain."

"What's a democracy?" Tim followed up.

"Where the people are represented in a parliament, listen, hear what's next, Croatian forces launch Operation Storm, sad business that war. After that will come the weather forecast, that's what's important for us at the moment. 'Auckland to Taupo including the Bay of Plenty and Central Highlands, sunny periods and light rain at times, particularly over the Kaimais, temperatures maximum 18, minimum seven degrees centigrade' not too bad," Will decided.

"Where's the Kaimais?" Gaynor asked.

"If you look at the map, not far south of Auckland on the left. If we get rain it could be after the first hour of travelling. Shall we see if we can find a family programme on television?"

There was a limited range of programmes compared with what they were used to back home, so Gaynor got from her room a story book called *Shrek!*, a humorous account of a monstrous green creature who leaves home to save the world and ends up by saving a princess. Gaynor's telling was funny and even Tim, who was inclined to be cynical at times, fell about laughing his head off with the others. Exhausted at the end, Gaynor felt they should take their children to bed as they wanted to get back together again to discuss their tour programme as soon as they could.

Meeting again in the lounge, Will got out what he had bought at the garage earlier in the afternoon when checking the oil level and tyre pressures. "I've got a *North Island Complete Drivers Atlas* with touring information. I've also taken from here an *AA Traveller for the North Island*, free to guests, which features places to visit and stay. When we've decided what we want to see and to stay for the first night, we'd better ring ahead before we leave and book two rooms in a featured motel or travel lodge. Depending on the layout, it might be possible to put the girls together in a double bed and accommodate Tim in a single bed a little later in another room as he's always complaining that he doesn't want or need to go to bed when the girls do. We've got used to all the room here."

"Now that's a thought," Gaynor agreed.

Will got out his engagement diary. "I've worked out dates, look, see what do you think? We left on the 26th of July, arrived here on the 28th, got the car on the 29th, went to Lake Pupuke on the 30th, sailed to Rangitoto on the 31st, Marine Drive and Zoo on the first of August, Rangitoto and earthquake on the second, MOTAT on the third. By leaving tomorrow, we've got two weeks and four days to visit both islands before we need to spend the rest of August near Ted and Layla's before undertaking the three hours' drive north to Paihia in the Bay of Islands next day. Once there we've got four clear days before we need to drive to the airport to catch the plane to Singapore and on to London next day, to arrive back home on the first of September. School starts on the fourth of September."

"Do we need that long in Paihia?"

"I would like to find out more about my elder sister's disappearance. From what Ted told me she became increasingly eccentric after returning to New Zealand at the end of the war, finally disappearing entirely about 10 years ago. The inquiry at the time was inconclusive. Ted went up Paihia in an attempt to speak to her best friend only to find that she was in Indonesia for an indefinite period. I want to locate this friend, if possible, assuming she has returned to New Zealand, and see what she has to say. It's especially important for me, and Ruth."

"Why Ruth?"

It was at this point that Will knew the conversation would become increasingly difficult. He did not want to appear ridiculously dramatic by saying he and Ruth, independently, had seen what at least could only be described at a spectre in Mrs Mill's classroom, which he found uncannily familiar as if he should know who it was, but did not.

"A spectre?" Gaynor questioned with incredulity.

"Well, at least a presence, which disturbed Ruth. I checked it out and discovered the same thing, but no other child or adult seemed aware of the presence that I knew about." Will decided he would broach the subject from a different perspective. "Your mother and other older people in Oftness say Vikant Primary was requisitioned during the war as a searchlight and ack-ack gun position, the classrooms being used for accommodation and training, particularly of Auxiliary Territorial Servicewomen, some coming from the White Commonwealth by their overheard accents."

"Yes," Gaynor agreed.

"I can't really remember what my elder sister Zoe looked like as I was very young when she left with our older brother, Ted, to emigrate to New Zealand in 1938. However, unlike Ted, she returned to Britain for the war period. Nevertheless, the..." Will hesitated, "presence, spectra, whatever, I felt I should know but didn't. What photos we had of Zoe was when she was young. While in Paihia in the Bay of Island, I was hoping that I could find and talk to Zoe's best friend, a mixed-race girl who Ted said was called Tawhaitu Tahu. After Zoe's disappearance, Ted and Layla went up to Paihia to see if Tawhaitu, who lived in Te Haumi Drive, could throw any light on what might have happed to Zoe but discovered that she had gone to Indonesia, a place called Arata Beach, 23 kilometres from Pariaman, for an extended period. Tawhaitu's likely by now to have returned to her Te Haumi Drive home. She could have a more recent photo of Zoe, for instance, and tell me about her increasingly disturbed and eccentric life before she disappeared, which might help resolve our mystery."

Gaynor gave Will a long, searching look and said no more.

"Anyway, let's get on with more pressing planning for the next few days. Everyone says we should see the thermal region of Rotorua and the lakes; you agree?"

"Yes."

"According to our *North Island Drivers Atlas,* the distance appears to be roughly 240 kilometres, distances are all in kilometres in New Zealand which, without stops, should take about three hours. Before we leave, we should look up the *AA Traveller* and book the two rooms I spoke about, hopefully accommodation won't be difficult at this time of the year."

"If they're open at all," Gaynor observed.

"Much accommodation must be as tourists come from all over the world, many from the northern hemisphere. New Zealand depends on tourism. What about this: 'Welcome Through Year Holiday Park, close to the city centre. Trout fishing and Wildlife. Motel Units and Cabins. Hangi and Concert Bookings. Two-Bedroom Flats, sleep up to seven persons. Indoor Heated Pools and Spa.' How about trying to book the two-bedroom flat?"

"Sounds ideal, we'll ring through in the morning. Finished with these references, I'll put them together to pack in the morning?" Gaynor began assembling the literature Will had strewn about.

Will leant back on the couch. Other than a few hiccups and glitches, the holiday had gone reasonably well, Will felt. He wondered, as they sat back together and put their feet up in front of the radiant heater, what the rest of their time in New Zealand had in store.

Chapter Eight

Gaynor and Will had agreed to set their respective alarms for seven thirty. When Will awoke, Ruth was sitting up playing with Yellow Ted, "I'm teaching him to dance, look."

Sleepy-eyed Will looked. Sitting on her knees, Ruth was gently shaking and singing to her teddy bear so that his legs moved in a credible dance fashion. "Very good, I'll run your bath in a few minutes."

"What are we doing today?"

"We're touring south."

"Leaving here?" There was disappointment in Ruth's voice. "I like it here."

"Me too," Will agreed, "but we've spent a lot of money and come a long way, so it seems sensible to see more of this lovely country. There are many wonderful things to see."

"All right, if you say so." Sometimes Ruth could sound very grown up.

Will showered and shaved then finished most of their packing while Ruth swam in their incredibly large bath. It was unlikely they would get a bath as large as this again so Will let her make the most of it. Eventually she needed to come out. Will helped her to dry and dress while she continued to croon to her teddy bear and make him dance.

Downstairs as usual Gaynor was found in the kitchen getting breakfast. "That bear's wet," she remarked after she had given Ruth a good morning kiss and Yellow Ted was thrust in her face.

"I'm afraid Yellow Ted got a bit wet while I was drying Ruth off after her bath," Will apologised.

"Yellow Ted can dance, look!" Ruth gave a demonstration.

"Amazing, excuse me, Ruth, but we need to get on this morning." Gaynor darted over to the oven top where bacon, egg, sausages and sliced kumara were sizzling.

"Like me to serve cereal and yoghurt?" Will asked.

"Yes please, if you don't mind," Gaynor replied, wiping her hands on her apron.

They pressed on. The car required strategic packing. At last, when the villa was locked and all was ready, Will said, as he bent over putting seat belts on the children in the back, "We need to drop the key into the office. You're driving the first 40 miles or so of motorway?"

Gaynor needed no guidance as they swept onto the motorway to begin their journey south, the children waving an emotional goodbye over the Harbour Bridge. Their whirlwind tour of New Zealand had commenced.

"We can turn off Highway 1 at Pokeno and take the more central Highway 27 or carry on to Hamilton, a big city by New Zealand standards of about 160,000, and turn left there," Will pointed out, looking at his driving atlas.

"What do you suggest?"

"I suggest we turn left at Hamilton for Rotorua."

"All right, straight on for the present then," Gaynor concurred.

After about another quarter of an hour, the children began to get fractious, Tim being an insidious tease. Finally, Gaynor said, "This is not working, Tim needs to be in the front seat away from the girls when travelling over a distance. It won't be so easy navigating from the rear seat, but I can see no alternative. I can stop the car now we've passed the motorway section."

Will agreed, they changed drivers while stopped and so for the rest of their trip, driving any distance, Tim occupied the front passenger seat. Gaynor, now navigating, saw that they needed to continue to follow Highway 1, crossing the Waikato River, New Zealand's longest, they learnt, at Cobham Drive. Not long after that, Gaynor directed Will to turn right onto the Cambridge Road. "Between here and Tirau I'll look out for one of those designated picnic spots. Some of them have proper toilets," Gaynor suggested, looking at the map. Away from Auckland the air temperature was perceptibly cooler. Will had the car temperature set at 22. In the rear-view mirror he could see the girls cuddling up to Gaynor on each side, their eyes opening and shutting, dozing in the warmth. Will was happy Ruth felt relaxed with Gaynor. She needed a mother.

"Before we left, I was reading that in the early days of settlement, before the building of roads, the Waikato River was the only practical route into the interior. Gun boats used it as well to establish the new colonial authority," Will observed.

"You know so much," Tim chipped in.

"Not really," Will countered. "but I like finding out, especially when it comes to new things, so that I can better appreciate what I'm looking at."

"That's the way Will is," Gaynor said to Tim.

"I guess that's so," Will agreed.

Before leaving the car to sit at a table at a wayside picnic location Gaynor had picked out, Will needed to dive into their luggage, hence the need for the strategic loading, for them all to put on warmer clothes.

"Why is it so cold?" Angela asked her mother.

"Because further south is colder in New Zealand, especially in wintertime, like further north is colder in Britain in the winter," Gaynor replied. "You've got your bobble hat on."

"I don't like the cold," Angela persisted.

"That's the way it is, eat your lunch," Gaynor insisted.

"Yellow Ted's not cold," Ruth commented.

For once, Will felt, Yellow Ted's thoughts as voiced by Ruth were helpful.

"The locals call Northland, where the Bay of Islands is, 'the Winterless North'," Will put in, "where we're going for the last four or five days in New Zealand."

"It's cold out here," Angela kept on.

"I'll cut up your tomato before you bite into it and squirt it over your face," Gaynor continued, ignoring the complaints. "You'll be back in the car before long."

Within 20 minutes they were back in the car again on the last leg of their journey to Rotorua. Will felt a bit sleepy in the warm car after lunch. Admitting this to Gaynor, she offered to drive while Will sat in the back with a girl on each side of him, his nose in the driving atlas, endeavouring to keep awake and navigate.

Approaching Rotorua on route 5, they knew in advance they were nearing their destination by the all-pervading smell of rotten eggs.

"What's the smell?" Tim asked, screwing up his face in disgust.

"Sulphur," Will replied. "The guidebooks say you can smell the place long before the 'Welcome to Rotorua' sign. I think you need to turn left at Pukuatua Street coming up," Will added, addressing Gaynor, "to get into the central business district and sort ourselves out from there."

"I don't like the smell," both girls joined in. It only needed Ruth to voice Yellow Ted's opinion to make the chorus of complaints complete but apparently smelling was not one of Yellow Ted's many remarkable attributes, to Will's relief.

"The advert said that the 'Welcome Through the Year Park' was close to the city so once in sight of the lake we'll ask a local exactly where," Will suggested.

The first person they asked proved to be a visitor like themselves so Will asked what looked like a Maori who pointed out where to go, which was not far away.

The park was spacious with its own system of roads. Seeing a sign saying reception they turned around and headed for it. They found they could get a two-bedroom flat. "Two nights?" Will asked Gaynor who agreed that to see anything they needed to book for at least two nights.

Their flat proved to be bright, painted in light pastel colours with a wide lounge fronting the lake, a kitchen-dining area on the left with two bedrooms behind the lounge overlooking gardens; ideal, they felt. There was a restaurant and store on site but rather than go out and buy food, Will suggested they order a couple of pizzas to be delivered to their flat for the evening meal, supplemented by what they had brought with them. He felt that there was nothing more daunting that having to turn round and get a meal at the end of a tiring journey with children clamouring for food, though he had to admit that their children were not particularly demanding in that way.

It proved a good decision as they were able to get a satisfying meal together relatively quickly. After they had washed up and cleared away, Gaynor said, "They're advertising hangi and concert party bookings, what's a hangi?"

"From what I was reading, hangi seems to be a traditional way Maoris used to cook their food, which was placed in pits on stones made hot by a fire, the food wrapped in leaves, covered with earth and then left to cook, only here they use thermal steam instead."

"We don't want to eat again, it's cold outside."

"I suggest we ring reception and ask if they can book a Maori concert only for tonight as it's winter," Will replied.

"Good idea, like me to see what I can find?" Gaynor offered.

"Go ahead, and if successful, ask where it is, time it starts and price."

There was such an event in a marae meeting house, not far away at eight, which proved to be colourful and a lot of fun. Maori men, women and girls sang in harmony, swayed and danced, sometimes the women using poi pois, light balls on strings, slapping their arms and thighs in time to the music. The haka, sung by the men to much grimacing and shouting, frightened the girls who clutched their parents' hands while Tim was in the aisle joining in.

Back at their motel flat, Tim asked why some Maoris were brown and others almost white. Will replied that he had learnt that, if a New Zealander had some Maori blood, such a person could choose what ethnic group he or she wanted to be associated with, Maori or pakeha, that is Europeans.

The girls were nearly asleep on their return. One room had a double and a single bed while the other, slightly larger, had a double bed and two singles. Will suggested that the girls could go to bed in the larger room right away, having either a single bed each or the double bed together, while Tim could go to bed a little later when he had calmed down which met with his approval.

Tim was persuaded to go to bed half an hour later as by then he was beginning to drop off. The three-seater couch was not as comfortable as their last but that was in a super home. In Rotorua it was cold enough for central heating in winter which, in their case, was in the form of circulating hot air. Somewhere, Will felt, there had to be a thermostat. However, the temperature seemed about right, and he and Gaynor settled down to watch television before turning the lights down low and cuddling up together.

Will was beginning to feel Gaynor had come to enjoy this quiet time together at the end of the day. Gaynor held his arm close when he put it around her. Inevitably they fell asleep before one of them woke with a start when they went to their respective rooms for the rest of the night to be there for their children. On entering his without putting on the light, Will found there were two girls in the double bed, so he fished for his bedclothes in his suitcase with a torch before tumbling into one of the singles, putting on his alarm for seven thirty next morning.

Waking with the alarm next day, Will was thinking they'd have to share the shower room in this more modest type of accommodation when, looking out the back, he observed steam arising from their plunge pool though there was frost on the ground. He went outside and tentatively felt the temperature of the pool. It was hot, almost too hot to swim in. He got out his and Ruth's swimsuits. "Come on," he said to Ruth, "we're both going for a swim before breakfast. Ask your mum," he added to Angela, "if you would like to come and join us. Perhaps your mum and Tim might like to as well?"

Opening the back door, Will took Ruth in his arms and moved quickly towards the steaming water, carefully climbing down the ladder with her. The water was hot, but immersing carefully, they got used to it. Before long they were joined by Gaynor and her two. It was strange, frost on the terrace but so warm in the water. They could have stayed there all day but too long would have been debilitating, though the mineral content was alleged to have health benefits.

Back inside, Will rinsed out the swimsuits, wrung them and put them in the airing cupboard. "They call swimsuits togs here," he announced.

"The term's Irish," Gaynor replied, cracking on with the breakfast.

"Is that so?"

"I do know something," Gaynor continued, "My former husband used it. He was originally from the Irish Republic."

They needed to get going as they wanted to see Whakarewarewa geothermal area in the morning and Lake Tarawera in the afternoon. As usual Will dished out muesli, yoghurt and juice while Gaynor cooked on the stove top. They took warm clothes as it would be cold out of the car.

Whakarewarewa was amazing, the innumerable geysers, pronounced 'guy-sers', were all named, the Pohutu Geyser erupting approximately hourly to a height of 30 metres. There were also fumaroles, bubbling mud pools, strangely coloured silicone terraces. It was like being in another world, or this one at the beginning of time. For safety it was important to keep to the marked pathways. Will and Gaynor held their children's hands just in case. Ruth clutched Yellow Ted tightly, telling him not to be frightened, revealing her own state of mind. Will and Gaynor felt it to be the experience of a lifetime.

Afterwards they looked at the *Drivers Atlas* to see how to get to Lake Tarawera and discovered they could by taking the very minor Lynmore Tarawera Orareka Road then branching south, running alongside Lake Rotokakahi before turning east to Ti Toroa beside Lake Tarawere from where lake cruises were available. They found they were just in time for the early afternoon cruise.

The cruise began by taking them south over turquoise waters during which they learnt, over the public address system, that in 1886 Mount Tarawera, overlooking the lake, violently erupted for six hours, causing the destruction and overwhelming by volcanic debris and ash of a number of villages and the world-famous Pink and White Terraces. These natural structures were created by the flowing waters of silica hot springs forming tiered layers of delicately coloured terraces containing hot pools in which people bathed. Approximately 120 people, mostly Maoris, died during the terrifying event.

The eruption, which began in the early hours of June the tenth, tore the mountain apart, creating a ten-mile rift in the mountainside extending as far south as Waimangu. The shattering sound of the eruption could be heard in Blenheim in the South Island.

Eleven days before the eruption, Maori and European visitors, famous Guide Sophia and a newspaper reporter observed a phantom war canoe of a style a hundred years earlier paddling across the lake in mist. Guide Sophia consulted her tribes' tohunga, Tuhoto Ariki, a priestly wise man, who interpreted the ghostly appearance as a very bad omen.

The gigantic eruption sent a ten-kilometre ash cloud bursting into the atmosphere in which lightning flickered along with fountains of glowing larva. Sixty people sheltered in Te Wairoa village in the strong house of Guide Sophia which survived the eruption; the village, later excavated, becoming a tourist attraction known as the Buried Village. Maoris who believed the prophecy of the tohunga fled the area and survived; those who had come under European influence and no longer believed in the powers of the tohunga did not. It has only been discovered in recent years that the tohunga was able to predict the impending disaster by observing the behaviour of insects and birds disturbed by ground tremors, too small to be detected by humans. Brother Ted, who fired up Will's enthusiasm to visit Mount Tarawera, Will remembered, had told him that when he first came to New Zealand, there remained the whitened shattered ruins of a tourist hotel on the mountainside which, when last time he visited, he said, he could see no longer.

When the boat drew up to the landing stage, under the shadow of the ominous mountain, Will and Gaynor discovered that they could trek up the mountain to see the craters and awesome rift and catch the next boat back but decided the route too long and strenuous, especially for the girls, and that the terrifyingly vivid account of the eruption coming over had unnerved Gaynor and the girls who were far from keen, so it was decided to take the boat back, leaving time for something else.

Disembarking from their cruise, they found canoes for hire in a bay nearby with one or two families having fun on the water. The gentle breeze was offshore making for still water along a scenic coastline. "Can we hire canoes?" Tim implored.

Gaynor did not want more rough water boating but the mirror-like water inshore was more to her liking, and she was competent when it came to small rowing boats and canoes. "All right," she conceded. "Will and I can hire a Canadian canoe each, taking our own girl, while you can have a child's covered canoe with double paddle if you are prepared to put on your light raincoat with gathered wrists, as water goes down your arms with a double paddle, is that all right with you, Will?"

"That sounds fun," Will was happy to agree, "as long as we stay inshore as the further offshore the stronger will be the wind, trying to push us out into the lake. Canadian canoes each and a child's single for an hour's fine."

It turned out to be an interesting experience. Grey teal and mallard ducks darted out now and then from behind clumps of reed and rounding one bend, they came upon a group of black swans sailing majestically by while they stopped paddling and silently watched. After half an hour, they turned back south for their starting point.

"My arms are wet and I'm cold," Tim complained, carefully getting out of his canoe onto the landing stage.

"Double-ended paddles have that effect, they tend to drip down the arms," Gaynor pointed out. "It was you who wanted to go out in canoes in the first place. When we're all in the car with the heater on you'll warm up."

Back at their motel flat, Will found the temperature control and turned it up by a couple of degrees. He offered to take them out to the site's restaurant or order a meal to be delivered, but Gaynor said she could quickly bake a nourishing meal from the food they carried which she began by turning on a preheating sequence on the oven.

Will helped her prepare the ingredients so that when the oven pinged all they had to do was to pop it in and then join the children in front of the television.

"Can I stay up late and watch the *Goodnight Kiwi* going to bed like I heard Uncle Ted talk about?" Tim inquired.

"If you'd been listening more closely you would have heard that it finished last year now that TVNZ no longer shuts down at night," Gaynor replied. "What he was saying was that he missed it as he thought it fun. Anyway, it would have been too late for you, we need to be up by seven thirty as we're moving on tomorrow."

"Where to?" Tim asked.

"Will and I will be discussing it tonight. You'll know in the morning."

"Grown-ups!" Tim said in disgust.

"Precisely," his mother replied with a grin.

Meeting in the lounge after having put their respective children to bed, Gaynor said, showing Will a brochure, "According to this brochure I picked up in

Auckland, the Waitomo Caves seem fascinating, magical glow-worms, stalactites and stalagmites."

Will took out his *Drivers Atlas*. "OK, let me try to work out a route, distance and approximate driving time." After some calculations he continued, "It's almost opposite on the other side of the island. The most direct route seems to be via a place called Arapuni, about 85 to 90 miles in all, take us about two to two-and-a-half hours driving time, but first I have to go to get some cash at the National Bank of New Zealand, it'll have a sign of a black horse."

"Does it have to be that bank?"

"Yes, my card is a Lloyds card, in the early days of settlement, Lloyds Bank, England, set up the National Bank of New Zealand as an offshoot. It still has some connection. Lloyds Bank back home in England has the sign of the black horse. Do you want to look at television?"

"No."

Will leant over, pulled out a stool, turned the lights in the lounge down low and they cuddled up together.

Next morning, a little reluctantly, they all arose at seven thirty. As they had to pack up as well as get breakfast, there was not time for the hot outdoor pool, so everyone had a quick shower in the twin shower bathroom instead. With lunches packed, they were away by nine forty-five, looking for a National Bank of New Zealand before driving out of town.

In the central business district, a National Bank of New Zealand was soon found, made prominent by a large black horse against a green background. While Will went in, Gaynor minded the children. Back outside it was decided that Will would drive first and, for journeys, Tim occupying the front passenger seat.

The route Will had worked out proved interesting, taking them through a variety of rural and wild central North Island scenery, beginning with the Mamaku Forest, followed by cultivated valleys with the occasional small town, separated by a jumble of low mountain ranges which the road wound through. Arapuni, with a population of about 2,000, they discovered, was next to the hydroelectric dam at Lake Arapuni, the adjacent power station of eight turbines being the largest on the Waikato River. They parked the car and walked over the wire-enclosed suspension bridge below the dam to view the awesome bursting out of the pent-up waters and the great river and gorge far below.

"I wouldn't like to fall down there!" Tim observed, in a subdued manner to which they all agreed.

Arriving at Waitomo an hour or so later, looking around for accommodation, they found a motel in a shallow valley along Mangarino Street off the main road within a reasonable distance of the caves' entrance. The motel had two bedrooms units, laid out much like their motel in Rotorua but featuring a wide porch, and a third smaller room opposite the kitchen/dining area which could be used as a day room or for whatever the occupants chose. They also found out in the night that it had a corrugated iron roof, unlike their Rotorua accommodation which had a roof consisting of light modern tiles. After their evening meal and the children asleep, Will and Gaynor were cuddling up comfortably on the sofa, nodding off with the lights turned low, they were suddenly startled by a vivid flash of lightning followed by a thunderous drumming on the roof. Concerned, they ran into the bedrooms to be with the children.

"What was that?" Angela asked tearfully of her mother.

"Heavy rain on the corrugated iron roof. This is a lightly constructed building, excellent if there was a strong earthquake but noisy in heavy rain. Aunty Layla told me in former times most New Zealand homes were wooden bungalows with corrugated iron roofs, increasingly less so today. She says Uncle Ted doesn't like heavy rain on the corrugated iron roof in Merani Street, but she says born and bred New Zealanders, like herself, find the sound soothing, reminding them of rain on the roofs when wrapped up cosily as children going off to sleep."

"I don't."

"I don't either," Ruth joined in.

"None of us here are born and bred New Zealanders," Gaynor replied simply. "It's becoming lighter now. Will and I will be with you for the rest of the night. Go back to sleep. I'll sit with you, Angela and hold your hand, good night." When eventually the three children were asleep again, Will and Gaynor sorted themselves out with the light of torches and turned in as well.

With alarms put on for seven thirty in both rooms, all were awake at much the same time, taking turns with the shower, both girls needing a little assistance dressing. At the age of seven, they could dress themselves quite well, but both tended to be dreamboats, taking their time, playing about. On the other hand, Tim liked to be thought of as grown up, could get on and needed no help from anyone for anything.

When all were in the lounge dining area, Gaynor picked up the 'Visiting the Caves' brochure from the side of the working top. "Escorted tours leave regularly on the hour and take a variety of time according to the tour booked. I'll ring up the centre to see what's available and whether we need to book today. Can I borrow your mobile, Will? There doesn't seem to be a phone in the place."

"Of course," Will replied, a little embarrassed, knowing he should make a greater effort to embrace modern technology.

Gaynor rang Cave Reception. "There's room on the eleven tour, so I've opted for that. Here's your mobile back, Will, I'll show you tonight how it works, much the same as in Britain, you must have forgotten." Privately, Gaynor felt Will probably had little competence in the first instance but wanted to be diplomatic. "We couldn't get on the ten tour as it was largely pre-booked by a big group of Koreans, which reminds me that Layla told me that you need to watch out for Asian visitors touring in hire cars in the South Island out of town where there is little traffic about as they tend to drift into driving onto the wrong side of the road on occasions, other than Japanese tourists as it's driving on the left in Japan. This is why you see lots of imported second-hand Japanese cars for sale as the steering wheel is on the right side. Layla said you can't drive a car in New Zealand with the steering wheel on the other side."

With the tour starting at eleven, there was more than enough time to get ready. Will took from the side of the working top the usual number of brochures he had come to expect regarding attractions in the area. He discovered that at Waitomo, as well as the caves, there was the Marakopa Falls, a gorge walk through a largely collapsed cave system with some natural bridges remaining, featuring spectacular scenes of tumbling water and luxuriant chasm growth. And Te Kuiti town, about six miles away, at the junction of State Highway 3 and 30, where there was a fabulous carved meeting house amongst other things. They would be spoilt for choice in the afternoon.

They found parking in a designated field and walked to the cave entrance. A family pass of two adults and two children came to 60 dollars, an extra child, as in their case, another 10. Strictly speaking they were two families, but Will especially had come to see themselves as a family when they were in reality two independent people, which Will was brought to realise only too well later in their New Zealand tour.

Waiting for the tour group to assemble, Will made sure Yellow Ted was secure in Ruth's bag as he hadn't been able to persuade her to leave him in the car, where Ruth insisted he would be lonely. The best he was able to do was to convince Ruth to let him carry the bag so that Yellow Ted was not lost down some dark, unreachable crevice.

Other than dim safety lights, it was dark in the caves with dripping water making pathways and staircases slippery. It was not particularly cold, Will estimated it was probably in the region of 12 degrees centigrade. They were conducted by a confident, well-spoken mixed-race young man who seemed to have some connection with the owners. His commentary was informative and not without humour. They went up and down steep staircases, through natural tunnels which opened out into spectacular caverns with glistening stalactites and stalagmites, some caves being subtly lit to bring out the delicate hues and reveal the many crystal-like formations. Other caverns were kept dark except for subdued pathway lighting for the visitors to gaze in awe at the myriads of glow-worm lights above.

In one of the large caverns, the guide stopped and asked if anyone knew which formations went up or down, stalactites or stalagmites? Nobody knew for sure, but Tim responded by saying that when the tights went down the mites went up, which made everyone laugh. The guide replied by saying it was a good one and asked Tim where he had learnt it. Tim said he learnt how to remember at school. Will made a mental note that he must congratulate Tim's class teacher next term, as it was not something he had taught him.

For the final part of the tour, they climbed carefully down to the present river created by water tunnelling through limestone over a great period of time and learnt that the glow-worms were actually fishing for midges, brought along with the flow of the water from outside. The worms let down spider web thread-like fishing lines on the end of which tiny bioluminescence lights adjacent to a very sticky substance attracted midges, which then got stuck in the glue and were drawn up and eaten; unlike fireflies, a sort of flying beetle, which dart about erratically at night, emitting flashes of light to attract mates or prey.

Members of the tour party were helped individually down into large open boats and were required to shuffle along to fill up the seating, the girls especially hanging on tightly to Will and Gaynor. When the boat was full, ready to leave, they were asked to keep quiet or the glow-worms would put out their lights, and not to use flash in their cameras for the same reasons. When they were all settled, the boat operator began to gently pull the boat forward by means of a fixed, overhead rope.

Before long what they saw above was breathtaking, a vast array of twinkling lights like stars in a cavernous heaven. They went slowly, the series of caverns dissolving one into the other, waterfalls appearing and disappearing like ghostly wraiths, along with the sound of splashing water. Quite abruptly daylight appeared ahead, and they emerged into dazzling sunlight. Spellbound, they stopped at a landing and were ushered carefully ashore.

"That was marvellous!" Gaynor commented enthusiastically as they sought to find their way back to the car. "Thank you, Will."

"I want to go to the toilet," Angela abruptly announced.

"I'll find a place for you in a minute. The only one who knew the difference between stalagmites and stalactites; well done, Tim." Gaynor gave her son a pat on the back.

"And well done, Mr Mathews. I'll have to remember to thank him when we get back," Will added.

After a suitable bush was found to take Angela behind, the car was eventually tracked down. "If we have our lunch in the car there'll be more time to do something in the afternoon, especially as it gets dark earlier the further we go south," Will suggested. This was agreed and they all sat in the car to have lunch, Will starting the engine to warm themselves up.

After lunch, looking at the brochures of attractions in the Waitomo area stored in a car pocket, Will said,

"Many of the walks like the Ruakuri Bush walk, the Waitomo Walkway and the Opapaka Pa Walk are too much for the girls especially, but this one's not nearly so long." He showed Gaynor a relatively short walk through a largely collapsed cave system forming a deep arrow gorge with fenced walkways constructed along the gorge sides giving spectacular views of a mysterious and beautiful semi-underground world. "It's not far away, what do you think?"

"The walkways are certainly well made and must have been expensive to construct, for short distances some of the former cave ceiling looks to be still arching over, fascinating. OK, appears doable."

There was a parking place near the entrance, and they started off. Very soon they were clambering up and down steel staircases with handrails and chain-linked wire sides secured to the vertical gorge walls. At times there were level sections making walking easier. All the while they were getting lower. Luxuriant ferns of every hue of green clung to the gorge sides while trees on the edges of the gorge cast flickering shadows. On occasions, trees had taken root beside the tumbling river at the bottom of the gorge, their tops coming up to meet them.

After half a mile, it was hard to tell, they had descended to the floor of the gorge onto a flat apron of rock. Twenty feet away a footbridge led across to the other side. Ahead, the gorge sides rapidly diminished showing blue sky, obviously the former cave system exit. Will let go Ruth's hand go to take photos with his trusty Fuji camera.

Suddenly Gaynor cried in alarm, "Where's Tim?" They looked around. He was nowhere to be seen. "Look after the girls." Gaynor ran back up the walkway,

Will following with the girls. "Tim! Tim!" Gaynor was visibly shaken. "He can't have just vanished. Tim!" She looked around in desperation.

A minute later they heard Tim's frightened voice, "I'm stuck! The ledge got narrow round the bend and I can't turn round to get back!"

Gaynor leant over the walkway as far as she could to see where Tim was as his voice appeared to come from immediately below. Then she screamed. "Hang on, I'll get help! Give me your phone, Will, I'll ring the emergency services!"

"Here's the phone but it's unlikely you'll get a signal down here. Look after the children."

"What are you doing, Will?"

"Look after the girls!" Will repeated, hurrying back down the walkway to the rock apron by the bridge. At the bottom, looking back, he saw what Tim had likely done. To the right of the walkway steps, a ledge led round a buttress. Acting on a hunch, he followed the ledge round the rock feature, squeezing past folds and cavities, climbing steadily. After a final unexpected turn back round a flank, the ledge abruptly narrowed to a couple of inches and Tim was on it, hanging on for dear life, unable to turn round. Speaking quietly so as not to startle him, Will said, "All right, Tim, I'm behind you, keep holding on. I'm going to shift your back foot further back onto a secure place after which you inch backwards, shifting one hand or your front foot at any one time. We'll keep doing that until you get sufficiently far back to be able to turn round."

Making sure he hung on as well, taking his own advice to move only one limb at a time, Will painstaking kept moving Tim's back foot backwards, talking to Tim reassuringly as he did so, until eventually he got him back far enough onto the widening ledge where he could let go and turn around, calling up to Gaynor, "Tim's all right now, we'll be up with you in three or four minutes."

Gaynor rushed towards Tim as he approached, giving him a tearful hug before standing him back and in no uncertain terms, telling him what a stupid, irresponsible, thoughtless boy he was while Will kept a straight face, remembering Tim's smirking countenance when he met with Gaynor's wrath. Gaynor then turned round to Will, gave him a hug before thanking him in heartfelt terms for likely saving Tim's life.

Will felt that the incident went a long way towards making up for his unintentionally putting them at risk on Rangitoto. "I think there's just time before dusk to see the Marakopa Falls. There appears to be a steep but wide track down, we might have to carry the girls back up."

"OK, I might have to put Tim on a lead."

"I won't go off exploring again on my own," a chastened Tim replied.

"I hope not, you frightened the living daylights out of us. When we get there, you can take your sister's hand and help her down the steep, slippery path to convince me you can act responsibly."

It was a thirty-minute drive to the well-marked falls. The track, as the brochure described, got steeper, descending through beautiful native forest with moss-hung trees. As they got nearer what the brochure described as a stream, but what Will felt would be a full-blown river, having come to realise that, in New Zealand, only the very largest rivers, like the Waikato, were known as rivers, everything else was a stream, they knew they were nearing the falls by the noise and mist in the air.

Rounding a steep bend to the left, there it was, a broad high waterfall, made even more impressive by recent rain. Will had never seen the Niagara Falls but felt what he saw before him more than made up for that. It was awesome. He said to Gaynor, "If you don't mind looking after the children, I'll scramble round to see if I can get a frontal shot," and began climbing round rocks at the foot of the waterfall.

Tim went to follow him, but Gaynor grabbed his collar. "You're staying here, young man, I've seen enough of you out on your own for one day."

The ascent was too steep for the girls, so Will and Gaynor put their seven-year-olds on their shoulders. "You go a little ahead of us, Tim, so I can keep an eye on you," Gaynor said to Tim, "but not too far, mind."

It was dusk by the time they got to the car and dark when they arrived back to their motel. Will put the television on for the children then, by now, a well-practised team, he and Gaynor swung into action, each contributing what they did best to get a meal as quickly as possible. After doing the dishes they looked at family television for a while. Before long, the girls were falling asleep and even Tim did not insist he should be allowed to stay up later.

Back in the lounge, Will and Gaynor cuddled up for comfort, Gaynor giving Will a kiss and thanking him again for getting Tim successfully out of difficulties. "You were right, Will, there was no mobile reception down in the gorge, thank goodness you could act," and gave Will another kiss. Later in the evening, a shower drummed on the iron roof and in case noise had woken the children, Will and Gaynor stumbled off to their rooms by the light of their torches, leaving a dim light on in the lounge.

Next morning after breakfast, they were off to Taupo to see the Huka Falls and the Aratiatia Rapids below the dam, a distance of about 95 miles, which Will calculated should take about two and a half hours driving time. Tim was in the front passenger seat and Will was driving first. It was fine but cold, Will had the car heater on. Gaynor started off by reading the girls a story. On the way they would pass through Kinleith exotic pine forest, a planted forest progressively cut down for timber with a large mill near Tokoroa. Will understood that native bush could not be cut down for timber like it was in the early years of settlement. They were going to spend the night at Waitahanui, eight miles south of Taupo, which Ted had told Will about. They had booked a lakeside motel the night before by phone.

Down where they were near the middle of the North Island there was little traffic about, what Will had thought driving in New Zealand was going to be like, not like the bottleneck where Ted lived on the Shore. They did not stop in the Kinleith exotic forest as both Will and Gaynor agreed they were more interested in the native forest, called bush, with its understory of fern. Will thought it logical to view the Huka Falls first, where the Waikato, one of New Zealand's longest rivers, drained Lake Taupo, the largest lake in Australasia. Will read they could eat their packed lunches in Wairakei Park to the north of Taupo where the Falls were situated.

This proved to be the case. There were adequate toilet facilities as well. Will said he could always take them to a café, but Gaynor insisted that the children did not want to wait about to be served and likely would not like what was on the menu in any event. Gaynor knew what everyone liked and tried to accommodate individual preferences in each packed lunch. She was very good and practical in many ways.

While eating, Will looked up more about the falls and learnt that the river, normally up to 100 metres wide, narrowed to 15 metres as it crossed a large, volcanic ledge and dropped 20 metres to form a beautiful blue-green pool; huka being the Maori word for foam. There was a viewing bridge over the top of the falls. Will made sure his camera was charged and at the ready.

After everyone had eaten and been to the toilet, they were ready to go, Gaynor determined to keep an eagle eye on Tim. They went first to the viewing bridge, where Will took photos, and then down a steep and winding pathway beside the falls where once again Will took photos of the turbulent water wreathed with spray, of which a number of the most dramatic he still features in the sitting room to this day. To give the children a rest, they went back to the car to drive four miles to the Aratiatia Dam, the next stage of the rivers' hurtling passage. The rock feature creating Lake Taupo, Will had read, was brought about by a series of eruptions, the last one, the Hatepe Eruption, occurring about three thousand years ago.

"Brother Tim said that when he used to go trout fishing at Waitahanui, while on leave during the war, the Aratiatia Dam and Power Station didn't exist. He said they were built in 1964. From about 1906 the Aratiatia Rapids were a great tourist attraction, along with Huka Falls. Now the sluice gates of the dam are open a number of advertised times during the day for tourist to once again see the rapids as they were before the dam was built. We'll drive to the dam, find out when the sluice gates are next due to open so we can go to a viewing station to see the rapids. Sounds good? All agree?"

Will did not expect any objections but felt it good policy for all to feel they were consulted. "Ted said that when he came here trout fishing on periods of leave during the war, there were experiments going on with thermal generation in the Wairakei Thermal Valley, but the Thermal Power Station we see today wasn't finished until 1958. It can be visited but we can't see everything in a day, and the girls especially would find it rather dull. According to Ted, the Wairakei Thermal Valley used to attract many visitors," Will informed them further as they drove along.

"What are rapids?" Ruth asked.

"A huge lot of rushing water," Gaynor answered in simple terms, not to be outdone by Will's extensive knowledge of the area, courtesy of brother Ted.

The parking area was clearly set out and they found that the sluices were due to open at two, giving them 20 minutes to get down to a viewing point. Dead on two, announced by a siren, a wall of writhing water came avalanching down the narrow, rock-strewn channel, causing the ground to shake and mist to fill the air. It was an awesome sight none of them would ever forget.

After the cascade passed and the rocks were again laid bare, they drove back to Taupo and, according to the driving atlas, saw they would need to drive west down the main street to the waterfront and for the next four miles at least follow the road along the lakeside before bearing a little inland for a period to come back to the foreshore at Waitahanui, passing over the bridge, their waterfront motel to be found lower down on a narrow service road soon after. They discovered their unit, as arranged, to be right on the pumice-strewn beach, their veranda a few feet above the gritty sands.

"White rocks floating in the water?" Angela exclaimed as they trooped into the living area, looking out across the vast lake.

"The seaside!" Ruth added excitedly.

"Looks like the seaside but it's a huge lake, like an inland sea," Gaynor explained.

"And those floating stones bobbing about in the water are pumice. It's what happens when hot volcanic magma comes in contact with water, the rapid cooling creating bubbles which makes pumice stone so light that it will float in water," Will explained.

"You read about it," Tim said accusingly.

"Of course," Will responded. "Like everyone else, I was born knowing nothing. If you can read, you can find out about most things. You're a good reader. There's a lot of information in the tourist brochures. You could be informing your sister and Ruth about many things."

"I read the brochures sometimes," Tim said defensively.

"Only about things you might think you'd like to do. Some of them give a lot of background information," Will concluded. "Let's go out onto the beach."

The children ran about freely, the girls trying to do cartwheels that looked more like bunny hops.

"We'd better get an evening meal going," Gaynor nodded towards Will, "then there will be time for a walk before dark. Stay in front of our bach," she called to the children.

"Our what?" Tim asked.

Gaynor laughed. "Our holiday home, get with it like Will said." The adults stepped back inside and swiftly got on with preparing an evening meal.

After washing up they put on warm clothes as at 1100 feet in altitude and in the middle of the island, Lake Taupo got cold in the evening. If the sky cleared there would be a hard frost tonight. Outside they headed back towards where the so-called stream entered the lake. Fifty feet down into the lake, strung along the edge of the apron of sand and silt brought down by the fast-flowing river, a picket fence of wet fly fishermen, including one or two ladies, all in chest waders, rods flailing, were determinedly trying to catch large rainbow trout coming up the river to spawn.

"Don't go too near," Will warned as the hissing back casts came close to where they were standing. "This is where brother Ted said he went fishing when on leave during the war."

"Looks boring, just standing there," Tim commented.

"Depends on your interests, but I must admit it doesn't grab me," Will replied. "Dusk is falling, look, lovely shades of red are forming over the lake, if you walk near the water's edge the sand's firmer." As they approached their motel unit, Will pointed to a rise on the other side of the road. "Ted said on that hump of higher ground opposite our motel unit there used to be a single classroom Maori school with an attached schoolhouse. Ted said he and his mate got to know the teacher in charge, Viti Harney, much respected by the local hapu, sub-tribe, basic unit of Maori society.

The local Maori schools between 1867 and 1969 had a special curriculum designed to teach Maoris and mixed-race children basic English and numbering during this transitional period. After 1969 such schools were no longer considered necessary. Ted said he and his mate used to camp above the bridge, with the schoolhouse behind them. Ted said he later learnt that where he camped there'd been a Maori massacre. Had he known it at the time, he said he wouldn't have liked to have camped on that exact spot."

"You do know a lot about Waitahanui," Gaynor remarked.

"Only because Ted went on about it. The trout fishing there seemed for him happy interludes during the boring war years. He hasn't told me anything else about further south. Apparently, he and Layla have had two trips to the South Island, but he never gave me any details of these."

"We'll have to read the brochures," Gaynor remarked.

"We sure will," Will agreed.

That evening they turned up the hot air blower and sat watching the sun sink out of sight in a brilliant red display, water lapping gently on the lake shore. Cuddling up together, Will considered it one of the nicest evenings of their entire trip. Tomorrow evening they needed to be in Wellington to take the ferry to Picton the following day.

They had the alarm on for seven thirty next morning, showering promptly, getting breakfast quickly and being off by ten to drive the 230 miles to Wellington Central taking, Will estimated, a driving time of about five hours. As was their custom now, Will started off driving with Tim in the front passenger seat, hoping to lunch somewhere between Marton and Fielding.

After Hatepe, State Highway 1 followed the lake side as far as Motuoapa, every bend bringing enchanting vistas in clear winter sunshine. Leaving the lake, the road climbed up onto the Rangipo Desert, east of the Tongariro Massive, created during a series of violent eruptions 20,000 years ago, which sterilised the region. Will and Gaynor observed that the road could be closed at times owing to snow, but today it was open, and they had great views of the brilliant snow-covered volcanoes of Tongariro and Ruapehu.

"There's skiing on Ruapehu," Will observed.

"Can we go skiing?" Tim enquired eagerly.

"We haven't the time or the gear," Will replied.

"You can hire skis," Tim protested.

"So you do read the brochures when you're motived, but we need the appropriate alpine clothing and the time. We have neither," Will replied with finality.

Passing through Waiouru, Will noted that it was home to New Zealand's largest military camp and training grounds. Will thought Ted must have known that well during the war as well but it was obviously not a place that he wanted to talk about. Will drove on through what had now become farming country, coming across the small town of Hunterville, the next signed town after that being Marton, after which they intended to find a suitable place to stop and have lunch.

They found a designated picnic area where, out of the wind at the height of the day, it was comparatively warm, and the children could run about for half an hour after which it was Gaynor's turn to drive. As usual, with the girls snuggling on each side and in the warmth of the car, it was hard for Will to keep awake. On one occasion, after nodding off, he could see Gaynor smiling at him in the rear viewing mirror.

"Navigating must be hard work," Gaynor said with a laugh.

"Sorry," Will replied, embarrassed.

"It's all one straight road at the moment, not easy to get lost, approaching Wellington will be a different thing."

Approaching Wellington was a different thing. After Paekakariki, routes coming on and off were more numerous, and Will had to concentrate to make sure they were following State Highway 1. By Tawa Flat, Will could see they were in a suburban area, driving through hilly suburbs with names like Broadmeadows and Ngauranga. Studying the map, he observed they were now sweeping along the Johnsonville Porirua Motorway. He had to make sure they kept on route 1 where the motorways divided, two carriageways bearing north to Lower Hutt. Before long they were running alongside Wellington Harbour opposite Somes Island before entering Wellington Central, the motorway ending near Kelburn Park.

"See if you can find some place to park," Will said, "while I sort out how we can get to our booked hotel."

"Easier said than done," Gaynor replied though not fazed by city driving like Will would have been.

When temporary parking was found, looking at the detailed inner-city map, Will said, "Sorry, it's back up again a short way, our hotel is off Barnard Street, Wadestown, we can leave the car there for collection, there's a hotel shuttle running to and from the Picton Ferry Terminal in Lagoon Road, I'll show you on the map."

Gaynor looked at the driving atlas, "No problem, leave it to me. I'll get us there."

Get them there she did, no problem as she said. Where there was a little difficulty was at reception. Typically, at international hotels, they had to produce their passports and Will his credit card of which an impression was taken. When the rather cynically disposed male receptionist saw the adults' different surnames and hearing Will's insistence that they must have communicating rooms, he adopted a wink, nudge, snigger manner when Will said that this was needed in the interest of the children, which made both adults cross.

"Why was he winking?" Tim asked.

"Because he's a silly, rude man," Gaynor replied.

"We need the shuttle for the ten ferry tomorrow, and we've arranged for Cars-for-All-Rental to pick up our hire car, getting the key from reception and the car from your car park."

"Will that be all?" the receptionist asked. "I'll arrange for your luggage to be taken up to your rooms on the fourth floor."

"I assume there are tea and coffee making facilities in the rooms with milk?" Will asked.

"And biscuits," the receptionist added as he pointed out their luggage to an approaching room porter.

"There is a lounge on the ground floor but it's too far for the children to find us if we're needed after they've gone to bed so we'll need to stay upstairs tonight," Will observed when they arrived in their rooms. "While it's still business hours we'll need to book places on the ten o'clock ferry tomorrow, arrange accommodation in

Picton for tomorrow night and for Cars-for-All Rental to deliver a car promptly next day to our motel."

"Do you think they will, their office is in Blenheim?" Gaynor remarked.

"We can but try, business can't be that good in winter."

"That cheeky receptionist made me cross," Gaynor added.

"Me too," Will agreed. "First time we've come across that sort of thing. We'll need to eat in their dining room, this is an old-fashioned hotel without room cooking facilities. I only booked it as it was near the ferry, where we could leave our car for pick up and they ran a free shuttle to the ferry. For the rest of our trip, it's going to be motels or travel lodges."

"The children won't like it," Gaynor shook her head.

"I've got some fruit and muesli in my suitcase which we could give the children for supper if they're still hungry. But first I need to get on with the bookings. I notice in the room information that there's no need to book a place on the ferry at this time of the year."

As Gaynor predicted, in the dining room the children only picked at their food and became impatient between courses, but it was a change not having to cook. They stayed down in the lounge for a while and tried to watch television, but the presence of other people was inhibiting. It soon became apparent that the children's interests especially would be better served up in their rooms. As they went for the lift, they were relieved to see that there was now a woman receptionist at the desk who smiled at the children.

There was room television, so they were able to pick a family programme. Will dished out muesli and fruit in the room's cups and saucers which Tim and Ruth enjoyed. Angela was in a whining mood, complaining of pains in her stomach. The larger room had a spacious en suite which, when the light was on and the communicating door open, provided enough light to get the children to bed and off to sleep. Will then had the brilliant idea of taking a chair each into the well-lit en suite so that he and Gaynor could look at brochures and maps for tomorrow.

The arrangement worked well until Gaynor heard Angela cry that she felt sick, requiring Gaynor to sit her on the toilet during which time she was a little sick and appeared to have a degree of diarrhoea. As Will couldn't help, he decided to join Ruth in the smaller of the two rooms and have an early night.

Will woke at seven thirty by the alarm, showered and shaved and gave Ruth a shower. It was decided not to go down for breakfast but to have the remainder of the muesli and fruit for breakfast along with hot cocoa in their rooms. They could buy snacks on the ferry.

"According to the blurb," Will said to Gaynor, his mouth full of muesli, "the ferry journey this morning is known as one of the best in the world and is rated as a New Zealand must-do experience."

"We'll see," Gaynor replied, trying to persuade Angela to eat something.

"We'd better wear all the warm clothes we've got. The Cook Strait part of the journey could be cold with heavy seas this time of the year. It's the Marlborough Sounds everyone raves about."

"Perhaps Angela might be better not to eat until we get into the quiet waters of the Sounds then," Gaynor observed. "We must remember to leave the car key at reception."

It was a rush to get their bags packed and sent down to reception to be ready for the shuttle, but they somehow managed it.

Infuriatingly, when they went to go down, the lifts were engaged as a lot of other guests were doing the same thing. Will toyed with the stairs but that too would take some time. In the end, just in time, they managed to squeeze into a lift, leave their room and car keys at reception before taking their place in the shuttle. Aboard the ferry, they sought inside seating with forward-facing seats giving the optimum view ahead.

After cast-off, the ferry moved initially slowly ahead into the calm waters of the harbour. Looking back, Will realised that for this departure, the ferry had left from Wellington Central, not far from where they first stopped upon arrival. Surprisingly quickly, the vessel gathered speed, going straight out into the harbour to clear Point Halswell before turning south down the harbour, the busy traffic of Seatoun on their right being in marked contrast to the sparsely populated East Harbour shore.

After clearing Barrett Reef at the harbour entrance, the ferry turned to head into an eight to ten feet swell sweeping down the Strait from the Tasman Sea out to the north. Will and Gaynor took hold of their children, Will ensuring Yellow Ted was secure in Ruth's hand luggage as the ferry crashed up and down, driving spray causing any passengers remaining outside on deck to scurry for shelter.

To everyone's relief, within an hour, passengers were pointing out Arapawa Island where the passage began to Queen Charlotte Sound. As soon as they left the open sea, turning left, the ship was in calm waters and they were able to relax and enjoy the glorious scenery, the weather cold and bright most of the time with occasional towering cumulus clouds. Will let go of Ruth and took out his camera. Gaynor got up and bought snacks from the now open canteen.

The rest of the journey was fabulous. There were so many hauntingly beautiful vistas opening up every few minutes revealing sounds leading off, some sheltering small settlements with a sprinkling of anchored yachts, as well as high mountains, at times reflecting in the water, forested headlands and romantic landings in sheltered inlets. On occasions they passed fish farms.

"Can we spend a day in the Sounds?" Tim asked.

"In view of all the other places we have in mind to see, it'll depend whether we have the time. I'll need to discuss it with your mother," Will replied.

At one thirty in the afternoon, the ferry began to slow down and passengers who had been this way before started getting their hand luggage together. Will and Gaynor assumed they must be nearing Picton. Then they saw the town, extending back up a shallow valley. To Will's surprise, the ferry gave one blast of its horn and began to turn right away from the shore and, after another three blasts, go astern into its berth.

"When we've collected our hold baggage, we'll need a taxi to take us to the Dusky Dolphin Motel which I was told was near a park. The taxi driver should know," Will said as they took their turn down the landing ramp. "I'll get it to stop on the way at a food market."

Their taxi driver, an Indian immigrant New Zealander, proved helpful, assisting in bringing in provisions and placing them where directed. Though not the New Zealand custom, Will gave him a tip.

"They don't seem to tip in New Zealand," Gaynor observed.

"I gather it's because of an egalitarian tradition and the fact that everyone by law, including waitresses, must have a living wage," Will replied.

"Good idea." Will knew Gaynor was keen on women's rights as he was himself.

"Now for a late lunch," Gaynor said after they had looked over their motel. "I think we need to stay here for two nights, Will, if you don't mind. I don't think Angela's well enough to travel on tomorrow. You might have to sightsee tomorrow without me. It'll depend on how Angela is. It's possible I might need to arrange for her to visit a doctor's they listed in the information pack."

Will had no option but to agree, if it were Ruth who was not well, he would be asking for the same thing. After they had eaten, rested and unpacked, Will took Ruth and Tim for a walk around the park and then along towards the waterfront.

"Look," said Tim, "there's a long train pulling wagons through the traffic!" Will looked to observe a goods train moving slowly through the broad road towards the waterfront.

"I have read that on occasions road traffic and trains have to share the same bridges. The railway lines are narrower in gauge than in Britain."

"Why?" Tim asked.

"Because of the mountains and sparse population, I understand," Will replied. "We'd better be turning back. It'll soon be dark."

Everyone was happier in accommodation of their own. Their two-bedroomed motel was laid out much as they had come to expect, with the dining room/living area looking out into a central courtyard with raised planting and a swimming pool, covered over at this time of the year. Gaynor went to bed early with Angela, Will looking after Ruth and Tim in the lounge, Tim being the last to take himself off to bed.

Their South Island hire car was delivered at nine thirty next morning from Blenheim, a beige Holden Commodore Executive VS, nearly brand new by the look of it with very few miles on the clock. Will went round it very carefully with the operatives to agree any imperfections, taking out full car hire damage waiver insurance before having Gaynor sign up as an associate driver.

Afterwards they agreed what they would like to do next day was a trip back up to Motuara Island, a bird sanctuary, at the mouth of Queen Charlotte Sound. As Angela had sufficiently recovered, Gaynor decided to go with them, reserving the option to stay on the boat if Angela was not fit enough to go ashore. There was a trip leaving at 11.

They drove to the waterfront in their newly acquired beige Holden, found where the Motuara trip left, bought tickets and clambered aboard. The trip boat was smaller and seemed faster than the ferry, making the island in a little over an hour. Angela was wrapped in a rug, lying across the seat. Gaynor decided she needed to stay aboard, out of the wind, where there was a toilet and washroom if needed. Tim was made to promise, if he wanted to land on the island with Will and Ruth, that he had to obey Will, being reminded that it was he who wanted to stay in Queen Charlotte Sound in the first place.

The island had initially been farmed, but in 1920 it was declared a reserve, was now predator-free and lush bush had grown back. Along with other trippers, they were taken to a special viewing platform where they were told it was likely they would be able to see tuis, bellbirds, robins, fantails and perhaps yellow-crowned parakeets, even a rare South Island saddleback if they were lucky. The guide told them not to feed the birds as the idea was to keep them in their natural state and not be dependent on handouts from visitors. But inevitably there was a family who had come prepared with bird feed and who, when the guide's attention was elsewhere, were putting their hands out with bird feed to feed especially the robins who, like robins in Britain, came particularly close. Tim asked the family if he could have some bird feed and was given a handful and was delighted to have a robin feed from his hand. Will said nothing as he had not disobeyed him, taking photos instead. When Tim told his mother, she was disapproving, pointing out to him it was not in keeping the environmental spirit and not a smart thing to do.

Will observed the robins had the same inquisitive characteristics of the British robin but were twice the size and were an overall light brown, not having the lovely red breast. After visiting the bird-viewing platform, they were taken to a lookout at the highest point of the island where Will took photos of the stunning three-hundred-and-sixty-degree panorama.

It was dusk by the time they got back to their motel. Will switched on television for the children and checked the room temperature. After their evening meal, there was much for the adults to do as they intended leaving for Kaikoura next day to undertake whale-watching on their way south. They didn't have a *South Island Complete Drivers Atlas* but Cars-for-All-Rental had provided them with a South Island map with road distances from which Will worked out Kaikoura would be about 160 kilometres and would take about two and a half hours driving time. They would need to ring ahead to book a motel in or about Kaikoura without delay.

Before the children went to bed, Will read them the true story of Pelorus Jack, a Risso's dolphin who, for 24 years, escorted the ferries between Wellington and Nelson from Pelorus Sound to French Pass and back again, a distance of five miles each way.

"Where's French Pass?" Gaynor interrupted.

Will explained that, according to the map, it was to the north-west of the Marlborough Sounds between D'Urville Island and the mainland where on occasions the tide raced up to eight miles an hour. He then went on to say that the dolphin appeared to enjoy swimming up against the vessels, riding the bow waves. Pelorus Jack became a tourist attraction, drawing celebrities like Mark Twain and the author Frank Bullen to the Sounds. The dolphin was protected by an act of parliament after someone fired a shot at it. Pelorus Jack was last seen in April 1912. Will added that Layla said her grandparents had seen it.

The drive to Kaikoura looked attractive, firstly through wine-growing valleys then along a scenic, precipitous coastline. When making inquiries, Will discovered that there was plenty of accommodation available in Kaikoura in August. He chose the Only Whale and Albatross Travel Lodge with a great ocean view as, rather than a motel, as it had a restaurant which was prepared to send meals to their two-bedroom unit to save Gaynor from always cooking.

That evening Gaynor took Angela to bed earlier than the others in the smaller of the two rooms and stayed with her until she was asleep, undertaking her packing for next day later in the larger bedroom. As it turned out, everyone had a comparatively early night as the day in the fresh air had made them all sleepy. By ten the following morning, they were on the road heading for Kaikoura, Will, as was now their habit, driving first.

The first town they came to was Blenheim, the largest in the Marlborough region and, according to the sign, the centre of New Zealand's wine industry, which Will could well believe by the large number of vines growing on north-facing slopes. At the small town of Ward, on State Highway 1, they decided to stop and have lunch with 82 kilometres to go to Kaikoura which, Will worked out, was about 51 miles. The local domain, right beside the road, was an excellent place for Tim and Ruth to run around in, Gaynor keeping Angela in the car with engine running and heater on until everyone gathered inside the car to eat their packed lunch. Following lunch, it was Gaynor's turn to drive. After the small town of Clarence, near a river of the same name, the Seaward Kaikoura Mountain Range, glistening in winter white, appeared towering above them to their right, contrasting to the blue of the Pacific Ocean on their left where serried waves crashed onto the beaches in lines of swirling foam.

Gaynor found their travel lodge on a partly bushed ridge above the town. It was well appointed and spacious with a lovely view over the town to the sea beyond. Having parked the car round the back, they trooped out onto the front veranda.

"We haven't had a view quite like this before," Gaynor remarked appreciatively.

"What's an albatross, Dadda?" Ruth asked.

"The largest flying bird with a wingspan of six feet. They range across the Southern Ocean."

"Do they attack you?"

"They might if you interfered with their young. According to what I've read, they feed on fish, squid and krill, tiny sea creatures. They will follow ships for hours. In the old days, sailors thought they brought good luck."

"Will we see any?" Ruth continued.

"We might."

"Will they bring us good luck?"

"I very much hope so. We'd better go back inside and unpack," Will concluded.

Halfway through, Gaynor stopped to find out the times of the whale-watching tours and discovered that being on winter schedules, they had missed the last one for the day but booked a tour for ten next day, finding out where the transport would be waiting to take them out to their boat. She felt Angela, who was getting better, would be all right to come as they would have access to toilets and a washroom. What they could do later this afternoon was view a seal colony at nearby Ohau Point.

At four, having got directions, they set off for Ohau Point. Upon arrival, after parking, they began walking along a boardwalk, but before long had to get off onto the rocks to avoid a large sleeping seal. Notices warned visitors not to get too close as seals' mouths, being full of bacteria, made a bite very hard to heal. They were also warned to beware of the tide. The girls especially needed no warning as they were very wary of getting too close and complained of the smell. In the end, rather than venture far out onto the rocks, they decided that it was more fun watching young seals frolicking round the freshwater stream near the road.

Back at their lodge at dusk, Gaynor liked the idea of having a meal being sent over from the restaurant providing she could find on the menu one they would all eat. Upon viewing, she found one so, after setting the table, the adults sat back and viewed television with the children until there was a knock on the door and their meal arrived.

After washing up, the children, including Tim, did not need persuading to go to bed as it had been a long day. Returning to the lounge after preparing their children for the night, Will and Gaynor decided to switch off the lights, open the curtains and watch the twinkling lights of the town below and the moon over the water, deciding to plan for tomorrow later. Inevitably they fell asleep, awakening with a start cuddled up together, the moon now on the other side of the bay, realising they would need to get up half an hour earlier than planned to do what they had intended to do later that evening. However, on reflection, Will felt that it was worth enjoying Gaynor's warmth and closeness and was glad the evening turned the way it had.

With two bathrooms, they were quick showering and then got cracking with breakfast and packed lunches. They took with them maximum clothing, as it would be cold on the water, and Will made sure his camera was fully charged. They left by twenty to ten to meet the bus that would take them to their whale-watching boat.

They found their vessel was a catamaran with a viewing cabin across the two hulls; also a railed viewing platform in front with additional railed viewing positions up on the prows of both floats. Once all were aboard, they were given a safety briefing and then told that the whales came to this part of the coast especially owing to a nearby deep ocean trench from which nutrients welled to the surface, attracting whales, orcas and dolphins. Amongst the whales, the sperm whales were the most sought after, coming to rest for 10 minutes on the surface before ending up with a spectacular lifting of their flukes high out of the water before diving deep down for 40 minutes or more. Other whales that could be seen were 16-metre humpback whales, less frequently 29-metre baleen blue whales, the largest animal known to have existed, and occasionally 10-metre-long minke whales.

At first, the children were wildly excited at the prospect of seeing these leviathans of the deep but as the vessel throbbed on, hour after hour, with the occasional shout of a distant sighting their initial enthusiasm turned to boredom.

"What's that stick the man's holding in the water?" Tim asked.

"It's a hydrophone," Will replied. "The crew member is listening to the chatter between the whales in an attempt to pinpoint their location so we can get a closer view."

"Can they talk then?"

"They can communicate," Will replied.

"Does he know what they are saying?" Tim persisted.

"From what I was reading, their clicking language has not been deciphered but I believe scientists are working on it," Will concluded.

"Can we go home now?" Ruth asked.

"I think we've another hour," Will replied, looking at his watch.

Suddenly, the crew member holding the hydrophone overboard, shouted a frantic warning to the bridge, pointing directly in front of their vessel. Almost immediately the sea churned. A huge whale surfaced right beside their vessel, causing it to rock violently, a massive fountain of spray with a stench like rotting cabbages thundering on the decks. The whale, blueish grey in colour, rolled on its side, seemingly as surprised to see them as they were to see it. The skipper turned their vessel away quickly, orders were not to get too close, but not before many passengers rushed to the side to take fantastic photos and videos, Will included. For a few seconds, the whale was so near a person could have jumped on its back.

"Can't have been part of a pod," Will said, "a loner coming up from very deep down. They're saying it's a blue whale, not often seen."

After what had been quite an exceptional close encounter, during their last hour on the water their ship tracked down a pod of sperm whales, enabling those aboard to get reasonably close views of the whales resting, preliminary to their once again diving, flukes sweeping upwards before resoundingly slapping the water.

At the end of the excursion, they climbed aboard their transport to be taken back to their parked car more than satisfied, after which Gaynor drove them back to their lodge for the night.

"Well, that was amazing," Gaynor said, putting on the lights and looking at the thermostat. "And you held up very well, Angela dear," she added, turning around to her daughter.

"I was frightened by that great big whale right beside the boat," Angela replied.

"We were all startled," Gaynor responded, taking her daughter in her arms and giving her a big kiss.

It was decided they would make their own meal tonight and buy more food tomorrow on their way to Christchurch. After the children had gone to bed, without fuss owing to their long day, Will and Gaynor put out the lounge lights, drew the curtains and for their second and last night felt they just wanted to enjoy the sight of the lights of the town, with the moon making a pathway through the water beyond, and the navigation lights of vessels slowly crossing the bay.

Cuddled up contentedly on the sofa, Will felt, as he, Gaynor and the children were getting on so well together, that this might be the right moment to ask Gaynor if she would consider marrying him on their return to Britain. He was just thinking how best to put the proposal into words when Gaynor heard Tim cough and splutter and scurried off into her bedroom. Will waited for her return for perhaps half an hour and, when she did not, looked at his watch. The time was two in the morning. He had better be off to bed himself.

In the morning, he learnt that Tim woke up, began eating a sweet in bed, which he was not supposed to, and got it down the wrong way and, following that, Angela had a nightmare about a great whale arising up in her bedroom and swallowing her up.

Christchurch was only a comparatively short distance, nevertheless, next morning before leaving, Will needed to book accommodation and look up the route. Taking the coastal route, the distance appeared to be about 112 miles. Will felt the journey would take about three hours, giving them part of the day to begin seeing over the largest city in the South Island, capital of New Zealand's distinctly English province of Canterbury, boasting an English-style gothic cathedral and square. By ten they were on their way, Will in the driving seat.

The sea was not in sight during their journey but at Rangiora, they crossed a wide river before coming into more built-up areas. After Kaiapoi, having crossed the similarly wide Waimakariri River, they entered Christchurch itself. Looking at a city map, the feeling was there was no better place to relax and have lunch than in Hagley Park, not too far from their booked motel in Addington. They found car parking nearby off Riccarton Avenue.

After lunching on a park bench, Gaynor felt she would like to see the much-acclaimed nearby botanic gardens. The gardens proved extensive and beautiful, even in wintertime. There were so many avenues, vistas and water features, all different with every sort of plant variety, form and colour. The children liked to climb the gently arched bridges and see if they could catch their reflections in the water. They ended up by having scones with cream and jam in the magnificent glass pavilion, after which it was time to find their motel, unpack and get comfortable for their two nights' stay.

The motel was more like the conventional two-bedroom New Zealand motel they had grown used to.

Gaynor spotted a corner shop near the entrance where they stopped first and bought from what was on offer enough to make their first night's meal which, when they got themselves settled and with Will's help, Gaynor had quickly on the table.

That evening they sat up late watching a programme about kiwi conservation and learnt quite a lot about the elusive bird, emblem of New Zealand, like it was the only bird known to have nostrils and it had the largest egg to body weight ratio of any bird. It was very vulnerable to predators such as stoats, ferrets, cats and dogs. A recent survey concluded that there were only 50,000 left of the four main species. On islands and on suitable peninsulas, which could be fenced off, particularly in Northland, predator-free zones were being established to help improve their numbers.

"Can we see a kiwi?" Ruth asked.

"I believe they can only be seen in special kiwi houses where the lighting is kept low," Will replied.

"Why the low lighting?" Tim asked.

"Because they're nocturnal creatures, that is, they only come out at night is what I've read," Will added. "We might be able to see one when we go up north."

"Goodie!" both girls chorused.

Tim was the last child to be persuaded to go to bed. When he eventually did, and Will and Gaynor had been sitting cuddled up together on the sofa for half an hour, there being no view out the window other than streetlights, it was Ruth's turn to cry out. Will went in to see what was wrong. She had tummy pains. Will gave her a warm drink and sat her on the toilet. When he eventually got her to sleep and went back into the lounge, he found Gaynor had gone to bed.

There was no need to get up particularly early the next day. They were first going to see the cathedral before taking in some of the other recommended sights of the town. It would be the day following, the 16th of August, they would need to be on the road early as they were going to undertake their longest day's drive, from Christchurch to Queenstown. Even so, they were off by ten thirty, Gaynor driving, as she was much more confident in a busy city.

"Christchurch has the reputation of being like an English cathedral town. The cathedral and square might be, and the canalised Avon River running through Hagley Park, but otherwise I don't see it," Will observed as he navigated with the city map from the passenger seat. "Near the centre of English cathedral towns there are generally rows of grey terraced houses but here the housing consists of detached brightly painted bungalows with red or green roofs, much nicer."

"I guess that's what the colonists came out here for, to build a better life," Gaynor replied. "The housing is nothing like we have back home."

"What are you talking about, Mumma?" Angela asked.

"The pretty houses, dear, we're not going far today. We'll be out of the car in 10 minutes," Gaynor reassured.

Being winter, Cathedral Square was not as crowded as it might have been. The stone cathedral did look like a typical gothic English cathedral. The building of the cathedral began in 1864, and they learnt that the spire, in particular, was damaged in a series of earthquakes in 1888, 1901 and in 1922. Had they known the extent of the destruction of the cathedral, the city of Christchurch and the countryside surrounding occurring in February

2011, brought about by a massive earthquake, including ground liquefaction, Will would have taken more photos of the cathedral and city than he did.

Will picked up somewhere that the first school in the city, perhaps the Cathedral school, he was not sure, was designed in Britain. Following the architect's design instructions, the school was dutifully built facing the sunless south, the architect forgetting that in the southern hemisphere the sun was in the northern sky.

The obvious place to have lunch was again in nearby Hagley Park. They found seats in a children's play enclosure in front of swings, slides and an ingenious climbing structure which, after eating, the children made full use of. Will and Gaynor had agreed on a number of places the brochures recommended seeing but when Gaynor announced it was time to go, they were told in no uncertain terms by the three children that they wanted to stay and play.

"Let them stay and play," Will said. "They'll be spending a long time in the car tomorrow."

Sitting shoulder to shoulder to keep warm, Will and Gaynor let the children play until it was time to take them home for the night.

The evening passed quickly. While Gaynor joined the children in viewing a family programme, Will booked accommodation in Queenstown and worked out the route. It would be 300 miles and would involve about seven hours at the wheel between them. When the children were in bed asleep, sitting by a radiant electric fire in the lounge, they agreed they would set an alarm and not fall asleep for half the night together but get to bed at a reasonable time to be fit for the long day ahead.

Next morning, awakening at seven, they noted there was frost on the ground though with the central heating and the heater left on low in the lounge all night, their motel was warm. With activities on hand for the children and with Will at the wheel they were on their way by nine thirty, Tim sitting beside Will in the passenger seat.

They made good progress. By eleven thirty they had driven through relatively flat agrarian countryside via Ashburton as far as Geraldine which, in distance terms, was two-fifths of their journey. After Geraldine, turning west towards the mountains, they stopped at Gapes Valley for lunch at twelve thirty where the children stretched their legs by a stream with lovely clear water, jumping from stone to stone.

"Don't get wet!" Gaynor warned. "It's too cold for that." In fact, it was the cold that drove the children back to the car for lunch which they had with the motor and heating running. After lunch, Gaynor took over the driving. Though the terrain was progressively less flat, Will noticed she was driving faster than he would have under the circumstances, exploiting the power of the car realising, not for the first time, what an experienced and skilful driver Gaynor was.

Coming suddenly to the end of Lake Tekapo, the stunning view before them compelled Gaynor to stop the car at the bronze statue of the collie sheepdog on a high stone plinth close to the Church of the Good Shepherd. They read that the statue was erected by Mackenzie Country residents in recognition of the indispensable role of the sheepdog in their livelihoods. Will took photos.

"I can't see the end of the lake. It's cold," Tim complained.

"We're getting into high country, the lake's 710 metres above sea level, it's bound to be cold in winter. Go back to the car," was Will's advice.

They all followed Will's advice, going back to the car. After a final gaze, Gaynor drove on at an increased pace. After five minutes, Ruth screamed, "Yellow Ted's been left behind!"

"Not again!" Will groaned.

Without a word, Gaynor spun the car around and went back. At the bronze statue of the sheepdog, Will leapt out of the car and searched about, finding Yellow Ted on the lakeside near the bottom of the rough stone plinth where he could not be seen when they drove off.

"What was Yellow Ted doing out of the car?" Will asked.

"Looking at the view, of course," Ruth replied as if Will was silly to ask. Not for the first time, Will had very dark thoughts of what he would like to do to that wretched Yellow Ted.

After Twizel, towering cumulus clouds started building, casting ominous shadows over their route. Before long, big snowflakes began falling, gently at first then increasing in intensity, driven by a rising wind. Soon Gaynor was driving through a swirling blizzard, and the road began to cover with snow. To make matters worse, the tarmac gave way to shingle in places on which the car swayed and slithered. Gaynor switched on the car's headlights.

"Would you like me to give you a spell at the wheel?" Will asked, secretly hoping the offer might not be taken up.

"If I stopped the car, we might not get enough traction to start off going again," Gaynor replied. "but thank you. I think this is just a heavy snow shower and it'll lessen, or we'll drive out of it. There's a patch of clear sky ahead." Will noticed through the driving snow that there was an area of lighter sky further on.

Gaynor proved to be right. By the time they reached Omarama, there was only the occasional snowflake with little snow on the ground. Gaynor drove on as fast as the conditions allowed, hoping to get to Queenstown before nightfall, Will marvelling at her skill.

The girls huddled beside Will, tired of the long drive and rather frightened. "When are we going to get there?" Angela asked. "I don't like the snow."

"How long? I want to be there. We've been ages in the car," Ruth continued on the other side of Will, squirming uncomfortably in her seat.

"You've all been very patient. According to the map, we must be nearing Cromwell where we turn west and then it's not far. Angela's mum's done a great job driving through all this," Will replied, putting his arm around Ruth. As if to emphasise that it was not all over, another swirling snow shower brought about white-out conditions, Gaynor not being able to judge whether the road ahead was about to go up or down. Doggedly she drove on.

Then, as abruptly as it began, the snow ceased, the sky cleared and there before them was Queenstown on Lake Wakatipu, the lights of the town reflecting in the water. Coming closer, they could see that the town extended along a bay divided by a headland at the end of a long arm of the lake with another arm extending off to the left, the water tinged red by the setting sun.

Their booked lodge, they discovered, was situated on higher land to the right of the town.

Swinging into Totara Motor Lodge, their car stood out owing to the caked snow on the roof, showing what they had been through. Trooping into reception, they could see it was a grand place with a dining room, extensive lounge and bar. They were given a key and directed round to their parking bay in front of their unit, the receptionist remarking on the state of their car, saying that they had only a few flurries of snow today in town, but she had heard that there was a good snow covering up on the Remarkables ski fields.

Their accommodation unit had a log cabin theme as suggested by the word totara, a southern hemisphere conifer, sacred to the Maoris, from which they made their war canoes and used for carving, they found out. Will and Gaynor especially were very tired and, not having bought food as planned, decided to eat in the dining room, the children on this occasion, having to get on with the menu.

"I like your food best, Mamma," Angela said when she saw what the waiter bought for her.

"Gaynor's food's yummy," Ruth agreed.

Tim, for once, concurring with the girls, joined in, "Mum's the best!"

"Gaynor's tired after all that driving in very difficult conditions, she needs a break from cooking," Will said.

"It's very nice of you all to say my meals are the best. My airport driving did not quite prepare me for today's journey." Gaynor gave them a tired smile of appreciation. "Thank you, Will, for insisting we use the restaurant this evening." At which the children got on with their meal without the usual complaints when eating out, Will was pleased to observe.

They were just finishing when, looking up, they were surprised to see a man approaching from a nearby table. "English people on holiday by your accents, let me introduce myself," he said with casual down-under charm, "Joe Jambeagle, entrepreneur."

Will observed him closely, curious that they had been approached by a stranger. He looked a flamboyant character of about 45, something between a Kiwi version of Crocodile Dundee and 007, wearing a between-the-wars flying jacket, jeans, high rodeo boots, his brown wavy hair down to his collar. He was carrying what Will first thought was a motorbike helmet but learnt later was a flying helmet.

"Why yes," agreed Gaynor as she was the one being addressed.

"You and your husband haven't picked an ideal time of the year?"

"We had to come at this time as this is the long summer school holidays back in Britain. Will isn't my husband, we're just friends from the same place of work."

"I thought not as one of the little girls called you mother and the other one Gay..."

"Gaynor,"

"Oh yes, Gaynor, pretty name, I haven't heard it before."

Will noticed Joe Jambeagle had no time for the rest of them, addressing and keeping his eyes solely on Gaynor. Tired as she was, Gaynor was an attractive woman, well turned out with a trim figure and a smiling, girl-next-door face. Will objected to the intrusion.

"Do you mind? Mrs McDonald is tired, she's had a very long drive, in trying conditions."

"That's all right, Will, I'm recovering," Gaynor replied quietly to Will.

Gaynor looked up at Joe Jambeagle. "Nice to meet you, Mr Jambeagle."

"Mind if I join you? I can give you a lot of advice about places to visit, save you wasting time." Joe Jambeagle drew his chair over to their table without waiting for an answer. "You may have heard of lake cruises aboard the 1912 steamer *Earnslaw*, it's a must for you all. Then there's the Shotover River, Skippers Canyon, Arrowtown, heritage mining township." Joe Jambeagle went on and on.

Finally, noticing the children becoming increasingly restless, Gaynor said, "You'll have to excuse us, Mr Jambeagle—"

"Call me Joe," Mr Jambeagle interrupted.

"Joe, but I need to get the children to bed, they've had a long day. Nice to meet you."

Glancing back as they left the dining room, Will noticed Joe Jambeagle looking hungrily after Gaynor.

"Funny name," Tim commented. "I've heard of the name Beagle but not Jambeagle."

"If that's his real name," Will observed cynically.

"Why not?" Gaynor replied. "We're in New Zealand now."

Will could see that Gaynor was impressed with him and thought it might be in his interests not to offer criticism which could well be construed as jealousy.

Back in their accommodation, Will and Gaynor busied themselves putting their children to bed, Will looking forward to a time alone with Gaynor, cuddling up on the sofa. Will returned to the lounge first, turned the lights down low and waited. When Gaynor appeared after 20 minutes and Will gently put his arm about her, he was about to say that they both needed to go to bed early but before he could do so, Gaynor got in first saying, "I hope you don't mind, Will, but concentrating all those hours peering through the snow has got me whacked. I feel tonight I need to go to bed before long."

Disappointed, Will said he completely understood, saying he appreciated her skill and determination, admitting he could not have managed the drive under the conditions experienced throughout much of the afternoon. Giving Gaynor a kiss, he reluctantly assisted her to her feet and said goodnight. There would be tomorrow night when they were more rested.

First thing next morning, while Gaynor got the girls up and showered, Will and Tim went to a nearby food market to buy from a list Gaynor had given them. After breakfast, as the day was cold but sunny, with a light breeze, they decided to take a cruise on the TSS *Earnslaw*. There was a cruise leaving at ten thirty.

According to the brochures TSS *Earnslaw* was built in Dunedin and then dismantled, its parts numbered and then taken by train to Kingston at the southern end of Lake Wakatipu. Arriving by car at the quay, still with some snow on the roof where Will had not knocked it all off, they recognised the *Earnslaw* by its sleek white hull and tall red funnel. They decided, for a start at least, to take seats on the lower deck, near the engine, to benefit from its heat, as there had been a hard frost overnight, though the prolonged snow showers of yesterday had been replaced by glorious sunshine which glistened on the snow-covered mountain ranges crowding the lake on either side. Today's trip was up the lake to visit Dan Angleford High Country Farm.

From offshore their first impression of the farm, backed by tall New Zealand conifers, was a cluster of white, single storied, red-roofed buildings, which Will thought looked more like a European spa than anything else he had come across in New Zealand so far. Ashore the children especially had a wonderful time, feeding the friendly highland cattle, deer, goats, and proud llamas. They watched sheepdogs in action while listening to an account of high-country mustering practices and saw sheep-shearing and wool-spinning demonstrations. Afterwards, they enjoyed a scrumptious high tea of hot scones, cream and jam in a warm lounge beside a roaring fire where the girls could take off their pixie hats and coats for the first time. On the way back on the *Earnslaw*, they were encouraged to take part in a jolly sing-along.

Back, tired, appreciating their warm lounge, Gaynor bustled about getting them all a creamy chicken and rice casserole which she said would take 40 minutes to bake, a dish the children especially liked. While enjoying their evening meal, Will, thinking this had been a much more relaxing day than yesterday and was looking forward to Gaynor's company later in the evening, was astonished by Gaynor's saying to them all that Joe Jambeagle had rung her room earlier in the day. He had invited her for a flight in his helicopter to see Lake Wakitipu by moonlight this evening, followed by supper at the skiing lodge of Jules P Huckleberry, his millionaire friend, up on the Remarkables, landing on the roof. Without further ado, she gave the children and Will a kiss, saying to Will that she was sure he would not mind looking after the children for the evening, that the children were to be good and that for Will not to wait up for her as she would be late, she was taking a key. With that, she was off. Joe would be waiting for her in the lounge.

Will could hardly believe his ears, no more could the children. They all sat looking at each other until Tim said to Will in indignation, "Why did you let her? You should have said no?"

"I'm not in a position to say no."

"You live with her."

"No, I don't. I'm not married to your mother or even engaged."

"You like her?"

"That's another thing. Your mother and I came to a business arrangement that I wanted to visit New Zealand and needed another adult with me for Ruth, and Ruth needed the company of friends. That's why we're together, enjoying this holiday. You notice we have separate rooms, one for each family. If I wanted to do something for a few hours not suitable for children, I would ask your mother to look after you all." Will had to say this to reason with himself as much as to inform Tim as he was hurt – he paused in his thoughts – and to think that two days ago he was about to ask Gaynor to marry him.

"I think Joe's a smarty-pants, I don't like him."

"I have to agree with you, Tim. Let's do the dishes and then see if we can find a programme on the tele you'd all like," Will replied, moving over to the sink.

They found on television a children's adventure story involving four children discovering a moa, an extinct giant bird, which led them to a fairy-tale Maori children's village after exciting adventures like going over waterfalls and finding their way through a thermal maze of erupting geysers and bubbling mud pools.

At the end of the programme, the girls decided they would sleep together for company after which Will and Tim sat looking at a documentary featuring back-country farming, appropriate after today's farm visit. At the end, Tim said to Will sleepily, "You're not a bad sort of chap considering you're a stuffy old headmaster."

Will felt like saying, 'And you're not bad sort considering you're a cheeky and impertinent boy,' but instead said, "Thank you, Tim," realising that if he said what he thought it would be relayed to Gaynor which, taken out of context, would not be helpful, after which Tim took himself to bed. Though Gaynor had told him not to wait up for her he did until by one, constantly nodding off, he too went to bed.

Chapter Nine

When Will took Ruth to the kitchen/dining area next morning, he found Gaynor already there, looking less fresh than usual, but otherwise cheerful and efficient. Giving her a perfunctory good morning kiss, he thought he smelt wine on her breath but was not sure. So as not to appear surly and put out, he mustered up a smile and asked if she had a pleasant evening out.

"Not bad, interesting experience," Gaynor replied, offering nothing more. Will, determined not to show curiosity or jealousy, refrained from any further questions. "Children good?"

"We watched television and had a happy time. I hope you did not mind finding Ruth with your lot. Angela wanted her with her for company as Tim went to bed later, though I found Ruth with me in the morning. I think I can remember her climbing in beside me a little before dawn."

"I'm pleased you all managed," Gaynor replied, sounding genuinely relieved.

In view of Gaynor's going out with this smooth-talking Joe fellow, Will decided he would map out the remainder of their New Zealand itinerary. Though he was open for discussion, in the end, the agenda was his, he was footing the bill. "If we're all up to it, I plan today to drive to Te Anau, then on to Milford Sound. After that I'd like to go on up to the Franz Josef Glacier.

I've never seen or been on a glacier. It's advertised that you can get a light plane ride and land at the top of the glacier right amongst the high mountain peaks. To get to the Franz Josef Glacier, we'll need to climb through the Haast Pass, which is under two thousand feet in altitude, not built until 1966. I'll get a weather report before starting out.

"Our drive today to Lake Te Anau is 110 miles, as we have to go right down to Lumsden before turning west and north. It should take us about two and a half hours, giving us the afternoon to sightsee. We need finally to return to Queenstown by the 23rd to be back at Ted and Layla's on the 24th, before going up north for the last four days as we catch the plane for Heathrow on the 30th, OK?"

"How are we going to get all the way back up to Auckland in time?"

"I intend to leave the car at Queenstown and for all of us to fly to Auckland, picking up another car either at Auckland Airport or have a car sent next day to brother Ted's," Will replied.

Having had only half her normal night's sleep, Gaynor was secretly relieved that Will did not have a long, tiring journey planned for today. "Sounds good," she replied. "Shall we aim to leave by ten, it'll give you time to book accommodation at Lake Te Anau." With that, Gaynor started on the packed lunches after which she brought out her bag and the children's, along with the carefully packed food ready for departure. By ten, they were off; Will driving, Tim beside him.

Will was able to book a two-bedroom bungalow set in Japanese style garden beside the lake, not so easy for Joe Jambeagle to find, he felt.

Though it was cold with patches of hard-packed snow in places, the driving was good in brilliant sunshine. At twelve twenty-five, they mounted a rise to see the deep blue lake before them surrounded by tall, snow-clad mountains.

After looking up what to see and do, it was decided that in the afternoon, they would take a motor yacht cruise with a stop-off at Fiordland National Park visitor's centre from which a guided walk was available. A notice said the cruise only went in good weather. Though cold, the day was calm and clear. The trip was on. As it was too cold to sit out on deck, they went down to the cabin, marvelling at the magnificent views through the windows. At the National Park, Will volunteered to take the girls round the visitor's centre while Gaynor and Tim undertook the guided walk through the bush as at their age the girls were not good walkers. Will thought he got the better deal as the exhibits in the visitor's centre he found fascinating, learning a lot about the geography and history of New Zealand's most remote and scenic province. By the time they got back to the bungalow it was dark. While the children watched television, Gaynor made them a meal of pot chicken and rice.

After the children were asleep, Gaynor cuddled up with Will on the couch in their usual manner, but Will felt that Gaynor's going out with that showy Joe fellow had altered their relationship, though Gaynor acted as if had not. Predictably she asked to be excused early as she was plainly tired. Will watched television for a while alone then, with nothing better to do, went to bed. Tomorrow they were going on to Milford Sound, a distance of about 75 miles, through the Homer Tunnel which, Will thought, depending on condition, should take about two hours.

As it turned out, it took longer to reach Milford Sound as there had been a substantial slip near the entrance to the Homer Tunnel with one-way traffic and a temporary shingle road surface. When they finally took their turn in the tunnel, they found it had rough, unlined walls, seemed about three-quarters of a mile in length, sloping gently downwards. The tunnel was narrow, Will fervently hoping to avoid a close encounter with an approaching large vehicle.

"Where are we staying tonight?" Gaynor asked.

"As we need to go food shopping, I felt a hotel where we could get meals would be better for one night. I managed to get two rooms in the old Tourist Department Hotel, which I thought might have the most atmosphere. It's featured as looking straight out towards Mitre Peak."

Arriving eventually at the hotel, they found it a wooden structure with large windows facing the sound. In its day it would have been the height of modern architecture, but now it was showing its age, damp and moss appearing in places on the windows. Its décor was luxuriant New Zealand bush and fern in harmony with its surroundings.

The children did their best with the menu, which was more to their liking than on previous hotel occasions. Not long back in their room, almost predictably, Gaynor received a telephone call. They had been tracked down. Will hovered near to the entrance to her room to overhear what he could of Gaynor's replies, "A supper cruise with a live orchestra... landing on the stern of your friend's superyacht... It's very kind of you, but I'd like my friend Will to have an opportunity... The invitation is for me only?... Your helicopter's waiting... I have a commitment here... if you promise I won't be back late like last time as we need to be off in in the morning in time to catch our booked four-hour cruise... No, I told you, I can't sleep in, and the following morning, we need to be up really early as we have a long drive ahead... I'm sorry, but that's how it is... All right, only if you promise, I'll meet you in the lounge in 20 minutes." Will heard Gaynor put down the phone. He retreated quietly back into his room as he did not want to be caught eavesdropping. Half a minute later, he heard Gaynor call, "All right if I come in?"

"Come in," Will called back, sitting quickly on his bed.

"You don't mind if I go out again tonight, Will. You did well with children last time?"

Having overheard much of Gaynor's conversational replies, Will felt better than on the previous occasion when asked the same question as he was aware that she had suggested to this Joe fellow that she would like him to have a turn going out but, of course, the womaniser was wanting nothing of that.

Tim, who had followed his mother into the room, made a face and said, "You're not going out with that smarty-pants again."

"Mr Jambeagle's a nice man," Gaynor replied defensively.

"He's a smarty-pants!" Tim repeated defiantly.

"You don't know him," his mother reiterated. Will was in agreement with Tim's assessment but said nothing.

The evening went well. Alone with Will, the children felt vulnerable, needing his security, and did not play up. Will gathered them into one room to watch television until the girls felt sleepy and went off to bed together, Tim following later when he too felt tired. Will watched television for a while alone, finally going to bed as well, not attempting to wait up for Gaynor.

The cruise next day was a mixed success. The views of fiords and mountains were stunning beyond all measure, the best in the world, but the girls had had enough of cruising.

"Are we going to see whales?" Angela asked anxiously.

"Not intentionally," Will responded to Angela's obvious relief.

Will and Gaynor took it in turn to amuse the girls, Will noting that Gaynor was obviously tired. He had asked her earlier if she enjoyed her evening. She said she had but had offered nothing further and Will refrained from asking more. Tim got more out of the cruise, exploring the vessel and appreciating the superb views. At one point, when the ship approached some incredibly high cascading waterfalls, the girls cried out in wonderment but for the rest they were not overly impressed. On the other hand, Will and Gaynor were; Will taking many wonderful photos. It was a day to remember.

After dinner, back in their rooms, the phone rang in Gaynor's room where they had had all gathered. Gaynor answered. "Not tonight, Joe," they all heard her say, "you got me back too late, I'm tired and we've got a long drive tomorrow." She hung up. Will gave a quiet sigh of relief.

"Smarty-pants!" Tim exclaimed. Gaynor ignored him.

The ring reminded Will, however, that he needed to talk to Gaynor before she became too tired. "I've got a confession to make, I didn't realise when I planned our South Island itinerary that there were so few roads. We need to fly to Auckland on the 24th to stay at Ted's overnight to be able to leave on the 25th to go up to the Bay of Islands. I would like to have four clear days there to find and talk to my sister's best friend to try to understand what disturbed her for the rest of her life after returning to Britain during the Second World War. In the meantime, to get to Franz Josef Glacier, we have to drive all the way back to Queenstown to then turn back up north to Franz Josef Glacier, a distance in all of about 395 miles, taking at least nine hours; too much for the children, too much for all of us."

"What's the distance from here back to Queenstown?" Gaynor asked.

"One hundred and eighty miles, taking about four hours over these roads," Will replied. "With snow it could be much longer."

"If you can afford it, I think I have the solution," Gaynor said. "I noticed at the airport, which is just round the corner by the way, where Joe's helicopter was parked, a light plane company was advertising taking parties of up to four climbers, skiers or sightseers to venues round about. I also noticed that a company based at Franz Josef's small airport was advertising one-hour sightseeing flights, landing for 20 minutes among the mountains at the top of the glacier. I'm sure the light plane company would take two adults and three children to Franz Josef Glacier and back. I'd like to see the region by air. I'd mind the girls if you'd then like to take Tim with you up on the scenic hour's flight, landing on the top of the glacier. I don't fancy it myself and I don't think the girls would either. You could book it all this evening from here. That's for tomorrow. The following day we could between us drive back to Queenstown. How about that?"

Will thought long and hard for a few minutes before getting up and kissing Gaynor on the forehead. "You're a genius!"

So it was arranged, the flights were booked and paid for by card, the alarm set for seven thirty, to catch the plane for Franz Josef Glacier at nine, Will and Tim then boarding the sightseeing glacier plane at 12 noon, afterwards lunching together at Franz Josef before returning by the light air company plane at four, leaving their car for the day at their Milford Sound hotel. The following day they would drive back to Totara Motor Lodge, Queenstown. After the children had gone to bed, Gaynor sat companionably with Will for half an hour before going to bed early as she was exhausted. For an hour, Will sat poring over maps and the revised itinerary before going to bed early himself.

With the alarm ringing in his ear, Will sat up and yawned. Ruth had started off sleeping with Angela but now she was with him. He was about to snuggle down again for a few minutes before remembering the tight schedule for the day. He promptly got up, shaved and showered in their bathroom before awakening Ruth. With the muesli and fruit remaining, they breakfasted in their rooms as breakfast in the dining room could be slow and they needed to be at the airport by a few minutes to nine. Will put in a daypack all the warm clothes he could find. He tried to persuade Ruth to leave Yellow Ted at home for the day, telling her Yellow Ted did not like the cold. Predictably Ruth said he did not mind the cold at all.

It was frosty and slippery as they walked the few hundred yards to the airport, their breaths condensing in the cold air. Fortunately, there was little wind.

"Where are we going?" Angela asked.

"We've already told you, to a small airport to fly in a light aircraft," Gaynor replied.

"I don't like flying in light aircraft," Angela complained.

"How do you know?" her mother contended. "You've never been in one."

"Yellow Ted likes flying in light aircraft," Ruth commented. For once, Will felt, Yellow Ted had made a helpful contribution.

Hurrying as best they could, they arrived at the airport steaming in the cold air as if they were on fire. The pilot, dressed for the part in an afghan coat with a fur collar, came out of an office the size of a garden shed to greet them. "G'day," he said, looking them over, "I could take five of your size, it's the weight factor. Good day for flying, just a few cumulus clouds about. Going to Franz for a glacier flight, I hear?"

"Just Will and my son, Tim," Gaynor said.

"Don't fancy it yourself?"

"Not really," Gaynor replied. "And the girls certainly wouldn't, they don't like the cold."

"It can be fair dinkum nippy at times up there," the pilot agreed. He helped them aboard a white and blue striped Cessna, seeing them strapped in and explained a few safety features. He seemed particularly concerned they did not fall out the doors, explaining he nearly lost a passenger in that way. Once they were all aboard, the pilot donned a light flying helmet, started the engine and looked up at the tower.

When the signal was given, the engine roared and the plane began to move down the runway, slowly at first then with increasing speed. Eventually they were off, climbing slowly in a circle, gaining height to clear the surrounding peaks, before following the sound to the sea. With the sea below them, they turned north along the coastline, the entrance to the Sound diminishing behind. Now and then they passed through fluffy cumulus clouds, blinking when emerging back again into bright sunshine. Before long, the pilot pointed out Mount Aspiring to their right then, after flying for some time, Mount Cook. The girls were beginning to get restless, wanting to move about, when the pilot, to their relief, said he was soon going to make their approach to Franz Josef Airport, undertaking a steep turn to his right.

Will admired the pilot's skill, descending between mountains affecting wind speed and direction. Bracing themselves for landing on the short runway, they were startled by a shrill alarm which soon stopped, the pilot apologising that he had forgotten to switch off the stall warning indicator. When the plane came to a stop, Will heard Gaynor give a sigh of relief.

As they had not a Franz Josef holiday address, Gaynor said that she and the girls were going to wait at the airport for the scenic flight company's call, after which she and the girls would inquire where they could get something to eat, leaving a note at the airport as to where they were so Will and Tim could join them on their return.

At twenty to twelve, Will heard his name being called over the public address system to go to the counter to pick up a phone call. It was from the glacier flight company, the caller's New Zealand accent amplified over the phone. He and his son would be picked up at the airport in 10 minutes to be taken to their aircraft.

The pilot, who approached them with another man, was dressed more like an alpine climber or skier, the man with him turning out to be a client. The high-winged monoplane Will and Tim were led out to was equipped with skis, wheels poking out though them. As Will climbed aboard, he had to admit to feeling nervous.

"We've not long got the snow report, first flight today," the pilot said laconically, "we're good to go. My name's Dermot. Make sure you keep your seatbelts on at all times, one of you with me the other two behind."

Will would have liked to have sat up with the pilot but indicated for the person on his own to do so as he felt he needed to be with Tim. Without further ceremony they were off, already having had clearance, the noisy aircraft climbing steeply towards the Waiho River and glacier terminal before passing over the seven-and-a-half-mile glacier, an awesome spectacle of slowly cascading and churning ice blocks.

At the top of the glacier, the plane circled around, the pilot searching for the best place to land, eventually touching down in a swirl of snow, the plane swaying and swerving alarmingly before coming to a halt. "It's this neve, snow that has partially melted, refrozen and compacted, tricky to land on. Don't go far, we can only be here for 20 minutes at the most. A snow shower could mean white-out, watch it," the pilot warned. With that he opened the door, and they climbed out onto a freezing plateau surrounded by forbidding peaks. Will and Tim had borrowed the girls' pixie hats which they pulled over their ears, banging their gloved hands together. It was unbelievably cold. Will fumbled for his camera. Vowing to keep the plane in sight, they went for a walkabout.

They had only gone about three hundred yards when a snow shower swept down, bringing with it zero visibility. For the first time, Tim grabbed Will's hand. He felt it quivering with anxiety. "We'd better follow our tracks back to the plane before they're snowed over, come on," Will advised.

Back at the aircraft, the pilot opened the door for them. They climbed gratefully inside. The front seat passenger was not to be seen. The pilot looked at his watch. As quickly as it came, the snow shower ceased, revealing the other passenger about four hundred yards away looking confused. As soon as he saw the plane emerging into sight, he waved gratefully and began stumbling towards it, sinking at times through the crust into deep snow.

All aboard the pilot increased engine speed, the plane slowly turning in a swirl of snow and began gathering momentum, heading towards where the plateau ended abruptly in what appeared to be a near-vertical thousand feet drop to the valley below, swerving and swaying over the unstable neve.

As the plane reached the edge, appearing to Will to be below take-off speed, it literally free fell, engine screaming until sufficient airspeed was built up for the pilot to be able to pull out of the dive within what seemed just a few feet of the glacier below. Will was unnerved by it, feeling like when he was taken on a funfair rollercoaster ride at too young an age. He felt Tim clutching him, shrieking with fear.

"I'll bank a bit so you can get some good photos," the pilot announced casually. "The glacier's catching the light at this point."

"Thank you," Will replied weakly. "Very good of you."

Back at airport reception, Will and the shaken Tim went to the counter to pick up a note from Gaynor saying that she and the girls were dining at the Green Kea Eating House and Bar. Will asked where that was and was told it was 10 minutes away on foot and given directions. On seeing his mother, Tim ran to her and held her tight.

"Enjoy your flight, darling?" Gaynor asked, surprised by the sudden affection, looking questioningly at Will.

"Super... a bit cold," Tim eventually replied in a quiet voice devoid of his usual bravado.

"And a bit challenging as well as on the cold side, I'll fill you in later," Will replied. "We both need a meal." Gaynor took the hint and signalled for a waiter.

While the children wandered about the shops back at the airport, Will quietly gave Gaynor an account of their mountain landing on the snow above the glacier, explaining how the neve made the landing and especially the take-off somewhat unnerving, as well as the cold and the temporary white-out episode.

"Quite an experience," Gaynor said, "the girls would have been terrified. I wouldn't have appreciated it either. I'm glad we didn't go."

"I wasn't expecting the conditions," Will admitted.

They were called for their Cessna return flight to Milford Sound dead on four, arriving back at their hotel after dark. Predictably, back in the rooms after dinner,

Joe Jambeagle rang. Will heard Gaynor reply firmly, "It's very nice of you to ask me, Joe, but I'm tired and have had quite enough flying for one day, another time," and rang off. Will smiled to himself.

After the children were asleep, Gaynor and Will spent only a little time together on the sofa as both were tired after their eventful day, needing to be up promptly tomorrow in readiness for their long drive back to Queenstown. Will wrote himself a note to get an early morning weather forecast.

Next day with Will at the wheel and Tim beside him, they set off for Queenstown at nine thirty with a weather forecast of occasional snow showers, a moderate breeze of between 12 and 15 miles an hour, with the highest temperature being quoted as six degrees. All went well until emerging from the Homer Tunnel when they were faced with single line traffic and repeated long delays. Looking at the car's ambient thermometer Will noticed the outside temperature had dropped to two. Ten minutes later it began to snow, the big Holden's handing, however, so far not being affected by the gathering accumulation. To Will's relief after 20 minutes the snow stopped. After another 20 minutes, the one-way ceased, and the road surface changed from shingle back to tarmac.

At Te Anau they stopped, went food shopping and then drove to the lake, the children having a run about before lunching in the car. At two, they started the second leg of their journey, Gaynor driving, experiencing only a further two light snow showers which were not intense enough to impede progress, arriving back at Totara Lodge as dusk was falling.

With a full kitchen at her disposal, and having bought the ingredients earlier, Gaynor produced a warming Creole Jambalaya with chicken. In the lounge after eating, Will was not surprised by the phone ringing. "Up on the cable car to the mountain restaurant for supper," they all heard Gaynor saying. "I can only go out with you, Joe, if you promise to bring me back in reasonable time as we're flying to Auckland tomorrow. All right, only if you keep your promise, see you in the main lounge at eight."

Before going, Gaynor helped Will book a flight for the next day and arrange for the collection of the car before hurrying off to the main lounge. Will felt bitterly that if Gaynor arrived back in the early hours overtired, he would need to speak to her about breaking their contract. In the event, she was not unduly late as he heard her come in and get into bed without putting on the light before he fell asleep.

Totara Lodge reception ordered a taxi to get them to Queenstown Airport to catch the 11 o'clock flight to Auckland Domestic Terminal. Before leaving they had to get rid of their food and some of their warm South Island clothes as all they had acquired would not fit in their suitcases.

Their flight was on time. Out on the tarmac they found their plane to be a light, turbo-powered Pilatus PC-12 with a high tailfin. Tim would have very much liked the adjacent larger, slim-lined Embradaer Bandeirante turboprop, but that was apparently scheduled for Christchurch for a greater number of Australian skiers destined for the ski fields.

"This looks a change from a Boeing 747," Will said, climbing the half a dozen steps onto the aircraft.

"Won't take time to load," Gaynor replied, seeing the girls up the steps.

"I don't want Yellow Ted up on the rack," Ruth protested as the attendant tried to stow her hand luggage at which the tiresome bear was taken out and secured within her seat belt.

Two hours later, they were walking up to Arrivals at Auckland Domestic Terminal to find Ted and Layla waiting for them. "Very nice of you to come out to Mangere to meet us," Will said to Ted as he came forward to meet them in his usual expansive manner.

"That's the least I could do for my brother and his family," Ted said as he swept the children up in his arms and gave them in turn a big hug.

The children, having got to know Uncle Ted and his genuine kindness, did not resist being hugged, nor did Gaynor. "As we drive back, tell us all about your South Island trip," Ted said, squeezing them and their luggage into his car. "Layla's got a late lunch waiting for you. I've booked two rooms for you at the Waterfront at Devonport for the night, you've seen the hotel, opposite the ferry terminal, it's nearer than Takapuna." What particularly struck Will as he got into the car was the mildness of the weather compared with the temperatures of the South Island in winter.

As dusk was falling, after a happy afternoon, lunch and dinner, they were taken to the Waterfront Hotel where they were warmly welcomed at reception. The hotel was different from any accommodation they had been in. Built in 1903, it had the character of an English hotel in a south coast resort like Torquay. After being given keys, they were taken up a long formal staircase with a polished wood bannister to a carpeted landing, their suitcases coming up in a lift to the right of the stairs. Here they were ushered into spacious rooms with large sash windows overlooking the harbour and city across on the south shore.

The children went to sleep early as they were tired after an exciting and varied day. Out in the corridor, noise came up from the bar below, but it was quiet in the rooms other than the occasional sound of traffic moving in Victoria Road below to the left. In one of the darkened rooms, Will and Gaynor drew ornate chairs up to a window and watched the reflecting lights of commercial and pleasure craft moving in the dark waterway, the city's high buildings across the water a twinkling and mysterious backdrop. Will listened for Joe Jambeagle's phone call but as yet he hadn't tracked them down.

"Brother Ted said he would like me to download our trip photos into a computer and then to a memory stick and send them to him. How do you do that?" Will asked Gaynor.

"You should have had a USB cable with your camera. I'll show you what to do when we get back to Britain." At that statement, Will felt heartened that Gaynor contemplated continuing their friendship back home and, sitting as close as two separate chairs permitted, the damaging shadow of Joe Smarty-pants, as Tim called him, for the present receded in his mind. After an hour or so they both got up together, arms around each other's waist and stood, looking out at the view. It was then Gaynor gave Will a long kiss, thanking him for the day, before they went to their rooms to look after their children as there was no communicating door.

In the morning they needed to take the children to breakfast which was served in a dining room to the left of a short corridor leading from reception to the street.

They were seated near a window where they could see passing locals mixing with tourists pouring off the ferries to view Devonport, the oldest and most charismatic suburb on the Shore. The menu was extensive with something for all. The girls chose pancakes with maple syrup, fresh fruit and whipped cream, Tim chose bacon and eggs, tomatoes, mushrooms, sausages, hash brown and toast. Gaynor said he would burst with all that lot, while Will, along with Gaynor, decided on eggs Benedict served on English muffins with spinach and hollandaise sauce.

While waiting for Ted to collect them to take them back to his place to wait delivery of their hire car, Will and Gaynor took the children across the road to Windsor Reserve where they played in and out of the roots of an enormous banyan tree adjacent to a modern library. As the children amused themselves, Will and Gaynor gazed up the ascending main street, with its shops behind colourful verandas, the footpaths on either side enhanced by floral planters enclosing cosy seating areas where street goers could rest and chat, to dormant 87-metre Mount Victoria volcano. Will thought Devonport, New Zealand, utterly charming and would have liked to have spent more time there.

Chapter Ten

Returning to their hotel to pay their bill and collect their luggage, the ever-helpful receptionist told them she had been able to book for them two rooms at the Settlers' Landing Motel on the foreshore at Paihia for the nights of the 25th to the 29th of August, leaving on the morning of the 30th. As Will was thanking the receptionist, Ted and Layla turned up to take them back to their home to await the arrival of their next hire car.

Promptly at half-past ten, two keen young operatives from Cars-for-All-Rental arrived with a silver Holden Vectra 2.0 GLS sedan. Will and Gaynor were pleased with the vehicle as they found Holdens very suitable for New Zealand roads. Will had observed the night before that the distance to Paihia was quoted as 230 kilometres, about 143 miles and would take about three and a half hours driving time. With that in mind, they left Ted and Layla's after a tearful farewell as they had grown fond of each other, intending to buy food on the way. With their large breakfasts, Will hoped that they could reach Whangarei before stopping, though Gaynor said she had read that the wharf at Warkworth was an attractive stopping place.

At the Esmonde Road interchange, Will managed to keep right then take the green loop leading up on to the Northern Motorway, turning off right at Orewa, Tim in the passenger seat beside him. The beautifully treed

Wenderholm Regional Park looked a lovely place to spend time, but Gaynor agreed for the need to press on.

Within a little over two hours, they reached Whangarei, stopping at the well-marked visitors' centre on a sweeping right-hand bend where there was an information area, toilets with washing facilities, a restaurant and recreational parkland beside the Raumanga Stream, a river by United Kingdom standards. Though it was winter, both Will and Gaynor commented on how warm it was. This was indeed the 'Winterless North'. Having bought sandwiches and drinks, they sat eating them on a bench beside the stream, after which the children ran about exploring, no need here to sit huddled in the car.

An hour later they continued on Highway 1, stopping at a food market before leaving Whangarei, an hour half after that turning onto Highway 11 at Kawakawa. A little before six, as dusk was falling, they turned right along the Paihia waterfront, completing their journey at the end of Marsden Road in the forecourt of the Settlers' Landing Motel, thankful that it kept lighter later than down south.

They found their second-floor rooms, accessed by an outside staircase, were on a veranda walkway overlooking the bay. Tired, they humped up their luggage. Before anything else, Gaynor unpacked the food and began making a pasta bake while Will helped the children unpack and stow their clothes. Half an hour later they were sitting together eating in one room looking out over the darkening water. It was still warm, Will, in shirt sleeves, estimating the temperature to be about 20 degrees Celsius. As they were eating, a scurrying breeze arose, causing the drawn-back curtains to toss and sway. Gaynor moved to slide the glass door across, leaving it two inches ajar.

"It's been strangely still up to now," Gaynor observed.

"I think the wind heralds a change," Will replied.

As Will and Gaynor sat close together on two chairs in the darkness, looking out across the bay, the children asleep in their rooms, Will turned the radio on quietly to hear a warning that residents in the far north should be prepared for an imminent tropical storm, the remnants of a force two hurricane that had recently caused widespread damage in Rarotonga and the Cook Islands. "Sounds a bit dire," Will observed.

"Won't be suitable for a boat trip tomorrow by the sounds of it," Gaynor replied.

"No, it doesn't, but firstly I need to see if I can make contact with my elder sister's Zoe's best friend, Tawhaitu Tahu. If you remember, Ted said that she was overseas when he attempted to make contact with her 10 years ago when Zoe first disappeared. I'll try to ring her in the morning, I have her address and phone number, that's why we came up north in the first place, as well as sightseeing, before having to fly back to Britain on the 30th."

"Of course," Gaynor agreed, "you must, I understand."

They sat close in silence, observing the increased swaying of yachts' anchoring lights. Gaynor's willingness to assist Will in his efforts to find the reason behind Zoe's disappearance and presumed death, which she did not fully understand, made Will warm to her, the shadow of Joe Smarty-pants coming between them receding in his mind. He felt that the time was right to attempt another proposal. Before he could put his intention into words, there was a cry from the other room. "Excuse me," Gaynor said, running out onto the landing and into the next room. When she came back 10 minutes later saying, "Angela had a pain in her tummy, I had to put her on the toilet," Will felt the spell had again been broken and he would try proposing to Gaynor another time. They sat close to each other for an hour, watching the rising wind, before agreeing they had had a long day and were tired, going to sleep in the rooms of their respective children.

At nine thirty next morning, Will ran Tawhaitu Tahu's number and was rewarded by hearing a deep, cultured Maori voice. Tim explained who he was and the reason for his ringing. After a long pause, Tawhaitu said that she would be very pleased to see him but that at the moment, as a lawyer, she was representing the local hapu in a Waitangi Tribunal fishing rights dispute and would let Will know in a day or two when she was available to see him. She would leave a message with the motel if they were out. Putting down the phone, Will joined Gaynor looking out at the storm causing trees to flail about as if shaken by a giant hand, rain squalls hurling walls of water at the windows blotting out the view.

"No sightseeing boats will be out today," Gaynor commented.

"Obviously," Will replied. "We have the choice of being cooped up here in the motel all day or going by car round to the other side of the bay to see what we can between the squalls of Kerikeri Inlet, the first settlement with the original Mission House and Stone Store. It's the 26th today, we fly back to Britain on the 30th."

"We'll see how it goes. I'll make packed lunches. We'll go down to the car during lulls," Gaynor replied after some hesitation.

Holding onto the children tightly, in a lull between squalls, they dashed down the outside staircase as quickly as they could, jumped into the car and slammed the door. Looking at the map, they saw they needed to take Highway 11 to Puketona, before turning north onto Highway 10, then having to take the first major turn-off right to Kerikeri. They started off slowly, Will driving with Gaynor navigating beside him, wind punching at the car as if they were a yacht battling a hurricane. When rain squalls struck, they had had to slow down to a walking pace to avoid torrents of water cascading down from higher ground.

Passing through Kerikeri, they needed to watch out for pedestrians being blown into their path, at the end of the town turning left to Kerikeri Inlet. Down by the water there was ample parking in designated car parks where they waited for a lull to dash into the Stone Store, the massively constructed building being impervious to the tropical storm raging outside. Inside, staff were dressed in the style of the 1840s, selling local produce in the manner of the period. After 20 minutes, during a lull, they made another dash of 200 yards to Kemp House, New Zealand's oldest building, constructed in 1821 on behalf of the London-based Church Missionary Society by local craftsmen and Maori. Will found it fascinating, but before long the children became bored. They needed to move on.

Looking outside, Will saw that the Kerikeri River was in turbulent flood, the churning waters cutting access to the footbridge across to Hone Heke's pa, or hill fort, so he drove round by the Kerikeri Heritage Bypass Bridge and parked in the partly flooded car park on the other side. The lulls between drenching rain squalls were becoming longer, allowing the children to get out of the car. Blue-fronted pukeko or swamp hen were striding about, delighted by their sudden increased habitat. The children wanted to get close to them but being birds of the wild, they kept their distance. Coming back to the car disappointed, they were confronted by the largest and most colourful rooster Will had ever seen. The bird was obviously domesticated, used to people, and followed them about. The children, who thought the bird to be native, were delighted but Will, who had a book on New Zealand birds, knew it was not. But whatever it made the children's day until a rain squall forced them quickly inside the car where they ate their packed lunches.

As Gaynor turned the car round after lunch, Will noticed that the track up to the hill fort was closed owing to the weather. Will had decided not to try in any case as the hillside was too wet and slippery with rivulets of water everywhere. Instead, they drove on to nearby Rainbow Falls. Finding it was a bit complicated, but when they did, there was ample parking. Waiting for another lull in the weather they took the children's hands and walked quickly for 10 minutes to a wooden viewing platform. What they saw was breathtaking, an enormous volume of water falling 27 metres over a basalt ledge, the spray reportedly rainbow-tinted in sunshine. After Will had taken photos, they hurried back to the car just in time before a further blinding rain squall occurred which lasted a good half an hour, buffeting and rocking their vehicle. When it had sufficiently lessened, Gaynor drove back to Paihia the way they had come.

That evening, for a change, they decided they would dine at a famous fish restaurant, four hundred yards back towards the wharves. Donning their light waterproofs, they made a dash for it, getting to the restaurant dry.

Inside they found the restaurant to be a long, green-painted wooden structure leading back from the street. With plenty to choose from there were meals to please them all. While they ate, they were aware of the gale outside rising and falling, gusts at times shaking the building.

On the way back they were not so lucky, being overtaken by a savage squall. With the wind behind them, the adults on the outside, they held hands so as not to be blown off their feet. Arriving back at their motel, they were absolutely drenched to the skin. Searching both rooms, Will discovered in cupboards two radiant electric heaters. They put all their wet clothes on a structure of chairbacks connected by broom handles around the back-to-back heaters, hoping the clothes would be dry by morning, there being no central heating in the far north. What they did not take into account was the high humidity which meant their clothes were only partly dry the following morning.

All three children, disturbed by the noise of the gale, took a long while to get to sleep, leaving Gaynor and Will little time alone before they needed to go to bed as well. By next morning, the wind and rain had lessened, though seas were still high, boat trips still not operating.

They waited indoors in case Tawhaitu rang. When she did not, Will decided they must do something with the day. He would have liked to have driven up by road to Cape Reinga where the Maori spirits of the dead leap off the headland by the roots of an eight-hundred-year-old pohutukawa tree to return to their traditional homeland of Hawaiki but decided it was too far, especially in this weather. Instead, Will thought he would settle for a visit to the Waipoua State Forest on the West Coast, a distance of about 95 kilometres, taking at least two hours each way in this weather. Sensibly, Gaynor said they must contact the local authorities first regarding possible road closures owing to slips or flooding. They were advised it was possible with caution but warned conditions could change. At eleven thirty they set off.

There were slips, flash floods and streams flowing across the road in places, where these occurred making for single-file traffic. Nevertheless, they managed to get to their destination by one thirty, on arrival eating packed lunches in their car adjacent to public toilets. While eating, Will read that the forest contained about three-quarters of New Zealand's remaining mature kauri trees which once clothed Northland and the Coromandel Peninsula. Watching the weather, they ventured up a track to look up at the astounding kauri, Tane Mahuta, Lord of the Forest. About them, every bit of foliage dripped.

After Will had taken a photo, they walked on quickly to look at Te Matua Ngahere, equally impressive, from a viewing platform. "I don't like the pixies," Ruth said, pointing down to the undergrowth of fern.

"There aren't any pixies," Will replied despite knowing that old-time Maori thought the forest was full of mischievous spirits and would not travel in it alone at night. "Yellow Ted doesn't see them." Having said that, Will knew he had made a mistake to drag Yellow Ted into it.

"Yellow Ted saw them first," Ruth countered. Not for the first time, Will realised that what was of interest to adults rarely held the same appeal for seven-year-olds.

"We'd better be getting back to the car before it rains again," Gaynor reminded them.

Will thought that might be wise. Once aboard, Gaynor turned the car and began driving back cautiously the way they had come while Will listened on the radio for road reports. With one diversion they got back to their motel as dusk was falling. Though the storm was now appreciably lessening they decided not to go out tonight, Gaynor immediately setting about making them all pomegranate chicken with almond couscous, a meal they all enjoyed.

After sorting through their clothes to see what was now dry, they turned on the television news. With further tragic events in Sarajevo again taking prominence, Will looked for lighter family entertainment, ending up playing rough and tumble games with the children on the rug as they had surplus energy owing to having spent so much time in the car. When they finally got the children to sleep, and Will and Gaynor got back in the sitting room, cuddling up together on the sofa, they both snoozed off, content with each other's warmth and closeness. When they did join the children for the night, Will felt that he and Gaynor were building up a sustainable relationship for the future.

Next morning at nine, Tawaitu Tahu rang. Will's heart jumped. Was he at last going to learn what occurred during his older sister's return to Britain during the war, resulting in her later disturbed life in New Zealand and eventual mysterious disappearance? The meeting was for ten at her home in Te Haumi Drive. Looking at a detailed street map of Paihia, Te Haumi Drive appeared about two miles to the south along Highway 11.

With Gaynor navigating they arrived in good time – and discovered what was meant by a pole house. Set amongst luxuriant trees and ferns, the house was situated on the side of a steep ridge, the far side being supported be incredibly long poles. Stepping out of the car they found themselves on a wooden platform spanning the gap between the road and house, the main entrance sited to the left of double garage doors. Before they could ring the bell, the door was opened by a cheerful Maori girl in a floral dress who led them upstairs to a large room, more like the bridge of a ship, with windows on three sides affording a panoramic view over the treetops out across the bay. To the left of a servery, a woman stood up to greet them from behind a desk beside a wooden filing cabinet. Will observed Tawaitu Tahu to be in her mid-seventies, her white hair gathered fashionably behind her. She wore a smart grey suit, had a discreet moko kauae, a female chin tattoo, indicating her to be, through her whakapapa genealogy, of high tribal rank. Will wondered if she would formally rub noses on each side, like the French kiss each cheek on greeting but, knowing them to be from overseas, instead shook Will and Gaynor's hands in the European manner. She then gave the children each a green koru necklace which Will understood to symbolise taking an important new step in life. Tawaitu took them as being one family. Will did not explain they were not, hoping that all going well, they would become one, which would be an important step for all of them. Will outlined to Tawaitu the reason why he particularly wanted to speak to her.

Hearing for the first time in detail why Will desired to talk, Tawaitu, noting the children looking around fidgeting, suggested that his wife and children might like to drive to Waitangi, five miles to the north, if they hadn't already been there, looking over the barque on the foreshore on the left just before the causeway before viewing Treaty House and gardens, coming back in two hours' time.

Gaynor and Will agreed, Gaynor saying she would be back at twelve. With that, Kaia, the maid, showed them out. Drawing up a chair for Will to sit beside her, Tawaitu, in a precise Maori manner, her aquiline features composed in thought, began telling him of her many years of friendship with the elder sister Will hardly knew.

Tawaitu met Zoe in the late fifties when, after Ted and Layla's marriage in 1956, she moved to Paihia near Kerikeri where she and Ted found employment when first arriving in New Zealand. Like last time, she sought employment in the prospering fruit growing industry. With accommodation in the rapidly expanding township of Kerikeri at a premium, she looked for accommodation further afield. It was at the time Tawaitu was advertising for a tenant for a self-contained flat she had built at a lower level on the right of her pole house. This had been intended for her widowed father, but her elder brothers' wives said that as Tawaitu was away half the time representing Maori claimants throughout the North Island, he would be lonely when she was away, and they would look after him in turn instead.

Tawaitu would have preferred a deserving Maori woman or couple for her flat, but when Zoe turned up on her doorstep with her lean, haunted face, she felt a compelling desire to help her. She could not explain why. Of about the same age but from completely different cultures and backgrounds, they nevertheless soon became firm friends. Maoris by nature are gregarious, Tawaitu's status, however, separating her in ordinary day to day life from whanau or kin. Zoe likewise missed her brother's company. When Tawaitu was at home and Zoe not at work, they spent their time together, other than when Tawaitu was involved in traditional gatherings with her hapu. Gradually, over time, Zoe confided in her what had occurred during her time in Britain during the Second World War, the reason, in Tawaitu's opinion, for her increasingly reckless and disturbed behaviour over the years, resulting 10 years ago in her disappearance and presumed death. This is what Will learnt.

In September 1938, Ted and Zoe travelled up to Paihia by service car, having arrived in Auckland on the *Rangitiki* two weeks earlier. They had heard that there were jobs for both sexes in the expanding fruit growing industry in the Kerikeri district where basic accommodation was available in wooden huts for the workers. As they urgently needed jobs and somewhere to live, they thought getting employment there would provide a start for their new life in New Zealand.

Before long, they could not help but become aware of a grass airstrip nearby owing to noisy yellow Tiger

Moths zooming overhead, especially on the weekend. It was the venue of the local flying club where well-off young men, and a few women, pursued the daring sport of flying. Zoe, an attractive young woman, began making her way down there in her spare time where she became known and increasingly offered rides in aircraft and invited to social functions by young men, keen to get to know her. Ted, on the other hand, in his spare time, was more attracted to dingy sailing in the Bay where he joined a sailing club and got to know the sailing fraternity.

To cut a long story short, it was not long before Zoe fell madly in love with a young flying enthusiast by the name of Brad Valentine. Brad was the epitome of the dashing young man in a flying machine. He was handsome with a broad smile and owned a red MG sports car in which he took Zoe to beach parties and romantic coves where they spent time alone.

Zoe was utterly devasted therefore when, in late 1939, without telling her, Brad, with a mate, suddenly left the Bay of Islands, catching the overnight train from Auckland to Wellington where they took passage on the Rangitata to join the British Airforce, which welcomed them as experienced flyers. After six months, hearing nothing from him and not knowing where to write, Zoe decided to go back to her homeland, join the Auxiliary Territorial Services, ATS, with a vague idea of finding Brad and in some way continuing the romance as she hurt so much.

Her brother Ted was very much against the idea as he realised that his sister was crazily infatuated and had heard that Brad had a reputation in the district as a womaniser. He said she could join New Zealand's

WWSA where she would meet many men. He said he had no intention of leaving New Zealand and would be joining the New Zealand Armed Forces when required to do so. Ted felt that, even if she could meet up in Britain with this Brad Valentine, she had no guarantee that she would be welcome. But Zoe was adamant, leaving New Zealand five months later, sailing to Britain via Panama on the Ruahine.

The next five months at sea, including the tropical wonders of the Panama Canal, the opportunity of a shipboard romance with an attractive fellow passenger and a young ship's engineer officer, both of whom asked Zoe out at Panama, gave her ample time for reflection. But the time the voyage took did nothing to put Zoe off her aim of reconnecting with Brad Valentine. Once back in Essex, she applied to join the ATS, hoping in that way to meet up with him. After basics, she was assigned to Oftness Training Camp at the requisitioned primary school.

She had been there less than a month when the women trainees got the exciting news via the grapevine that some off-duty fighter pilots of the Fighter Command Squadron based at the Group Eleven Airfield at Debden, 30 miles to the northwest, were having an unofficial knees-up in a nearby parish hall and the girls had been invited to attend. It had been arranged that an ATS-driven Royal Army Service Corps vehicle would make a delivery to their training camp early evening, and after leaving, stopping around the corner for all the girls who could get an evening leave pass to board in front of the load, go on to Debden Airfield, where it would make a similar delivery, and then hang round in the vicinity to take the girls back at eleven – highly irregular proceedings. Zoe could hardly believe her ears. It was a long shot, but there was just a chance that Brad Valentine might be there.

When the girls arrived, the party was in full swing, having been going for some time. The hall was full of tobacco smoke, the heavy blackout curtains reduced ventilation to the minimum. With eyes watering, Zoe looked around. At first all she saw was a mass of people, singing, dancing and swaying about, glasses in hand. At the far end, a piano was playing in front of a stage.

Then she saw him, her Brad, glass in hand at a table loaded with beer bottles, with a girl on his knee. On a chair up close to him, another girl was fawning for his attention. He was more than a little drunk. Dismayed, choking back tears, she went towards him. "Brad," she said as she got up close.

Blearily he looked up at her, his hand on the bared thigh of the girl on his lap. "What are you doing here, girl, I thought you were back home in New Zealand?" He turned away to squeeze the girl on his lap who gave him a kiss.

As if she had been stabbed by a knife, Zoe staggered back from him. He did not even call her by her name which he knew so well. He clearly was no longer interested in her. Sobbing, she ran blindly for the door where, in the foyer, she flung herself to the floor and sobbed her heart out.

She did not know how long she was there when she felt a hand on her shoulder and a gentle male voice with a New Zealand accent saying, "Zoe, can I help you?" Surprised, she looked up. A pilot officer, indicated by the thin green line on his sleeve, was looking down on her. Who was this New Zealander who knew her name? "You don't remember me, but I was a member of the Kerikeri Flying Club, one of the many, name of Sam Bretson. You were involved with Brad at the time. I wasn't a particular friend of Brad, but we decided to go to Britain and join the RAF at the same time." He gave her a clean handkerchief. Zoe observed him to be of slight build with a sensitive face and completely sober. "I have a BSA Blue Star outside. Like me to take you back to your barracks?"

Tearfully she agreed. She did not want to go back inside. "Could you ask back in there for a large girl from Northern Ireland with glasses and tied-back hair called Pat and tell her I'm going back with you please, I need to let someone know. And if you want directions, ask the Service Corps driver."

Fifteen minutes later, he came back to her. Gently Sam helped her to her feet. Outside in early October, there was a chill in the air. He took off his uniform jacket and helped her put it on over her uniform. Barely taller than her it fitted her exactly. She protested that he would be cold but smiling he took out a leather jacket, leather helmet and goggles from a side pannier on his bike. Though she felt she did not ever want another male to touch her again, she appreciated the warmth and sympathetic feel of his arm about her as he carefully lifted her onto the pillion with the bike on its stand. "Hold onto me," he said, "tight and don't let go." Despite herself, after he had swung his leg over the petrol tank and settled himself in front of her, she cuddled into him, putting her arms tightly about his waist. She had not ridden pillion on a bike before and did not want to fall off. Sam looked back at her, but she could not see his face. Did he give her a brief smile? She did not know.

The bump as the bike was edged off its stand made her start. Rising off his seat, Sam put his weight on the kick start. On the second attempt, the bike started, spluttering in the still air. Once the engine settled, he pulled away slowly, the air beginning to pull at Zoe's hair as the speed increased. The noise coming from inside the hall faded. They were on their way.

The hour and a half's ride back to the camp passed like a dream. Zoe was aware of arcing searchlights in the distance, the occasional bursts of ack-ack fire and thuds of bombs, the dimmed bike headlight probing ahead. She held onto Sam tightly, swaying with the bike as it turned a corner, pressing into him for comfort and security. She awoke from the dream when the engine finally stopped, the bike leant on the side stand, and she was carried off. They had arrived at the outskirts of Oftness.

For some reason, they stood holding on to each other, not really understanding why. Zoe gave a big sob as she had been doing every so often on the journey back. "Unless you want to go in now, the others won't be back for some time." Zoe nodded but made no move. Sam led her to a nearby bank and sat down. Zoe sat beside him, holding his hand.

For a while they said nothing, Sam understanding Zoe was in a state of shock and knowing why. He felt that the story told itself and, unless Zoe wanted to talk about it, he would let it be. But after a while it was Zoe who felt that Sam had something on his mind. "How has it been for you, fighting in the skies for the RAF? Do you miss New Zealand?"

"Back home, we have a free outdoors lifestyle, the Brits are up against it at the moment, life's tough for them."

"I mean for you personally?"

Sam took some time to reply. "As it happens, from today I'm on a month's leave."

"I guess you deserve it," Zoe replied, warming to Sam's quiet and modest manner. "There can't be any job more stressful than that of a fighter pilot."

"Group captain says I've sortie fatigue just because I asked Squadron Leader Howard if I could have a different flying role. For that he referred me to the station commander." Sam sat with his head in his hands. Zoe put her hand on his shoulder in sympathy. "That's not the case at all. Group captain didn't seem to understand. I tried to explain but he wasn't listening," Sam went on.

"No?" Zoe could see Sam was perplexed, seemingly mystified and angered by the response. "Warm enough?" he asked suddenly, turning to Zoe, "We could swap jackets, my riding jacket's warmer than the one you've got on?"

"No, I'm all right," Zoe replied. "Didn't understand?"

For the next half an hour he told her why, appearing grateful that he could speak to someone outside his unit, who were the only people he knew in Britain. What he said was that, though a member of the Kerikeri flying club, his ageing Tiger Moth was not a recreational machine. Older than Brad, he was a professional flyer when he could get work. He loved flying. It was in his blood. He took people on joy and sightseeing rides, surveyors and expedition leaders on air reconnaissance flights and gave local communities one-man air-shows, flying under bridges and power lines, but always in other ways shying publicity. An aircraft was an extension of himself, he could do anything with it.

At Debden Airfield, which flew Hurricanes, he was far and away more experience than the other hastily trained young Battle of Britain fighter pilots – and the equally young opposing German fighters. In the air he was one step ahead of hostile aircraft, able to keep in blind spots, not getting caught himself. By not drinking or partying late, his reflexes were good and, being fit, he was better able to withstand the G-force of tight manoeuvres. Consequently, to date, he was a survivor and had many downed aircraft to his name. But he wanted a different role, a challenging flying role, but not his present one, not any longer.

He was not fatigued. He had become sickened of seeing, for a fleeting second, the horror in his young adversaries' eyes when they realised Sam had them in his sights and they were about to be shot down and likely killed. Swerving instantly away he got no satisfaction seeing them spiralling downwards in flames, bits breaking away from their aircraft. He had been criticised for staying too long in the vicinity when what he was doing was hoping he would see a 'chute open.

Zoe could see that Sam was sensitive by nature, utterly different from Brad. Though devastated by her own rejection, her heart went out to him. "Are you getting nightmares?" she asked, then wondered if she had said the right thing.

"Sometimes," Sam admitted in a dejected manner, his face still in his hands.

For some while they sat together companionably, shoulder to shoulder, listening to the sounds of the night. “What are you going to do for the month?” Zoe eventually asked.

“I don’t really know, I’ve got nowhere to go, flying is my only interest.”

Though Zoe did not really understand why, she said on impulse, “If I can get out some evenings would you like to meet, perhaps go to a pub? I lived in Northland for a year, remember? We have that in common.”

“Do you mind? I’d like that, though I’m not great company. Where could I meet you?”

“Here at eight to start off with, it’ll be dark by then, Oftness is just round the bend. I could wait back in the trees till you appeared on your bike.”

“You might not get an evening pass or have evening lectures?”

“I’ll sneak out if needs be. I think that’s the Service Corp truck returning. I’d better walk to the gate and go in with the others.”

Sam got up and helped Zoe to her feet. “I’ll walk to the gate with you.”

Arm-in-arm they walked to the school gates where the truck was letting the girls off round the corner. Zoe did not know whether Sam would kiss her goodbye. Instead, he held her close for two or three minutes. “See you at eight tomorrow,” he said then turned away into the darkness.

“You’re a fast one,” her friend Janet said as the girls walked across the playground together, “a pilot taking you back. I hope you didn’t do anything I wouldn’t have, given half the chance?” Zoe did not reply, dazed by the unexpected turn of events. Sighing heavily from her long period of crying, she walked inside. She had much to digest.

During her training next day, Zoe was reprimanded for not paying attention. She apologised, making an effort to concentrate, not wanting to jeopardise her request for an evening pass. At the end of what seemed a long day, warmly dressed, leave pass in hand, Zoe walked quickly to their rendezvous on the bank outside Oftness, arriving there just before eight. Two minutes later she heard the sound of a motorbike and Sam's dimmed headlight appeared round the bend. She stepped out to be seen.

Carefully pulling his bike onto its stand, Sam went forward, putting his arms round her waist, drawing Zoe close for a full minute, saying nothing, appearing to obtain comfort from just holding her. "How's your day been?" Zoe asked.

"Long," Sam replied, "I spent part of the day along the south side of the Blackwater Estuary. I found much of it out of bounds, especially around Bradwell. I was stopped on occasions, but for my uniform I'd have been arrested. And yours?"

"Long, so much happened yesterday. You need to be careful, at Southend-on-Sea, Southchurch Road to the seafront is all a military restricted area. You don't know England. There're no road signs. Where would you like to go?"

"Somewhere quiet."

"There's the Boar along Bridgewick Road," Zoe suggested.

Though it was only two miles away, Sam stopped at every intersection for Zoe to indicate which road to take. Inside the Boar, they took a seat away from the fire in a dimly lit corner, Zoe sipping a white wine while

Sam would only drink tonic water, he did not consume alcohol.

"There's quinine in that," Zoe laughed.

"Long-distance flyers use it for leg cramp," Sam retorted.

They did not say much, sitting close, companionably, enjoying being together. Suddenly Zoe sat up, looking at her watch, putting it to her ear to make sure it was going then winding it up to ensure it kept going. "It's getting on for ten, I have to be back by ten thirty."

Snuggled up behind, Zoe directed Sam back to school. Round the corner they hugged until Zoe, looking at her watch again, said, "I really must be off, will I see you tomorrow?"

"Same time same place," Sam replied, looking after her as she ran across the playground.

That is how their relationship started. For a precious month they met as often as they could. In Oftness, Zoe spotted a schoolfriend who was now a land-girl on a farm owned by an old couple not far out of town. When Zoe told her of her romance, saying she would like a really private place where they could be alone together out of the cold, her friend suggested that, if they met at the farm's boundary, away from the farmhouse, she would quietly show her the barn, accompanied by the dogs. There she could spend time with her Sam in the hayloft, the dogs, having got acquainted with their scent, not creating a fuss.

To her dismay, Zoe learnt next day that evening leave passes were not going to be issued to her group training to be Predictor operators. They were to be examined in turn through the night for their skill and their understanding of the procedures involved in synchronising with area aircraft locator devices. As her group were not going to be tested until after midnight, Zoe decided to skip out anyway. As soon as it was dark, she slipped out of her classroom dormitory, leaving the window ajar and, in stocking feet carrying her shoes, ran quickly to the men's latrine block, the women using the former children's toilets inside, where she waited under cover until the night patrol passed; after which she ran to the tall iron railings and nimbly climbed them, finally running panting to their rendezvous by the bank just as Sam's motorbike arrived.

Sam was intrigued with the idea of their spending time together in a hayloft. He got on well with her land-girl friend, Janet, along with dogs, as they walked together to the barn for the first time. From then on, when not going to local pubs, Zoe and Sam curled up amongst the hay. Unlike Brad who, whenever possible, wanted to lie down with Zoe whether she felt like it or not, Sam was in no hurry to have his way with her, obviously liking her for herself. It was only after a week or so, with her encouragement, that he went any further.

Their growing fondness became increasingly more precious as the end of the month drew closer when Sam would have to report to group captain to find out whether he could have another flying role. By now they had been to all the pubs on the Dengie Peninsula or Hundreds, still called Hundreds owing to the fact that in Saxon times the peninsula supported one hundred families who sent one representative to the Witan, later renamed Parliament by the Normans.

At the end of each succussive evening, parting became more difficult. As the last days of the month approached, they clasped each other longingly until Zoe, shoes in hand, waiting for the patrol to turn the corner, wrenched herself away to run through the playground and slip through a window. One evening, right near the end, she found her trestle bed had been dismantled and sheets and blankets hidden by pranksters, taking her an hour trying to find everything in the darkness without waking the dormitory lance corporal.

Their last evening together was bittersweet, weeping in each other's arms, promising after the war to meet again and be together forever. They walked in silence to the school gates. Without looking back, Zoe moved slowly through the playground, not caring if she was seen. Sam stood looking at the window she disappeared through until dawn, tears running down his face. Inside, Zoe flung herself on her bed and cried her eyes out.

That evening Zoe, having passed for Predictor Operator number three, was going on active duty for the first time, hoping for a quiet night. She was tired, having been out with Sam much of the night before, and apprehensive. She had often peeped out through the blackout windows at night at the girls up there operating the searchlight with the men alongside manning the gun, knowing that before long, at the completion of her training, she would be taking her turn before being transferred to a battery somewhere else. This was her night.

Up until ten, all was quiet. Suddenly, without warning, sirens sounded. A number of enemy aircraft had been spotted approaching at speed from the sea. What was unusual was their height. They generally passed high overhead to attack targets inland, but tonight they were very low indeed. Within seconds, all hell was let loose. Oftness and their battery were under attack. They were being strafed, lines of shells throwing splinters over them. Zoe heard the gun commander swear and a girl scream in their own air-raid shelter as it took a hit. The gun fired continually, their crew frantically trying to keep the gun on target. Then another sound joined the cacophony. A number of their own planes were diving on the enemy, twisting and turning in furious aerial combat directly above them. The searchlight momentarily flicked on a plane onto which the synchronised gun fired, scoring a direct hit. For a fleeting second, as the aircraft spun to earth, hitting the ground nearby in explosive flames, Zoe saw that it was a Hurricane.

Devasted, Zoe could hardly believe what she saw. How many of the others realised they had hit one of their own in the melee she did not know. Those who might have were not saying. Oftness and the gun had never been under direct attack before. Previously they had only fired at passing enemy aircraft. Being a target was beyond their experience.

Zoe froze in shock. This was Sam's first night back on duty. He had been hoping for another role but felt his superiors were likely to refuse his request, owing to his being so successful as a combat flyer. For his life to be ended by friendly fire, by a gun she was helping to direct, was more than she could bear. Like a zombie, she was led away by an ATS medic, her shock being put down to the terrifying attack on the site.

Zoe was so traumatised she was sent to Colchester military hospital. There she eventually came across a badly wounded pilot from a flight based at Debden. She asked him if he knew a Pilot Officer Sam Bretson and what had become of him. He said he did know who he was but did not know him in person, or what happened to him, only that he was no longer based at Debden. Over the next few weeks, Zoe made every effort to find out what happened to Sam. Personnel from the Oftness Camp and people living in the area were not allowed near the crash site to know if a body had been found in the plane or nearby.

When Zoe was eventually discharged from hospital with what the medial authorities described as an obsessive depressive condition, she was declared no longer fit for service with the ATS and assigned to the large munitions factory at Bridgend, in South Wales, to work as a Canary Girl. There she remained through the remainder of the blitz and for the next two years, hoping in some way to learn what had happened to Sam. With her health deterioration in the toxic factory atmosphere, in the end she applied to return to New Zealand to join her brother, which was granted as, though she was a British citizen, it was conceded she had emigrated to New Zealand before the war, had New Zealand residency, but had returned to Britain to join the ATS in Britain's hour of need. This being granted, Zoe went back to New Zealand late in 1943 only to find Ted was in the services but stationed in New Zealand. She went back to Paihia, working in an orchard, as it was the only place she knew.

Tawhaitu told Will that from the time she knew Zoe, her behaviour became increasingly reckless and disturbed as if possessed, haunted by something she was unable to escape from. She bought an old Harley-Davidson motorbike which she drove at increasingly high speeds until she came off in the shingle and spent months in hospital with multiple broken bones and skin grazing needing rotation surgery. When microlight flying became possible in the late seventies, early eighties, Zoe took it up from Kerikeri airfield, flying with abandon through the skies as if escaping her haunting memories by joining feisty aerial spirits, soaring and swooping with them. She liked to fly down to Auckland to stay with her brother.

There she was particularly fascinated by Rangitoto Island, considering it a primeval deity from the deep. She used to buzz round it like a frenzied maenad, getting into trouble with civilian air traffic control. It was while flying 10 years ago that she and her aircraft disappeared. Knowing her fascination with the island, it was thought her disappearance could be in that area, but her body and plane were never found.

With a start, Will realised that he might have unwittingly come across Zoe's last resting place. "I think I might know where her plane came down!" he abruptly said to Tawhaitu.

Tawhaitu looked at Will with incredulity. "You do?"

"Yes, in an area of scoria outcrops off Rangitoto, about 30 metres offshore, not far west and south of the lighthouse, where vessels wouldn't go."

"How was it then you discovered this wreckage? While I was away in Pariaman, I was given to understand that a thorough search was made all round and over the island?"

"By accident," Will replied, not wanting to give further details about the embarrassing episode when he let Ted's boat float off the island during his stay near his brother and his wife in Takapuna, and he unwisely tried to swim after it, to be rescued by resourceful Gaynor. "The water happened to be very clear at the time owing to the wind direction. Normally wave action on the reefs stirs up the water."

"Well, that's incredible. I'll certainly get the area you described checked out by scuba divers and, if the microlight remains prove to be Zoe's, the kikokiko that possessed her could be released, combined with the information that I obtained from a New Zealand flyer while staying at Arata Beach in Indonesia 10 years ago at the time of her disappearance. We couldn't have a tangihanga at that time without a body which would have helped her spirit leave her so that it wouldn't become a restless wanderer. Hopefully, when you and your brother, her nearest relatives, hear what I'll tell you next, her spirit will rest in peace."

"I'd be extremely grateful," Will said, immensely relieved that one of the main reasons for his coming to New Zealand was about to be realised.

"Well, 10 years ago, the demands of my job necessitated that I have a few months' break, right away from New Zealand and the demands reconciling our two cultures were making on me as a lawyer, so I went for an extended holiday to West Sumatra, Indonesia. After staying for a couple of months at Arata Beach, long enough to get to know the locals, I got to hear of a New Zealander, in his sixties, flying with great skill as a part-time archaeological surveyor for the provincial government. On hearing this, I became curious and, after further inquiries, discovered he lived with a local girl about 10 miles away on the other side of Pariaman.

"I sent him a note saying that I was a fellow New Zealander and would very much like to meet him. I eventually got a reply back asking why, saying he would meet no journalist or give no interview. I responded in turn by asking if, by any chance, he'd served as a pilot in Britain during the war and, if he did so, had he'd ever met a girl named Zoe Whitby. To my surprise, he agreed to meet me to answer that question only."

Will learnt from Tawhaitu that the New Zealander she got to see was named Sam Bretson, had flown in Britain during the Second World War with the rank of pilot officer and admitted that he had known a girl named Zoe Whitby for a month or so. Sam had survived the war. Though he felt his request for a transfer to another flying role would be refused he was, in fact, assigned to an elite aerial reconnaissance unit flying a Spitfire without armaments for lightness and range with a trimetrogon camera configuration plus a rear-facing camera for very low flying called dicing.

He would be on his own, often flying low, using every tactic to avoid interception including escaping into clouds where possible when pursued. He acquired a considerable reputation for the quality of the photos he brought back. Incredibly he survived the war though on one occasion he actually landed on the far end of an enemy airfield briefly to attend an oil leak, taking off again before it was realised his machine was a British aircraft. He remembered Zoe and their bittersweet affair but did not return to New Zealand for many years after the war, selling his services to a number of countries where he was able to pursue the flying he loved. He felt, with the passage of time, his month with Zoe was one of those wartime romances which, though deeply felt at the time, were soon forgotten. He had no idea that she thought she was instrumental in shooting him down. He did not know that a Hurricane had been lost over Oftness and was concerned to hear that the incident had affected her mental health for the rest of her life. Brad Valentine, Sam said, was shot down a month or so after his rejection of Zoe, was quite badly injured, eventually marrying his British nurse. The couple returned to New Zealand after the war but soon moved to Australia. Sam had never heard from him since. They went together to Britain from Kerikeri at the beginning of the war but in other respects were not friends.

At that point, Gaynor and the children were ushered back into the room by Kaia. "Had a good time at Waitangi?" Will asked.

"Great," Gaynor replied, "the children found plenty to do and see. Was Miss Tahu able to help you with your quest?"

"Indeed, she was," Will said, looking and smiling at Tawhaitu. "From what I heard and will tell Ted, I feel the problem at the school will be resolved. Time will tell, but I feel hopeful."

"I'm pleased to hear it," Gaynor replied, still looking rather mystified. She turned to Tawhaitu, "Thank you, Miss Tahu, you seemed to have taken a load off Will's mind."

"It's been very interesting meeting your husband, Zoe was a dear friend. During his visit to New Zealand, Will may have come across the missing link, solving the mystery to my friend's, his older sister's, disappearance."

As they were being ushered out, Gaynor said, "I noticed, now the wind's died down, the sea's much calmer. Could we go for a Bay of Island cruise for our last afternoon before flying home?"

"What a bonza idea!"

"You're acquiring Kiwi speak," Gaynor laughed, giving Will a nudge.

"Let's do it!"

"Whoopee!" the children endorsed, jumping up and down.

Chapter Eleven

At the cream-beige weatherboard ticket office to the right of the long wharf, they bought tickets for an afternoon's cruise which included calling at Russell, going up to Cape Brett, the Hole in the Rock, seeing seals, afternoon tea at Otehei Bay, Urupukapuka Island, returning at dusk. Beginning their walk up the long wooden wharf to their boarding bay, the first thing they saw on the left was a large sunken catamaran, a witness to the power of the recent storm. Boarding their cruise boat, they climbed up the steep stern stairway to the upper deck, choosing to sit just behind the bridge near the funnel exhaust to be out of the wind.

Where they sat proved a good choice, other than when Gaynor had to struggle down the steep steps to the lower deck carrying Angela when she wanted to go to the toilet.

"Got Yellow Ted safe?" Will suddenly remembered to ask Ruth, who nodded, pointing to her bag. After all this time away, Will did not want to see Yellow Ted, on their last day, floating away on the tide with all the ensuing drama. Three loud hoots made them jump. They were off, heading north-east at good speed towards Russell, initially known as Kororareka, briefly New Zealand's capital before Auckland, later Wellington. With a permanent population of 760, it was a small community, prettily set in a bay. From the boat, its historic buildings, like white-painted, wooden Christ Church, constructed in 1835, New Zealand's first church, and Pompallier Mission, a larger building, set amongst trees up on a hill to the right, could be identified. More people joined the cruise and then they were off again, to round Tapeka Point, before threading through romantically beautiful islands, large and small, towards Cape Brett with Motukokako Island beyond.

After a time, the steady beat of the diesel engine slowed and the boat came up near a rocky islet, rising up and down on the swell for passengers to observe the pointed nose, whiskered kekeno, or fur seals, who stared back curiously. Will took out his camera, balancing precariously to take photos. "They've lovely brown coats and little earflaps!" Ruth exclaimed with interest. "Better than those last ones." Will could not see much difference but was glad Ruth was happy, perhaps being in the boat gave her more security. He marvelled at the skipper's ability at being able to bring the boat in so close.

Twenty minutes later they sped away up the west side of the Cape to be joined by a pod of bottlenose dolphins who surfed and gambolled on the bow waves. "Careful, we don't want you overboard!" Gaynor warned as Will grabbed the rail at the last minute to stop himself going over the side as he leant over to take photos.

The pod left as quickly as it came as the boat cleared Karkarpa Point on its way north. Not long after that they passed Cape Brett to head on again north to craggy Motukokako or Piercy Island. Will could see how it got its name, the end bastion of rock was pierced by an eighteen-metre hole, forming a natural arch, a formation of great cultural significance to the Ngapuhi Iwi or tribe. Swaying with the swell, their boat entered the arch, which narrowed at its further end, remaining for a few minutes for photographs before going astern.

With the afternoon getting on the boat turned back for the sightseers to have an island afternoon tea. Halfway towards Russell, their boat stopped alongside a long wooden wharf where everyone disembarked. Holding on to the children, Will and Gaynor walked towards a bay backed by an informal garden. Ashore they were directed across a lawn to a pavilion where a sumptuous meal awaited them of exotic salads, pavlova cake, strawberries and cream and lots more.

"Look, there's your favourite coffee coconut cake," Gaynor pointed out to Angela. "Don't eat too much though, as it's difficult to take you to the toilet on the boat. And there's some of your vanilla sponge cake with what looks like pomegranate jam," she indicated to Tim. Afterwards, as dusk was falling, the children ran about in the garden, the air comparatively warm in 'the Winterless North'. Tim wanted to climb a volcanic peak nearby. Will said he would go with him as he did not want him missing the boat and for the view. Gaynor heartily concurred as she would not be letting him go without Will accompanying him in any case, which did not please Tim. It was a good job Will did as they had barely reached the top before Will saw their boat returning, took a hurried photo and they both ran down to meet Gaynor and the girls on the wharf.

"You've just made it," Gaynor light-heartedly scolded.

"Why did the boat leave in the first instance?" Will queried.

"I overheard it was for crew safety training. I think we should travel in the downstairs cabin coming back, be warmer and the children may need the toilet."

"So might I, the pavlova cake was delicious." Will made a face.

The light was fading as their boat threaded back through the chain of islands, silhouetted in the sunset, Russell appearing mainly as twinkling shore lights when they called to let off passengers before the final leg to Paihia.

"I don't think I need to make a substantial evening meal tonight, but we'll need to pack what we can for tomorrow," Gaynor commented on their return to their motel on the Paihia foreshore.

They were sitting together in front of the right-hand unit, watching the moon rise over the water when the phone rang. Gaynor answered, "This is our last night in New Zealand, Joe. No, I won't be seeing you again unless you ever come to England. No, I didn't know you owned one of the islands which was your home base. We all have to be at Auckland's International Airport by five pm tomorrow for the flight home. No, I can't stay longer in New Zealand, I have commitments, I'm sorry." Gaynor turned to Will. "I'm going out tonight, you'll be all right with the children? Joe said if there were any unforeseen hold-ups, he'd fly me straight to the Domestic Terminal at Mangere, just across the way from the International Terminal. His speedboat will be at the wharf in 20 minutes. In an emergency, Tim would always be able to navigate for you, but I expect to be with you in the morning."

Gaynor rushed into their other unit to finish packing. "Joe Smarty-pants," Tim exclaimed.

"Precisely," Will agreed, really disappointed they were not going to spend their last night in New Zealand together, which he was much looking forward to. Not knowing why he did it, while Gaynor was in their other apartment, he took up Gaynor's jacket, which was lying on a chair, and slipped into her inside secret pocket, where he knew she kept her passport and return flight ticket back to Britain in a light plastic envelope, 500 New Zealand dollars in 50-dollar notes, much of his remaining New Zealand money, before Gaynor flew back in again and gave them all a brief kiss. Sadly, Will and the children watched from the balcony as she ran back up the road towards the wharf until she was lost to their sight.

Will took the children back inside. "What would you like to do before bedtime? You can keep me company for a bit longer, Tim, if you can stay awake."

"I like it better when Mummy's home," Angela said sorrowfully.

"We all do," Will replied, picking the girls up and giving them a hug. He asked the children what they might like to do. The girls said they would like to hear him read from A.A. Milne's *Now we are Six*. Will dug out his old copy which he kept from when he was first a teacher. Though frowned on these days as being politicly incorrect, Will found children still enjoyed the song-like cadences of the poems. Tim opted for trying to find programmes he liked on television. By nine the girls were falling asleep and he put them in bed together in the other room. Tim took himself to bed in the other room. By eleven, Will found himself nodding off and lay down where he was.

When Gaynor arrived breathlessly at the wharf, Joe was waiting for her impatiently. He gave her a hungry kiss then hurried her off along the deserted walkway to where an ultra-smart speedboat lay. Without offering her a lifejacket or putting one on himself, he went off at top speed, bouncing over the waves in clouds of spray, ignoring the harbour speed limit. How far out into the bay he went, Gaynor had no means of knowing in the darkness. Eventually they arrived at a darkened island. Switching on a powerful searchlight, Joe steered the boat through a cleft into a secluded rock pool. There, on a ledge, a man in a white jacket was waiting for them who handed them carefully ashore and then, with the aid of a powerful torch, led the way up a steep path to a forbidding mansion, light shining from a range of upper-storey windows.

Inside Gaynor could only describe it as being like a set from a James Bond movie, all stainless steel and glass, or from a space odyssey. The man led them into a surreal upper room designed like an airport control tower with a panoramic view across the bay where a table was laid for dinner for two.

"Take a seat by the window," Joe said. "You get a great view from there. Supper will be served in a few minutes." Gaynor looked out into a starry night, the moon creating a silver pathway through the water. A plane's twinkling lights appeared overhead, moving quickly through the sky, in contrast to a vessel's navigation lights, moving slowly through the water. In this place, Joe had it all. She felt him edging very close to her.

A man entered. It was the same man who met them on the stone quay. Unlike most mixed-race people in the far north, he seemed neither Maori nor Islander but Chinese. With deference, saying nothing, he served a meal of lobster, clams, mussel, sweetcorn and new potatoes. It looked delicious but Gaynor, who had eaten already, could only manage a little lobster. "I'm sorry, Joe," she said, "it looks delectable, but I've already eaten very well this evening."

"Never mind," Joe replied in a charming manner, "try this Chardonnay." He took a bottle out of an iced bucket and delicately poured her a glass.

"Aren't you having any?"

"I'll finish the bottle after I've navigated you home."

"Of course." The wine was the best Gaynor had ever tasted. She thought it must be a very expensive vintage. She knew Joe only liked the best. It relaxed her. It had been an enjoyable but tiring day.

"Another?" Joe inclined the bottle to her invitingly.

"Just one more or I'll be falling asleep." Smiling, he poured her another.

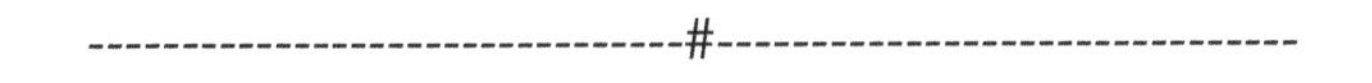

Gaynor woke up slowly, she felt very sleepy. It was a struggle to surface. She opened her eyes. The sun was shining outside, high in the sky. She lay, looking out the range of windows. A gull flew nearby, for an instant blotting out the sun.

Suddenly she sat bolt upright, startled. Where was she? It should be dark. She tried to remember. She had been dining with Joe on his island pad. She was not in their motel with the children. She must be still on the island, on a couch next to the windows where she dined the night before. She felt stiff and cold. She must have drunk far too much. Her trouser bottoms were half off as if she had gone to the toilet in a hurry and was too sleepy to pull them up properly afterwards.

But she had not drunk too much, only two modest glasses of wine. That would not have made her drunk. The awful truth began to dawn on her. The last thing she could remember was Joe over her with his erection out. That was not right. She did not have that sort of relationship with him. She had been drugged and, with her clothes in the state they were in, likely date raped. Fortunately, at this time of the month, it was unlikely she would become pregnant. She felt defiled and disgusted. She must get back to her children and to kind, patient Will who was looking after them. What would they all think? By the look of the sun high in the sky, they should be well on their way to the airport. She looked at her watch. It was not on her. She looked for her handbag. It was nowhere to be seen. Panicking, she felt in the secret pocket of her jacket for her passport and ticket. They were there. She opened the pocket to make sure. They were there all right along with, she counted, 500 New Zealand dollars in 50-dollar notes. She did not put the money there. It must have been ever-thoughtful Will.

She got up and straightened her clothes. She felt awful, as if she had a dreadful hangover. Quietly she slipped out of the room. There seemed no one about. She made her way downstairs along eccentric walkways and galleries. On the ground floor, the few doors she could find to the outside were all locked. She fought down panic. She opened a door and found herself in a small garbage room where she felt a breeze. It came from a chute leading to outside bins. She was desperate. It took great courage, but with her arms above her head, she slid feet-first down it to land in a pile of stinking trash, but she was outside.

What next? No use trying to find the rocky basin where they landed. She would not be seen there. It would be better to go in the other direction to attract attention. She hurried off. From the outside, the building looked quite an unremarkable squat tower. She entered a stand of trees, feeling more secure under cover. On the other side was the sea. It was a small island. She climbed down to the water's edge.

Half a mile offshore, two racing dinghies were flying about in a stiff breeze, at times coming within three hundred yards of the shore, their crews practising their skills. Taking off her white blouse Gaynor got on a rock and began frantically signalling, feeling like a dishevelled Robinson Crusoe. Eventually she was seen, and a dinghy came closer to investigate.

"Help!" Gaynor shouted. "I'm stranded on the island and have to get home to my children!" The dinghy headed for the shore and an 18- to 20-year-old boy came over to her, leaving his mate to hold the dinghy.

"Are you all right, lady?" he asked.

Putting on her blouse, Gaynor quickly explained she had been abandoned on the island, that she had to get back to her family at Paihia, and at five, catch a plane to London. She said she had money to pay them. To her relief, though, the boy did not seem interested in the money, and, after consulting with the crew of the other dinghy which had now come ashore as well, agreed to help her. Gaynor was put on one of the dinghies and told to hang on. The boys pushed off, jumping aboard, the yachts speeding away, heeling to the wind, skimming through the water, the young sailors leaning outboard on trapezes, dressed in wetsuits, spray, on occasions, sweeping the boat, racing with each other towards Paihia.

Cold, wet and exhausted, Gaynor hung on for dear life. A helicopter appeared overhead. Joe must have learnt of her escape. It came in low but, as it was easily recognised, dared not blow them over with its downdraft. Looking over to the other dinghy, Gaynor realised that one of the crew of two, who she took to be a boy was, in fact, a girl. Hectic though it was, Gaynor felt secure then, feeling they were the best of New Zealand youth, eager to please and come to the rescue. The regulations were that being under sail, powered boats had to give way to them. She gathered a mid-reach was their fastest point of sail.

At Tapeka Point, they came about. Gaynor was dragged unceremoniously to the other side of the boat. The cold and exertion were beginning to clear her head and now, facing the coastline, she saw they were passing Russell with a ferry leaving. Paihia was not far away. The wind was becoming fluky. The yachts bucked and swayed, responding to the changing pressure on their sails. Recognising Motumaire Island, Gaynor indicated that she would like to be landed on the south end of the beach across the road from their motel. With the beach fast approaching, one of the crew went up on the prow, ready to jump overboard and drag the boat ashore. It all ended with a sudden rush and jolt; Gaynor being helped off onto the sand. Barely being able to stand up, she expressed her extreme gratitude, again offering them money which they refused. Then they were cheerily off again, seemingly happy with the challenge and being able to help.

Gasping with anxiety, Gaynor scrambled up the metre bank, holding onto a root of one of the pohutukawa trees spaced evenly along the foreshore.

Struggling over the grass, stiff from the boat ride and still drugged from the night before, she staggered across the road to their motel. Their hire car was gone. Cleaners were in their rooms. Will with the children had left for Auckland's International Airport. With a cry of desperation, Gaynor began running the half mile to the wharf where she knew there was a taxi rank. She heard the buzz of a helicopter overhead but did not care.

At the shore end of the wharf, there were toilets. She needed the toilet and to straighten herself up, but without her handbag with her hairbrush and everything else a woman carried in a handbag, she could make little effect. Her blue, salt-encrusted trouser suit was drying with the sun and wind, and she had warmed up to some degree with the running, but she did look a mess, her clothes crumpled, her hair a bird's nest. But she had to move on. Nearby a kiosk sold fish and chips. She bought a packet and a bottle of mineral water. Clutching these with her money in her hand to show she could pay, she ran along a line of waiting taxis, asking to be taken to Auckland's International Airport.

Every taxi in turn refused. They were local taxis operating locally. Gaynor was becoming desperate. Overhead the helicopter droned. Joe said that in an emergency, he would fly her to the airport, he would fly her if given half a chance but not to the airport. The last taxi was a rather aged Holden with a large overweight Maori at the wheel. Disillusioned she asked him the same question. To her surprise, his eyes lit up. "That will cost you something."

"I have the money," Gaynor said, showing him a handful of 50-dollar notes. "I have to be at the airport by four thirty at the latest in time to join my children and partner for a flight to Britain. They've gone ahead. I've been unexpectedly delayed. They need me. I've got to catch that flight for the sake of my children at all costs!"

"Hop in the front seat," the driver replied, "I'll have to leave a message for my wahine." He returned puffing. "I have whanau in Papakura. Pai eh, I'll stay the night. Pai eh. My name's Hemi."

"Gaynor," Gaynor replied, dismayed by the only taxi that would take her but what else could she do? "I have to be at the airport by four thirty at the very latest," she repeated.

The driver looked at the taxi clock. "Take us about three hours, fifteen minutes. I drove a taxi in Auckland for many years, eh. We'll make it. No hanging about eh. You have fish and chips, eh."

"Like a chip?"

"Later." They were off, breaking the urban speed limit, heading for Kawakawa. Gaynor found Hemi a good driver, fast but skilful.

"You're fair dinkum cold?" he observed.

"Yes."

"I'll put up the heater." As Gaynor warmed up, she warmed to Hemi as well. He talked. She found he had a wife, his wahine, and children, he loved his children. Like all Maoris, family was important. He was delighted with the opportunity to see his extended family, whanau, in Papakura, returning next day. He might even get a fare back if a passenger off an international flight wanted to travel directly to the Bay of Islands. A helicopter still hovered overhead. Gaynor felt that if Joe and his henchman landed and tried to intercept Hemi would be more than a match for them. He was also perceptive.

"Had trouble in the Bay, Taniwha, eh?"

"Something like that." Gaynor only learnt some time later that taniwha were unpredictable water monsters, sometimes in disguise, making her reply entirely appropriate. "How do you know?"

"Salt on your clothes, you're wet. English?"

"Yes."

"Know Princess Di?"

"Know of her, I don't move in her circle."

"Beaut, eh. Given a bad time, eh?"

"She has charisma. Like a chip?" she asked again.

"Will have gone cold. I'll heat them up." Hemi squealed the taxi to an abrupt halt, placed the fish and chips in the engine compartment, and then drove on fast. After Kawakawa, the helicopter disappeared. Ten minutes later, Hemi stopped again, retrieved the fish and chips and gave them to Gaynor.

Gaynor admired Hemi's skill as a driver. Having been a part-time professional herself, she recognised ability in another. He drove hard and fast but did not take risks, particularly at the end of the New Zealand system of two lanes up the hills on major roads and one lane down, when risky drivers were inclined to not get into lane in time for the single lane down. At Waiotu he stopped for petrol. Gaynor handed him a 50-dollar note, assuming he would likely be out of cash. "First instalment."

"Thanks," Hemi replied, grinning. Before entering the business district of Whangarei, he stopped at a relatives' café for them to go to the toilet and for him to buy cans of beer for his relatives in Papakura where he would be spending the night. While there, Gaynor rushed next door to a pharmacist to buy a hairbrush and a make-up set before returning hurriedly to the café. Hemi recognised there was no time to sit down for a meal, they would have to make do with Gaynor's fish and chips, which in New Zealand always came in generous portions.

He drove on fast, watching out in his rear-view mirror for road cops. The car powered up the Brynderwyns from the plains impressively, showing it was not as clapped-out as it looked. Gaynor looked at the car clock. It was getting on for three in the afternoon. Would she make it in time? Boarding gates would shut at twenty to five.

Wellsford held them up, but after that they flashed through Dome Valley, well exceeding the speed limit. Gaynor hoped Hemi would not collect a speeding ticket over her. Warkworth and Orewa, larger urban centres, inevitably took longer to negotiate but, turning right at Owera, Hemi gained the Northern Motorway where he once again he opened the throttle, the Holden sounding like a Le Mans twenty-four-hour racer. Gaynor was on tenterhooks, expecting to hear the screams of police sirens behind them at any moment. What a stranger would do for another was humbling. Hemi was indeed the proverbial Good Samaritan. There was so much good in the world to offset evil.

The Upper Queen Street interchange Hemi took in his stride, he knew exactly what lanes to take to go south for the airport, having made the same journey many times before. Gaynor's heart was pounding. Would she make it? Hemi sensed her anxiety. He patted her knee reassuringly. "You OK? I get you there. Got ticket and passport? What Airline?"

"Air Singapore."

"Far left, make out departure card, check in, upstairs for departures. OK. Kia ora."

Gaynor took out four more 50-dollar notes, putting them on the dashboard. "Is that enough?" She grabbed the money as the car swung briefly right onto route 20, before turning left again for the straight run into the airport along an avenue flanked by tall palms.

"OK. OK." There was no time for change if there was any owing. Hemi drove the car as far up to the departures entrance as far as he could.

"Goodbye and thanks." Gaynor would have given him a kiss but there was not time.

"Haere ra," Hemi called after her.

Sobbing with anxiety, Gaynor ran into the large departure hall, looking about her to see if she could spot Will and the children ahead. As Hemi had said, Singapore Airlines check-in was at the far end. But first there was the tiresome departure card. Taking care not to scribble so as not to have to make it out again, she wrote it out, trying to stop her hand from trembling. Then she ran to the check-in desk. Her appearance with no luggage made the operative check her passport and ticket with great care, causing Gaynor to almost cry out with frustration. Finally, she was given a boarding card. Desperately she ran for International Departures. It was upstairs on the right. She sprinted up the escalator.

Next was security. It was slow. Though she only had a recently purchased toilet bag and a hairbrush she had to take her turn in the queue, where most passengers carried much that had to be x-rayed and examined.

Gaynor could have screamed at the delays. Through at last, she looked up at the electronic departure board. Wringing her hands with impatience, she waited for her flight to appear. Eventually it did, boarding now, gate B3, where was that? She had to sprint downstairs to the main concourse, through the shops, on to a central hall. Where was her gate? She scanned the signboard. "Last and final call for SQ308." Her flight. Hell! Upstairs again! Along an endless covered walkway interspersed with travellators. She sprinted madly, taking advantage of the travellators, looking to see if she could spot Will and the children ahead. "Gate shutting," the public address system warned. Panting fit to burst, shrieking, she gesticulated towards the operatives standing ready to close the flight. They saw her, waving for her to hurry up.

The operatives briefly examined her boarding card and passport and pushed her into the tunnel where she staggered to the far end, turning left. Waiting stewards, none too impressed by her lateness and appearance, helped her, gasping for breath, aboard where she held onto rails to stop herself falling to the floor. When she had sufficiently recovered, she showed her boarding card with her seat number and was directed to the far end of the plane. Looking frantically around her, she staggered along the aisle, trying to spot Will and the children. Where were they?

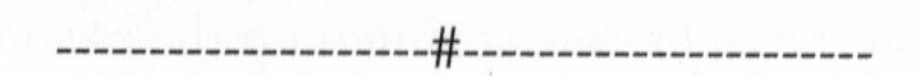

Will woke with the alarm at seven thirty. He was on his own, the children next door in the other unit. He got out of bed, going to their room via the balcony walkway.

They were all asleep, the two girls together where he had left them. He looked around for Gaynor. He could not find her anywhere. He looked in the shower and toilet, not there. He ran out onto the balcony and looked about to see if she was outside, getting a bit of fresh air which was not like her as she always wanted to attend to the children first, wake them up, get them showered, followed by breakfast for all. Where was she? Then Will remembered her saying that in the event of any unforeseen delay, Joe-Smarty-pants, as Tim liked to call him, would fly her to the domestic airport next door to the International Airport. He could not quite imagine what the delay might be, perhaps seas getting up again, making travel by water dangerous, application for a private flight plan taking time for approval by the local air authorities. Whatever; Gaynor was not with them. What should he do? He had better get himself and the children to Auckland International Airport to catch their flight back to Britain, scheduled to take off today, the 30th of August, at five in the afternoon, local time, very much hoping Gaynor would be there to meet them.

He got the girls up, putting them in the shower together. "Where's Mummy?" Angela asked.

"She seems to have been delayed. We'll be seeing her later," Will replied, trying to conceal his concern. "Get up!" he called to Tim. "Take a shower. We need to be going soon." Sleepily, from his bed, Tim asked the same question as his sister and got the same answer from Will. While the girls were showering, Will went to Tim's bed, gently pulling back the bedclothes. "You need to help me, Tim, and your mother, by pulling your weight, assisting us to get away on time, helping with the packing, getting the suitcases into the car, helping with the navigation, especially through Auckland. Your mother was very good at that."

"Right oh," Tim replied to Will's relief, getting out of bed and taking himself to the bathroom.

"Good lad, I'm relying on you," Will said, going back to attend to the girls. Once he had got the girls dried and dressed, he took out bowls for all, put in an assortment of fruit and yoghurt and called them all for breakfast, saying he had not the time to give them a cooked breakfast, putting suitable items at the same time into a plastic bag to eat on the way. While the children were eating, he looked up the road atlas. It was a distance of about 255 kilometres and would take Will at least four to four and a half hours driving without stops. He would need to be on the road by ten.

Gaynor had largely packed the night before. He just had to collect her toiletries from her dressing table and shut her bag up. He then packed his own and the girls, assisting Tim to pack his. Finally, after looking in all the drawers, he dragged the suitcases out onto the balcony walkway, lining them up at the top of the stairs, after which he drove the car round to the bottom.

Though the girls wanted to help, he would not them play a part in getting the suitcases down the stairs in case they got out of control and fell on them. He then looked in everyone's hand luggage to check what was in was appropriate like toiletries and games, especially looking out for Yellow Ted. Without Gaynor, there was a bit more room in the car and Will managed to get everything stowed. He did not need to go to the motel office as he had paid fully on arrival, opting to leave their keys in the doors instead. "I want Mummy!"

Angela complained as he arranged the girls in the back seat alone.

"We all want her," Will replied. "We'll be meeting her at the airport," he added with more confidence than he felt. What would he do if she were not there for any reason? He would have to take the children on alone to Britain, hoping Gaynor would be on a following flight. He could not stay in New Zealand a day longer as he needed to be back for the start of school term and was running out of money. He had used all the credit on his Lloyds Bank credit card and practically all the credit available on his back-up Barclay's credit card. He would have a lot to pay back when he got back to Britain. He was absolutely dreading the prospect of, in the last resort, taking them aboard with Angela and Tim crying out for their mother. He desperately hoped that would not happen, that they would meet Gaynor at the airport.

With their luggage aboard, the girls in the back of the car, their games and comforts around them, Yellow Ted in Ruth's hand luggage, Will drove off. "Yellow Ted doesn't like Smarty-pants," Ruth announced in a voice of suspicion, inferring she did not trust him. Knowing Yellow Ted spoke Ruth's thoughts, Will realised he and his daughter were of the same mind.

At first the journey went comparatively well. New Zealand, away from the cities, did not have the complexity of roads like the heavily populated South of England. Looking up at the green road signs and down at the open road atlas on Tim's lap, Will covered the 45 miles to Whangarei by eleven thirty. "Keep looking out for the red shield with number one on it," he said to Tim. "I don't want to go off onto side roads. We'll stop at the visitors' centre at the other end of town. I think from memory it'll be on the right, on a long, left-hand bend."

It was well signed. Will saw it in good time and drove into the parking bays. "I want my mum," was the first thing Angela said when Will went to take the girls out. So far, the girls had been good and patient.

"We'll go the toilets and then perhaps you'd like a run around by the river," Will replied brightly, taking with him their plastic bag of food. He could take the children into the cafeteria but, helping themselves to want they wanted from a picnic table, he felt, would suit them better. Fortunately, the weather continued mild. After three-quarters of an hour, he felt they should move on. "How much longer?" Tim asked.

"I want Mummy," Angela complained.

Will looked at the road atlas. It seemed like about 110 miles to go and would take him at least three hours, longer if he missed his way. He thought that he had better not tell them. "Some time yet. Come on. We want to see Gaynor."

To Will's relief, having gone to the toilet, the children climbed back into the car without too much fuss. Making sure he stayed on route 1, Will progressed south, the girls, tired after their run about, quiet in the back. "Have we come to Mata yet?" he asked Tim, having remembered it was the next township of any size.

"I haven't seen it yet," Tim had been fiddling with the glove pocket and not paying attention. Will prayed he would concentrate and be of help to him when driving through Auckland. After a while, the coast appeared on the left. "I want to go to the toilet," Angela announced. He stopped the car in a layby. A sign read Uretiti Beach, a good place to stop. He took Angela behind a dry bush which had what looked like peapods with little black peas. When Will brought her back to the car, she threw a tantrum and would not get in, crying that she wanted her mother. Will's heart fell. Fortunately, Tim rose to the rescue, taking her hand saying, "Well, you won't see her staying here," and coaxed her back in the car.

They were off again, Will looking anxiously at the time. He remembered the long climb up the Brynderwyn Hills and knew he was on route 1. Towns like Wellsford and Warkworth had routes going off but Will managed to keep with route 1 heading south, so far so good. "It's a long time," Angela complained, missing her mother keeping them amused. At that, she began to kick the seat and throw herself about. *Oh no*, Will thought.

"Stop it," Ruth said sharply. "You're behaving like a baby!" at which, to Will's surprise, she stopped. Life without Gaynor, particularly travelling, was not easy.

After Orewa they joined the Northern Motorway. "Once across the Harbour Bridge, we've got to bear left. I won't have time to drive and watch the map, I'm relying on you to help me find the way to the airport," Will said to Tim. To add to Will's concern, Angela started crying again. "It won't be too long, Angela dear," Will called back, feeling sorry for her. Signs for Takapuna and Devonport were appearing ahead, after which there would be the Harbour Bridge, Will remembered, when he had looked at the Auckland City map. If he just stuck to route 1, he would be taken near the airport where prominent signs would tell him where to turn off.

The immense structure of the Harbour Bridge appeared ahead. He kept to the left-hand lane as he thought that, before long, he would need to bear left. He so wished Gaynor was at the wheel. He really was not up to city driving. "It's a great view!" Will called, trying to sound enthusiastic.

"I want Mummy," was the only response coming from Angela. Will groaned inwardly.

"Turn off here," Tim announced. Will took the slip road off.

The overhead gantry said 'Fanshawe Street'. Then Will saw a sign saying, 'Viaduct Harbour'. It seemed familiar, after which he caught sight of a red shield with six on it. Oh no, this was not route 1 southbound. Where was he? The old Customs House appeared on his left. Will remembered he had seen it before. He dithered. A car tooted him. Of course, Ted had brought them this way when he first picked them up from the airport. It must be possible to get to the airport this way. He was tooted again. There was no place to stop the car and look for himself. "We're going to the airport," he reminded Tim. He saw he was coming to Tamaki Drive with water to his right and left. He had been here this way with Gaynor. He knew he did not want to go down Tamaki Drive but over the causeway crossing Orakei Basin.

"Keep looking for an airport sign," he said to Tim who was desperately trying to work out where they were. Will felt sorry for him as well as himself.

"I want Mummy!" Angela whimpered.

"Stop being a cry baby. You're wetting Yellow Ted," Ruth commanded.

"Look after Angela," Will said gently. "She's upset." Route 6 took them under a motorway going south, which Will suspected they should be on, and through an old suburb, by the appearance of the shop fronts and verandas, called Onehunga. Then they both saw the sign together, 'Airport' left.

"Whoopee!" Tim cried. Filtering left they observed they were on a major route with a red shield saying '20', before long crossing Mangere Inlet on a substantial bridge. Will recollected Ted pointing this out when picking them up from the airport on their first arrival. The airport was at Mangere. Soon route 20 divided, the left-hand fork saying 'Airport'. They were not far away. They had made it, at last, in reasonable time.

He drove up a long avenue flanked by stately palms. As he neared the airport, he saw a sign saying, 'Rental Car Returns'. He must go there. On the left was a stack of airport trolleys. They would need two with all their luggage plus Gaynor's main suitcase. He loaded the trolleys, hand luggage on top. "Take a girl's hand on each side of you and don't let them go. We don't want to lose them when we get into the crowded terminal," Will asked of Tim.

"I don't want to hold Tim's hand," Ruth complained.

Oh no, don't you start, Will thought then out aloud said, "Yellow Ted will feel very lonely on his own in the crowds."

"He'll have me," Ruth replied.

Sometimes, Will felt, one could never win. "Take both girls' hands and don't let them go," Will commanded again with a sense of urgency. "We'll miss the flight if one of you gets lost." Tim got the message and took both the girls' hands despite protests. Then Will began to push two trolleys, one in front of the other.

Inside the main hall, he looked around. Where was Gaynor? He hoped she might be waiting. "I want to go to the toilet," Angela said. Gritting his teeth, Will looked for the 'Mens'. Despite security, he would have to leave their luggage outside unattended and hope for the best. He squeezed them all into a closet and asked Angela and Ruth to go, after which he asked Tim. Tim refused in front of the girls. Will looked at his watch. Time was getting on. *Oh, no, not another performance*, he thought, *there isn't time for that.* He took the girls outside. "Go now," he said to Tim. "Don't lock the door." Tim went inside and tried to lock the door, but Will had his hand in the jamb. Tim tried twice, hurting Will's fingers then gave up and did what he was asked. "Little horror," Will muttered to himself. He then directed Tim to hold the girls' hands and went in himself.

Outside, pushing two trolleys, he followed the signs to Singapore Airlines check-in, which was at the far end, looking around for Gaynor as he did so. He could not see her anywhere. "Keep looking out for Gaynor," he said to the children. There were departure cards to be filled in for all. Will looked at his watch. It was getting on for four, he had better hurry up. It took time, carefully copying passport particulars before adding departure details, stopping every few minutes to look around for Gaynor. The children were getting restless. "I want my mummy," Angela whined.

Finally, he got them all to a check-in desk, waiting their turn. When it came, he was asked to put in turn all hold luggage on the transporter.

"You're overweight," the operator announced, looking at the weight calculator.

"I want my mummy," Angela whined.

"I want her too," Tim chipped in.

"Are all these children yours?" the operator asked suspiciously.

"Only one is, Ruth Whitby, you can see by the passports," Will replied patiently. "Mrs Gaynor McDonald, the mother of the other two, is booked on this flight. She's been delayed. Including her, I'm sure our luggage is not overweight. Could a seat with us be reserved for her?"

The operator checked the passenger list. "Nevertheless, as she's not here in person for this check-in, you're in excess, one hundred dollars."

Will checked in his wallet. He did not have one hundred dollars. He had slipped practically all he had left into the concealed pocket in Gaynor's jacket. Desperately he gave the operator his emergency Barclaycard, praying there was enough still left on it. It took a long time being approved. The clock was ticking.

Now, with only their hand luggage, he hurried them all to International Departures which he found was upstairs, looking around for Gaynor as he did so. He could not see her anywhere. He bundled the children on to the escalator as the lift was ages in coming, telling them all to hang on. Halfway up, Angela lost a shoe, necessitating Will to scramble down frantically to retrieve it.

Will looked around. Security next, that was bound to take some time. Gaynor was nowhere to be seen. Showing their boarding cards, he was directed inside. There were long queues. He scanned them for Gaynor. As far as he could see, she was not among those patiently waiting. Where was she, time was getting on? The children were getting impatient.

It came to their turn to put their hand luggage and coats in the trays. Will had to remove his wallet, phone and house keys to be scanned separately. "Yellow Ted's not going in there!" Ruth said defiantly.

"All possessions must," an attendant replied, grabbing Yellow Ted. Ruth screamed and snatched him back. Everyone looked their way, startled. Will's heart fell, not another scene. To his great relief, a woman attendant stepped in, likely a mother herself, and directed Ruth through the scanning arch holding Yellow Ted, hiatus resolved.

Will helped the children put their coats back on and ensured they had all their hand luggage. He looked at his watch and around for Gaynor, hoping he might see her ahead. He could not. He led the children down to the main concourse, stopping to look up at an electronic departure board. "Look for SQ 308," he said to Tim.

"It says 'boarding now B3'," Tim replied.

"Gee, so it does, we'd better get going!" Will grabbed the children's hands, hurrying them downstairs through the shops. He stopped in a central bay, looking to see where Gate B3 was. It was upstairs again, along a seemingly endless covered walkway. He led the children onto a series of travellators, holding the girls' hands to stop them falling, looking at gate numbers and up and down for Gaynor. B3 seemed to be at the very end. Arriving breathlessly at the assembly area, he found most boarding categories had already boarded and they were soon directed to board. Looking back to see if he could see Gaynor, Will showed their passports and boarding cards. Asking for their hats to be taken off, the children's faces were examined carefully against their passport photos as was Will's. It seemed a man on his own with children of different surnames was considered unusual.

"Where's Mummy?" Angela asked for the umpteenth time.

"Behind us," Will replied, hoping against hope this was the case. Aboard they were directed to the rear of the aircraft where Will found their seats and began to stow their hand luggage, keeping out games, a light rug, and Yellow Ted. Having got them all in their seats, belts on, Will stood up, scanning the remaining boarding passengers for Gaynor.

"Where's Mummy?" Angela whimpered.

"Where's our mum?" Tim insisted.

"Coming," Will replied, wondering how on earth he could cope if Gaynor did not make the flight. The number of boarding passengers drew to a trickle and finally ceased. All had boarded. Will put his head in his hands in despair.

There seemed some commotion up forward in the cabin. A distraught passenger appeared. Then Will saw a dishevelled woman in blue rushing, staggering up the aisle towards them. "Mummy!" Angela and Tim cried, struggling out of their seatbelts. Gaynor rushed towards them, hugging her children emotionally in turn, before sinking down in the reserved seat beside Will.

"I thought you'd gone off with Joe," Will blurted out.

"No, no, it's you I love."

"Will you marry me?" Will hardly knew what he was saying.

"Of course, I will."

To Will's embarrassment those passengers near enough to hear the conversation clapped and cheered.

Then Gaynor put her head on Will's shoulder and cried. Will had never seen Gaynor cry before, neither had her children. He looked at her, so different from her usual well-groomed self.

"You've had a bad time."

Gaynor nodded. Will held her close.

--------------------------------#--------------------------------

By autumn half term, staff and governors had been informed of Will and Gaynor's engagement. Gaynor had gone back to her part-time airport car-driving job, feeling it was easier for Will not to have a wife on the payroll. Will was grateful. He, in turn, felt it was time to find out if one of his major reasons for going to New Zealand with Gaynor had been resolved. He decided to spend another night in Mrs Mill's classroom, choosing a Friday night this time so he did not have to go to school the next day. Like last time, Mr Macnamara, the caretaker, was suspiciously resentful when Will sent him home at six thirty, saying he would be working late at school. In Mr Macnamara's opinion, headmasters were not capable of locking up their own schools. Feeling sheepish but at the same time apprehensive, leaving only the office lights on, Will walked silently to Mrs Mills' classroom, determined to stay awake till dawn.

After a time, it became extremely difficult. Will walked up and down, slapping himself, whistling tunes under his breath, even trying a bit of solo ballroom dancing, anything not to fall asleep. On occasions, he fell over chairs which he did not mind as this jerked him awake. It was the longest night in his life, but in the end rewarding, the ghost, apparition, whatever you might like to call it, did not appear. Zoe's restless spirit had been put to rest.

In the spring, Will and Gaynor got married, honeymooning in the south of France. Gaynor's mother said she would look after the children. In the end, they decided to take the children. It was the children that had brought them together.

Back in Peckingly, six months later, Will found Yellow Ted, dusty, lying forlornly in a heap in the corner of Ruth's bedroom. He was no longer Ruth's most needed, inseparable companion. She now felt secure with a mother, a sister and brother, as well as a devoted father. Will picked up Yellow Ted, turning him over. At one time he would have liked dearly to strangle him, cut him into many pieces, throw him in the rubbish bin. But now he felt a strange nostalgic affection for the discarded bear. He dusted him off carefully and put him on top of the wardrobe to watch over them. Yellow Ted had played his own unique part in bringing them together.

About the Author

John Chudley, is of dual nationality, being born and brought up in New Zealand and having spent much of the later part of his life living and working in Great Britain. Visiting New Zealand regularly, he is intimately acquainted with the New Zealand scene where much of the story unfolds.

Lightning Source UK Ltd.
Milton Keynes UK
UKHW042242051121
393428UK00013B/284